THE SECRET ANIMAL SOCIETY

LUKE GAMBLE

ILLUSTRATED BY JANE PICA

TO GABRIEL AND ALL OUR
FURRED, FEATHERED AND
SCALY FAMILY MEMBERS,
PAST AND PRESENT!

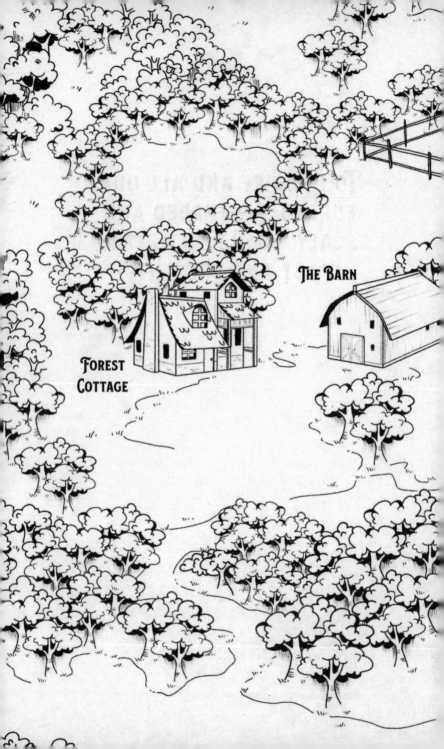

THE BARN

FOREST
COTTAGE

DOCTOR'S
STUDY

CHAPTER ONE

In which the indomitable Edith receives some extraordinary news, and must face up to the possibility of an altogether different kind of life, and a summer holiday like no other...

The halls of St Montefiore's School for Girls were enough to terrify any girl. In the playground there stood a big bronze bust of Margot Montefiore, who had founded the school many centuries ago. Along every wall were hundreds of paintings – Margot Montefiore's face peered down from all of them. Sometimes she was staring. Sometimes she was glaring. *Always* she had her finger raised, as if to reprimand every single girl who passed by, under her steely gaze.

Outside the headmistress's study, her oil-painted face was a perfectly gruesome grimace – for any girl sitting here must *surely* have demanded the worst telling off.

Or so thought Edith Wight.

Edith had been sitting here for hours already, while the school emptied around her as girls left for the summer holidays. Perched on the edge of a hard wooden bench in the gloomy, windowless corridor, her blonde hair pulled back in a painful school regulation ponytail, she glanced up at the clock beside Madam Montefiore's most fearsome gaze with sharp blue eyes. There it hung at a crooked angle, its large pale face framing two spindly black hands. Edith willed its hands to move, but the time was passing with aching slowness.

A short burst of laughter echoed through the old building from the front hall – another girl being collected. It died away abruptly as the thud of the heavy front door reverberated with finality. That was it: the last of the pupils had gone for the summer.

Well, *almost* the last.

Edith sighed and screwed up her eyes, hoping a phone would ring, for someone to tell her that it was OK, that her parents were coming after all.

They couldn't have forgotten – not twice in one year.

A sudden scurrying noise made her look sharply to her right. It took her a moment to see anything in the dim light, but then she spotted a small dark shape chasing along the edge of the skirting. The mouse seemed panicked, racing first one way and then another. Edith watched, wondering why the creature was so distressed. Then she noticed someone had placed a large box against the wall. It must be obstructing the spot where the creature needed to go. It had been blocked out of its home.

Edith bit her lower lip. If the teachers caught her getting up from the bench she'd really be in for it – at St Montefiore's, the school motto was OBEDIENCE MATTERS – but there was no way the mouse would be able to move the box. If anyone else saw it, they'd kill it.

Edith made her decision. With a quick push, she propelled herself off the bench.

"EDITH WIGHT! WHAT DO YOU THINK YOU ARE DOING?"

The raised voice echoed sharply in the confines of the walls.

3

Edith looked up to see the angular figure of Madame Entwhistle, the French mistress, looming at the end of the hall.

Edith wasn't the only one who'd heard. The voices within the headmistress's office had abruptly stopped as well.

Something inside made Edith fight her instincts to obey and she dashed towards the box, hitting it full tilt and causing it to spin away from the skirting.

"EDITH WIGHT, GET BACK ON THAT BENCH AT ONCE!"

The sound of Madame Entwhistle's footsteps matched the anger in her voice.

Edith looked down. But the box had slid into the middle of the corridor and the mouse was heading towards sanctuary. Uttering a little squeak, it disappeared from sight.

"EDITH WIGHT!"

Madame Entwhistle was almost on top of her. Edith looked around. The door to the headmistress's study opened and then. . .

Then the world was an explosion of incandescent light.

The pain that suddenly exploded in Edith's head made her clutch her temples with both hands.

Clamping her eyes shut, she doubled over and staggered backwards, reeling as if she had been struck full in the face.

As the pain began to ebb away, Edith slumped to the floor, her chest heaving for air and sweat running down her face.

"EDITH WIGHT!" Madame Entwhistle roared. "YOUR BEHAVIOUR BEGGARS BELIEF. GET BACK ON THAT BENCH IMMEDIATELY!"

"She's had another attack, Madame Entwhistle." A more authoritative voice spoke from the study's doorway. "Give her some air. I'll see to this."

"As you wish, Headmistress."

Edie registered the sound of Madame Entwhistle's footsteps retreating and other footsteps approaching.

The sound of softer footsteps approaching faintly registered in Edith's consciousness.

"Child, are you all right?"

Edith opened her eyes, bracing herself for a resurgence of the pain. Nothing happened. She nodded up at her headmistress and got to her feet.

"Come into my office, Edith Wight. We have things to discuss."

* * *

The headmistress's study was small and square, and every inch of its walls were covered in yet more portraits of St Margot Montefiore. The woman in the pictures looked surprisingly like the headmistress who directed Edith to an upright leather chair, and this was no surprise; St Montefiore's School for Girls had been passed down from one generation to the next, ever since its founding.

The headmistress, as round and plump as her ancestor, sat behind her antique oak desk and paused to regard the girl in front of her. Edith was small for an eleven-year-old and she sat there clasping her hands together, looking pale, thin and drawn.

"Sorry, Headmistress," she said quietly once she had fully regained her senses.

"Edith," the headmistress said, with a hint of a sneer. "Child, you seem to have had another of your ... *episodes*. I need to speak to you about your parents."

Not for the first time, Edith wondered if the headmistress really cared about the tumble she'd taken. She looked up, expectantly.

"Have they forgotten again?" she asked. The disappointment tasted sour in her mouth.

"Not this time." The headmistress paused with relish. "Your mother and father will not be here to collect you today, nor any other day. They have gone missing."

Missing. The word was so simple and yet so bewildering. Edith's eyes darted around, as if she might even find her parents hiding under the headmistress's table. It suddenly seemed so long ago that she'd last seen them.

"Where are they, Headmistress?"

"Well, if that was known, they would not be *missing*, would they, young lady?" The headmistress smiled. "This isn't like half term. *Then* they simply got the dates wrong – well, when your lives are as busy as your parents' lives are, off trotting the globe looking for natural 'wonders', it's quite easy to forget a little girl you left halfway across the world. What is it they're looking for this time? Tree frogs? Rare butterflies?"

"Flies, Headmistress."

"*What?*"

"They're studying bluebottles. It's my mother's speciality."

The headmistress gave Edith a look of disgust. "I dare say *some* people find flies fascinating, but what those people might be like, heaven knows – and, good gracious, just to think that they've left you behind while they're gallivanting across the world looking for *bluebottles!*"

"My mother says insects will save the planet," Edith said defensively, suddenly emboldened. "Without insects, there wouldn't be any other life on earth."

7

"Well, whatever they're up to, we've had no word from them and neither has anyone else. This latest expedition of theirs, well, suffice to say it's been a little more remote than usual. It's thought they've been cut off by floods and are stranded in the Amazon rainforest."

The Amazon. Her parents had been there before. There was more to investigate in the Amazon rainforest than anywhere else on earth. There were still corners of the Amazon where new animals lurked, undiscovered by humans.

Edith's mother and father had first met when they studied Natural Sciences together at the University of Cambridge. From there, life had taken them all over the world. They'd spent summers in the Sahara, studying desert hedgehogs and hopping jerboas. They'd over-wintered on an Antarctic island, documenting the lives of penguins and leopard seals. They'd even been to the bottom of the ocean to take pictures of the strange, shapeless jellyfish who live on the seabed itself. When Edith was small, they'd stopped roaming for a while and all lived together in their flat overlooking Kensington Gardens in London – but when Edith was old enough to go to boarding school, they'd set off again. Edith would thrill to get letters and postcards from places as far away as Mongolia and the Solomon Islands, Yosemite Valley and the fjords of Iceland – but none of it seemed so thrilling today. Edith thought immediately of the mouse trying to get back into its hole.

"Doesn't anyone know where they are?" She had always tried not to show any fear in front of the teachers at St Margot Montefiore's School for Girls. They loved it when you showed a little fear. "Are they still alive?" she said quietly.

"Here," the headmistress said. She picked up a letter from the big oak desk and tossed it on to Edith's lap. "Now you know as much as we do. It seems the Peruvian authorities last had radio communication with them a week ago when they issued a warning about heavy rain. But now the rivers have broken their banks and the floodwaters are rising. Well, if you will go trotting off to heaven knows where, you're bound to come a cropper one of these days. It's their own silly fault, if you ask me."

Edith fought back the urge to shout out, *"Well I didn't ask you!"* and instead said, "Is anyone looking for them?"

"Read it for yourself," the headmistress said dismissively. "There's another expedition, the Syndicate, in the same region. They're missing too. The only difference, it seems, is that this Syndicate didn't leave behind a troublesome little girl whose headmistress now has to find *some* way of accommodating her over the summer."

The headmistress gave a dramatic shake of the head.

"Where will I go?" Edith asked, panic creeping into her voice.

The headmistress produced a little card.

"Your emergency contact. Every parent has to leave one. Just in case they, you know, get eaten by a crocodile, or fall overboard at sea, or go missing in a jungle."

Edith shivered as she looked at the card being pressed into her hands.

PILGRIMS VETS PRACTICE

FOREST COTTAGE

OGDEN'S COPSE

NEW FOREST NATIONAL PARK

A Sanctuary for Nature's Wonders!

For the longest time, Edith just stared.

"I... I... I'm not sure who..."

The headmistress's eyes flared in panic. Then she let out a little sigh of relief.

"For a moment there, Edith Wight, I thought you were about to have another of your turns! And I've got a plane to catch. Now, it seems this Pilgrims Vet Practice is run by an uncle of yours. His dearly departed wife was your mother's sister or some such. But, whatever he is to you, he's to be your keeper this summer."

Keeper? The word sounded perfect for an animal doctor, but not for a child.

Edith paused. She was stunned into silence. She had never had much contact with anyone in her family other than her parents and grandmother. She wasn't sure if her uncle would even know she existed. Her mother had never even mentioned that she had had a sister!

"I don't know him. My parents have never talked of him. Or an aunt."

"We've managed to speak to someone at this address," the headmistress continued, "and explain the situation. We didn't speak to the man himself. He was out on some expedition of his own, I understand. Must be a family trait – being too busy for you. Still, his housekeeper seemed reasonably understanding." She stood and picked up a suitcase and parasol from behind the desk. "I'm sure it will work out just fine. So, if you wouldn't mind. . ."

Edith watched the headmistress's hand dart behind

her desk, and come back up carrying a suitcase and a parasol.

"Tick, tick!" she declared, using the parasol to shoo Edith back towards the door. "Oh, and don't you worry –" She reached into a drawer under the desk and handed Edith a bulky envelope – "the expense has been added to your school account to be settled before the beginning of next term."

Out in the corridor, Edith stood alone, listening to the click of the headmistress's heels march away to her holiday on the Costa del Sol. Too many thoughts were buzzing in her head. Her parents – lost amongst the rising floodwaters of some faraway jungle. A whole summer stretching out in front of her – in the company of a man she'd never known. And. . .

Her eyes panned down. The little hole in the wall was still exposed, and out of it poked the mouse with its little whiskery snout. It squeaked once, sending another shockwave through Edith's mind – but this time she didn't faint clean away.

He was wishing me her good luck, she realized. He was wishing her "bon voyage". She wasn't sure how she knew it, but there it was in her head, as clear as day.

And, as Edith tramped away, she was grateful.

She was going to need all the luck in the world.

CHAPTER TWO

*In which Edith is abandoned in the middle of nowhere,
and follows a brambled path straight into her future...*

Edith woke up with a start. She'd been vaguely aware
of the taxi leaving the main road and heading down a
bumpy track, but that was ages ago. The car was now
motionless and the engine idled.

"This is it," said the driver. He was a big man with a
shaved head and a no-nonsense attitude, but despite his
tough appearance, he sounded strangely rattled.

Rubbing the sleep from her eyes, Edith looked out of
the window. It was already dusk, the darkness hardening,
and worryingly she couldn't see any sign of a house or
even a light.

"This is the address?" she asked. "But we're in the middle of a wood!"

There was no doubt about it. On every side, the trees crowded round. Their boughs, heavy with leaves, reached over the taxi to make a great shadowed tunnel through which the car had been driving. All around was thickening darkness.

The driver peered out through his windscreen. The car headlights picked up a crooked little wooden sign, roughly staked into the ground by the side of the track.

"That sign says that this is Forest Cottage." He pointed with his finger.

Edith's forehead wrinkled as she leaned forward to see the sign. She could just about make out the large black letters which read FOREST COTTAGE, but that was all. There was no building, no path or driveway in sight.

"We've been driving down this track for ages," the driver said. "I thought we'd end up in a village or something, that it was a cut through – but the track ends here. But look." He tapped the satnav on his dashboard and shrugged. "This thing can't be wrong. This is where that headmistress of yours said I should drop you."

Edith pressed her face to the glass. Surely, *surely*, this couldn't be the place. But the taxi driver was already stepping out of the cab, collecting her rucksack from the boot and opening Edith's own door. Her eyes flitted nervously about as she climbed out of the car. Tall trees loomed ominously in every direction and, as she stood on the edge of the track, dressed in fashionably ripped jeans and wearing a pair of sparkly purple trainers, she realized she was more geared up for a trip to a city shopping centre than an ancient wood. They weren't even her clothes; her best friend, Anita, had lent them to her for the holidays because she couldn't carry them all the way back to her family home in India. Edith suddenly felt incredibly self-conscious. She'd wanted to make a good impression for her uncle, but now she felt silly.

"This place has a funny feel to it," the driver said, as he slid the bag at her feet and slunk back to his cab. "I wouldn't hang around too much outside if I was you." When Edith said nothing in reply, the driver gave a polite cough and held out his hand. "Sorry it's cost so much love, but you're in the back of beyond out here and I've got to get on. Look, are you sure you want to be left here? This is the furthest you can go into the New Forest before you're leaving it again, and it's an eerie place. Lots of stories about these old woods."

Lost in the moment and a bit overwhelmed by the ancient faces that seemed to be etched into the gnarled bark of the trees, Edith had completely forgotten she was supposed to pay the taxi driver. She bent down and quickly unzipped the top pocket of her rucksack. Pulling out the envelope the headmistress had given her, she turned back to the car with an embarrassed expression.

"I'm sorry," she said, flushing. "How much do I owe you?"

The taxi driver glanced at the meter on his dashboard. The journey had taken over three hours and a line of big red numbers glared at him. "Sorry, love. My boss will have my guts in a bucket if I give you a discount."

Edith pulled out the money in the envelope and flicked through the notes before handing the entire contents over to the taxi driver.

"Look, here's my card," he said, climbing back into the driver's seat. "If you find yourself stuck, give me a call."

He looked concerned. They were empty words and they both knew it. Edith could tell by the way he kept nervously darting his eyes into the shadows, the way he started each time one of the magnificent boughs of the tree tunnel shuddered slightly in the gloom; this taxi driver couldn't *wait* to get out of this wood.

"I'm sure it will be OK," Edith whispered – though, if the taxi driver had cared to listen at all, he would have noticed that her voice was trembling. "My headmistress spoke to my uncle's housekeeper. He's expecting me."

"Seems a rum sort to be living in these woods, if you ask me."

The taxi's engine gunned back into life. "You got my number. Give me a call if. . ."

But the taxi had already burst into life and sped off before she could hear the driver finish his sentence. For the first time, Edith was alone in the wide, wild forest, with the branches of the trees overhead blocking out what little light was left.

As she watched the taxi's red lights bump their way down the track and out of sight, she looked at the taxi driver's card, crumpled it into a ball in her hand and thrust it into the recess of a trouser pocket.

It was no good to Edith.

She didn't even have a mobile phone.

After a little while, Edith zipped up the top pocket of her bag again and took a deep breath. There was no good fussing, she told herself, as she adjusted to the silence of the forest. There was nobody coming to help her.

There hadn't been since she had sat down outside the headmistress's study. She would just have to get on with this and toughen up.

It was the first time Edith had been out of London by herself. The silence was almost deafening. She couldn't remember ever not being able to hear the noise of a car engine or a horn. Standing in the middle of the New Forest, enveloped by trees, with not a single building in sight, she couldn't have felt more out of place had she been standing on the moon.

And yet . . . it wasn't really silence. Not if you listened *carefully*. She could hear something scurrying in the leaf litter on the forest ground. Birds were skittering, up there in the trees, looking for the best roosts for the night. To Edith, it was like a chorus of a thousand – no, a million – voices. You simply had to listen.

She absentmindedly rubbed the sides of her head, hoping she didn't get one of her headaches. She could feel the buzzing now she'd got out of the taxi and she tried to shut the sensation out. It felt like a persistent hum just behind her eyes. It was always harder when she was in a new place. The pitch of the noise seemed to change when she was somewhere unfamiliar, making it more difficult to tune out.

It was one of the reasons she rarely went out and her

teachers didn't like her going on school trips. Especially as the doctors had never been able to explain it. Too often, people regarded her as a ticking time bomb, counting down until the next "episode".

Edith walked up to the crooked sign and traced the words FOREST COTTAGE with her forefinger. The letters seemed somehow fresh against the aged wood on to which they were painted. Behind it, she saw that what she had first taken for just another part of the forest was actually a tall hedge of hawthorn and privet – and no sooner had she spotted this than she noticed a little wooden gate squeezed amongst the leaves.

Nothing about getting to her uncle's house had been easy. He lived in a place inaccessible by buses, miles from the main road and totally disguised from the track outside. Why was the entrance so hidden? Did he even own a car? If he did, Edith thought, it must be one that could fly, because there was no way it would fit through the tiny gate.

Fighting back the foliage, she dragged her rucksack through the narrow gap before hoisting it up on to her shoulders. As she did so, a little moth flew up from the top of the gate, its wings shimmering in the fading light. It fluttered close to Edith's face. A smile crept on to her lips. . .

FOREST
COTTAGE

. . .and a sharp stab of pain lanced behind her eyes. Screwing her eyes shut, Edith took a deep breath of air and the pain seemed to go away. When she opened them again, the moth had gone. She must have frightened it.

Edith looked up. The thin mossy track she was following disappeared into yet more bushes as it snaked up a slight incline. Right now, there was no sign of the house, just an overgrown path weaving into the unknown.

The night was growing darker by the second.

Shrugging off the dull ache in her head, Edith started forward. She'd always been tough and good at coping – but when you spent most of your time alone, that's what you had to be. She had a "plucky spirit". At least that's what her dad had told her a few years ago. It was definitely being tested today.

A bramble whipped at her. Something dark and furry scuttled across her path, taking fright with an enormous squeak as it brushed against the side of her foot. More than once, Edith thought to turn back – but all that was waiting down there was the empty dirt track, the tyre marks the taxi driver had left behind and the deepening night.

No, she thought, there was nothing else for it but to carry on.

She had all but given up on finding the cottage when a new sound erupted.

First there came a crash. Then a shout. And, finally, a large snorting noise. This cycle kept repeating itself, almost in a rhythm, and Edith felt a wave of nervousness bubble up in her tummy.

CRASH!

"No!" came a low, booming voice.

SNORT!

"No!" the voice shouted again.

CRASH!

"I'm telling you. The Doc says this will make you better!"

SNORT!

Edith waited for the crash – but this time it didn't come.

"That's better," said the voice. "Good boy. The Doc will be pleased. You've done us both a favour!"

SNORT!

Edith wondered if she dared go on, but with a deep breath, she found the courage and ploughed on through the brambles. All of a sudden, the path burst out of the bushes and she floundered into a large clearing. Surprised by the sudden sense of open space, Edith stopped and stared in wonderment at the scene in front of her.

The lawn, perfectly manicured, would have done justice to any cricket pitch in England. There was a picturesque old cottage with a thatched roof and a perfectly manicured lawn in front of it, like something out of a fairy tale. Its thatched roof snugly hugged a red brick chimney that puffed wisps of white smoke up into the night sky. On the opposite side of the clearing, clearly ancient in construction, was a huge wooden barn. Warped timbers weaved themselves up the walls to support a rolling slate roof. It faced the cottage, with its two huge doors standing slightly ajar, framing a cavernous entrance big enough for a team of cart horses to pass through.

Through the gap between the barn doors, Edith saw . . . *lights!*

That was where the noises were coming from. And, as Edith stood there, one of the doors started to move. A huge hand appeared, gripping the edge of the door as it swung further outwards.

Taking an involuntary step back, Edith watched as the largest man she had ever seen in her life emerged from the barn. His chiselled features gleamed in the twilight, accentuating the shaved sides of his head, which was topped by a mohawk of wild, brilliant blond. His hair, tamed by a strong leather band, flowed into a ponytail down his broad back. And with intricately patterned tattoos wreathed up his muscular arms and a plaited beard that seemed to spear forwards as he walked, the man looked for everything like a Viking warlord.

Yet, there was something undeniably *friendly* about the way the starlight cascading into the glade twinkled in his eyes. He wore a pair of worn green trousers and a simple shirt that stretched over his massive frame, his bulging arms straining it at the seams. In his free hand, Edith noticed he clasped a large jug which he quickly preceded to shake out on to the grass as if it were a thimble.

"Just because he's big, he thinks he can get away with anything," the man muttered to himself, in a deep, gruff voice.

Slightly uncertain, Edith cleared her throat and the man looked up in surprise. They stared at each other for a moment, before the man's face split into a massive grin and he barrelled forwards.

"You must be **Edie!**" he boomed. "We're all so excited to meet you!"

But then Edith's attention was drawn from the giant before her to a creature, standing half in and half out of the barn. It seemed at first to be a magnificent horse with the most dazzling white coat – but it was bigger than any horse she'd ever seen. And there was something else too. Wings.

Horses didn't have *wings*.

As the thought registered in her mind, and to Edith's increasing incredulity, two majestic wings unfolded from the horse's back, bedecked in resplendent white feathers.

The creature gave a snort and Edith found her eyes locked in its gaze.

The look lasted barely a millisecond. Then, without a moment's warning, a pain seemed to explode inside her skull and Edith's hands shot up to clasp each side of her head. She'd never experienced anything so severe before.

A thousand bolts of fire lanced through her brain and she screwed up her eyes in agony.

"Help!" she managed to gasp.

It was a good job the giant man was already in front of her, because at that moment Edith fainted clean away and she felt the man catch her just before she hit the ground.

CHAPTER THREE

*In which Edith wakes to find herself
at the heart of a most unusual family
of two- and four-legged friends...*

The sound of a kettle was the first thing Edith registered. She blinked hard, squinting through half-closed eyelids as she took in her surroundings.

Wincing as her vision came into focus, Edith found herself staring up towards a window. Outside the glass, the darkness was absolute – though whether it was the same night, she could not say. She thought back and remembered a giant man and a winged horse. Surely that had just been her imagination. She shook her head, certain her mind had been playing tricks on her...

The warm glow that bathed the room was coming from a single light in the ceiling. Thankfully, the sharp stabbing pain in her head had gone, but there was a loud buzzing in her ears and she shook her head as if to clear it. No matter how hard she tried, the noises persisted, and Edith gave a little sigh of frustration.

Taking in her surroundings, Edith realized she was lying on a large sofa inside the sanctuary of the cottage. Her head had been propped up on a cushion of the deepest ruby red and she saw a huge kitchen that immediately felt both homely and safe.

Piles of books lay everywhere: on shelves, on the kitchen table, on the floor. Stacks of maps, magazines and papers haphazardly lined nearly every surface. On the mantelpiece, above a large open fireplace, sat a single framed photograph. It was the only space that wasn't cluttered. In the frame was the pretty face of a blue-eyed young woman, her hair the colour of gold, her nose the exact same shape as Edith's own. Edith wondered if she might have been some sort of distant family relation – perhaps she was even her aunt.

A door creaked open and Edith turned to see a little old lady wander into the room, her kind twinkly eyes framed behind a pair of round tortoiseshell spectacles.

"My dear," she said, in a voice as light as feathers,

"you had quite a shock. Poor Francis didn't know what to do. He felt dreadful!"

Edith gulped, uncertain what to say.

"So, do you feel better now? How's your head? I gather you fell with a bump?"

Edith managed a weak smile of thanks as the old lady handed her a glass of cool water.

As she took a gulp, a hundred thoughts clattered through her mind: where her bag was, when the headache was going to go away, what she had *really* seen in the barn...

The old lady's words brought her back to the present. "I expect you're wondering where your uncle is?" she said, bustling over to the sink. "Well, don't worry my dear, he'll be back soon for dinner, he's just out on his rounds."

"How long have I been asleep?"

"Oh, an hour, maybe two. You took quite a tumble!"

So it *was* the same night. Edith felt a sense of relief that she hadn't been unconscious for too long. She propped herself up on the sofa and watched as the old lady started to peel potatoes with quick flicks of her wrist.

"I didn't realize my uncle lived here, or..." *or even existed*, Edith thought to herself, but caught the words before she said them aloud. "Or had a housekeeper, until the headmistress said she'd called you."

The old lady laughed, uproariously. "The thought your uncle might live here alone! Haha! He should be so lucky! Your uncle wouldn't survive a day without the rest of us! He'd forget to eat breakfast, lunch and dinner – always so tangled up with these 'cases' of his. Why, without us, he'd forget his own head!" She paused. "Not to say your uncle isn't intelligent. Why, I'd venture to say he's the smartest man I've ever met. But head smarts and common sense, sometimes they don't go together. Once I was ill for a week, and he ate nothing but apples plucked from the garden. He had stomach cramps for a month!"

She laughed again – and then Edith's attention was pulled away as a massive brown dog burst into the room. At first, its amber eyes sent a sudden chill of fear through Edith, but before she had a second to react, it planted a huge slobbery lick on her face and dipped its tongue in her glass of water.

Edith squealed in surprise. She'd never really had much to do with dogs, let alone been kissed by one almost as big as herself.

"Oh, that's Arnold. He takes liberties I'm afraid, there's no telling him."

Realizing he was being talked about, Arnold had started to wag his entire body. Despite the feeling of pressure in her head threatening to worsen once more,

Edith couldn't help but reach out to cautiously pat him, his jowls spraying her with yet more slobber.

"Arnold, do leave the poor girl alone!" exclaimed the housekeeper who, having finished the potatoes, walked over to wrestle the dog away. "Honestly, that dog doesn't have any manners!"

As if in reply, Arnold promptly sat down in front of the sofa with a sigh and rested his big head on Edith's lap.

"He likes you! You'll have to be firm with him though, my dear, he can be a bit wilful. Like all the other occupants of this cottage."

"What sort of dog is he?" Edith enquired, tentatively reaching out again to stroke his massive head.

"A bit of this and that. Mainly Wolfdog, watered down with a bit of Great Dane, maybe some St Bernard, and there's definitely a hint of Rhodesian Ridgeback about him.

Some of his ancestors were probably used for hunting lions, but the only thing Arnold likes to hunt is whatever I cook in this kitchen. He really is hopeless. Big lump that he is, he won't go outside in the rain and is frightened by loud bangs. In short, he's very sweet but, despite his somewhat frightening appearance, he is undeniably the most useless dog I have ever encountered. He's been with us for about four years, I should think. He was a rescue, you see; his original owners didn't anticipate he would get so big, so your uncle took him in. That was that – he hasn't left since!"

Now that she was finished with the potatoes, the little old lady brought two cups of steaming tea over to the coffee table and eased herself into an armchair at the sofa's side.

"Have a sip, Edie, dearest. You don't mind me calling you Edie, do you?" Edith nodded, and the kindly woman beamed as she carried on talking. "That tea should help you get over your shock. It's a special leaf from a remote part of Thailand. Your uncle brought it back from one of his travels. You'll find it quite different to what you might normally be used to, like much of your stay with us, I suspect."

Edith picked up the cup and looked inside. It certainly didn't look like any drink she had ever seen before. The tea had a greeny-pink tinge, there was no milk and a blue swirl seemed to snake around inside the cup. Knowing it would be terribly rude to refuse, Edith raised it to her lips, gave a little blow and took a tentative sip.

Almost immediately the most amazing warm glow started to spread through her body and the buzzing in her head seemed to go quiet. She looked up in surprise at the housekeeper, who was watching her closely.

"Delicious, isn't it? Now, before we discuss the finer points of Thai tea, we should be introduced properly. My name," she announced, "is Lady Elizabeth Beatrice Violet Thornfrulnaught ... but since you are allowing me to call you Edie, please call me Betty! As you correctly deduced, I am your uncle's housekeeper – although, looking at the mess in here, you'll no doubt be wondering what I do all day!"

"Not at all," Edith quickly said, her good manners kicking in.

Betty gave a little chuckle and waved a hand around the chaos of the kitchen. "Sweet of you to say, my dear, but all will soon become apparent. Francis, the man you met, is my son. He's never been one for academic studies, but he is sweet, loyal and he helps with the animals we look after."

Betty's eyes crinkled in amusement as she saw Edith's expression of surprise.

"Haha! I can see you wondering about the lack of family resemblance, but I adopted Francis, you see. The story goes that his father was a famous Icelandic strongman. You'll like him, I'm sure. Aside from his great strength, Francis has a certain way about him that puts jumpy creatures – and people – at ease."

Edith could hold it in no longer. Where this courage was coming from, she did not know. Maybe it was the strangely coloured tea that was emboldening her. She set the teacup down and said, "When I met Francis there was an . . . *animal* coming out of the barn. What *was* it?"

Betty's eyes narrowed. "What was it you saw?"

Edith hesitated. "I'm not totally sure. It all seems a bit blurry – and then my headache started and . . . I think it was some sort of horse, but. . ."

"Of course! What else could it have been, my dear?"

Edith held her tongue. It seemed so preposterous. *HORSES DIDN'T HAVE WINGS!*

Her silence lasted too long, because Betty gently reached over and touched the back of her hand. "Don't be alarmed, my dear. You know your uncle is a famous vet, don't you? This is Pilgrims Vets Practice."

Edith nodded, although in truth she hadn't known that her uncle was famous.

In fact, she didn't know him at all, but something made her hold back blurting that out. What if Betty thought she was an imposter? Where would she go then?

Sensing Edith's hesitancy, Betty smiled. "He's not famous in the way you might think – he's not on TV shows or in newspapers, but in his field of work he is very highly regarded. He certainly isn't a normal vet. Not in the traditional sense – we don't have a walk-in clinic or take appointments with pet owners. We do, however, look after all types of animals here – patients come from all over the world for his services. They have done so for the best part of thirty years. Some of them are very valuable – you could say rare or unusual creatures. We have to keep ourselves to ourselves, as they could attract the wrong sort of attention."

At Edith's feet, Arnold lifted his enormous head and set up a mournful whimper. Betty reached down to tickle his ears and he quietened.

"You mean . . . people might want to steal them?"

Arnold gave a single, terrified howl.

"Yes, my dear," Betty replied. "It can be a dark world sometimes. But you must always remember the golden rule – you can't have shadow without light! Nevertheless, that is the reason why we live where we live. It's why you have never visited us before. We don't generally allow visitors, even family. Not that we aren't delighted to have guests here – it's just too risky. We can't have the public getting wind of our work and popping round, disturbing our patients. In fact, unless you knew exactly where you had to go, no one could ever find us."

"But the sign?" whispered Edith.

"Oh, we only put the sign out for you, my dear. Francis will have removed it by now. We try to keep ourselves very much to ourselves." She paused, a look of concern flashing across her face. "Now, your headmistress told me a little about the situation – she mentioned your parents are stuck in some floods?"

"They're in the Amazon," Edith said. "Apparently there's another expedition in the area that's out of contact as well – the Syndicate or something. That's all I know."

Betty's face seemed to twitch ever so slightly. "Syndicate, you say?"

Edith's rucksack was lying on the floor. She had to shift Arnold's enormous, jowly head to reach it. Producing the letter from its pocket, she handed it over to Betty – who, squinting through the thick lenses of her spectacles, read it closely.

Betty's silence was full, it seemed to Edith, of apprehension.

"What's a Syndicate?" she finally asked.

Betty put down the letter and said, "It's a group of people who share a common interest." But her voice was level, almost guarded.

Edith was stopped from asking Betty what she thought of the letter by an ear-splitting shriek and a crash. The noise startled Edith out of her seat, Betty out of her boots – and panicked Arnold so much that he picked himself up and promptly hid beneath the kitchen table, which rocked and rolled as he tried to squeeze underneath.

Edith's eyes darted around the kitchen. On the other side of the windowpane, dazed from where he'd crashed into the glass, there stood a huge black bird with a white bib and a massive bright orange bill.

"Oh, Gerry!" Betty exclaimed, once she saw the bird. "Honestly! Get to the front door, you stupid creature!"

The bird, still reeling, picked itself up and vanished back into the night.

With a dramatic roll of her eyes, Betty shuffled out of the kitchen. Edith heard her open the front door. There came another ear-splitting shriek, and then the ball of black feathers, lit up with that luminous orange beak, hurtled into the room. Edith watched it swoop in circles then land on the arm of the sofa where she sat.

It was only then that she saw the piece of thread around its neck, and the tiny roll of paper tied up at one end. The bird seemed to be presenting it to her proudly.

As Betty came, huffing and puffing, back into the kitchen, she nodded at Edith, who tentatively reached up to pull the note from the thread.

"Unroll it, my dear, and tell me what it says," Betty urged her, casting a quick scowl towards the feathered intruder.

Betty, hopefully Gerry can find his way back in the dark! Have been called away on urgent business. One of the ponies is hurt. I don't know what savaged him, but there may be more of them out here. I'm taking him back to his herd, but I may be some time.

Save dinner! And wish me luck...

Edith had needed to focus all her effort on reading the words and keeping her mind clear as her headache threatened to return. She had scarcely finished reading it when the bird hopped across the sofa, plucked the note from her hand with its beak and passed it to Betty. The old lady nodded, as if to say she'd received such notes a hundred times before.

"It's OK, Gerry, you can go to bed, there's no need to send anything back. I'll put his dinner in the Aga. Thank you for bringing the message."

Gerry gave another loud squawk and then hopped off on to the floor.

Betty returned her gaze to Edith.

"Well, that's that. I suppose you'll just have to meet your uncle in the morning."

Edith didn't reply at first, because she was fixated on the bird. He had started to hop across the sofa, along the window ledge, to the kitchen counter – and there he was busy trying to insert himself into a grocery bag.

"Oh, that's just Gerry," Betty explained, as if it was the most ordinary thing in the world. "After he's been out in the forest with your uncle, he gets tired – so he likes to go in the bag. It's a pain because, once he's in there, it's almost impossible to remove him. He's what you might call a very stubborn old bird." She flashed Edith a smile. "Some might say they seem to hang around the place."

"Is he a toucan?" Edith asked, looking at Gerry's huge yellow beak and distinctive colouring.

Suddenly realizing he held her full attention, Gerry

gave another squawk and hopped out of the bag. It was only then she noticed that Gerry was hoping on just one leg.

"He is indeed a toucan – or a '*One*can', in Gerry's case. Your uncle met him on one of his expeditions, but ended up having to amputate his leg. Got himself caught in a glue trap, poor chap. He'd been stuck in that tree for nearly a week when he was found. Half dead and his leg rotting off." Betty paused for effect.

"Oh, you poor bird!" cried Edith, horrified.

"Yes, he was rather. Your uncle had to bring him back here to patch him up and, after that, he decided to stay. The jungle's not the easiest place to get about with one leg. He couldn't really balance on the branches, and one leg makes him fly at a funny angle. Now he's part of the fixtures here at Pilgrims. Useful for sending messages in a place with no mobile phone reception. Do make yourself acquainted." Betty gave a wry smile. "Only watch him at breakfast; you wouldn't expect it for a toucan, but he's very partial to baked beans. . ."

Edith eased herself up from the sofa and walked towards the big bird. Putting her hand out towards Gerry, she crouched down and waited. The bird, watching her intently, hopped away from his bag towards her and bowed his head for a stroke.

"My, my!" exclaimed Betty. "I've never seen him come out his bag to greet anyone, let alone do that before!"

"He's so handsome," said Edith.

Gerry gave another little squawk and, daring to come even closer, settled down on the countertop.

FIZZZZ!!!!!!!!!

It was like some invisible hand had suddenly descended and taken hold of Edith's head, squeezing it like a vice. She winced. She shrank back, her hand flying up to clutch at her temple.

"Edie, what's wrong?" In a second, Betty was on her feet, reaching over to put a hand on Edith's forehead. "You're burning up! Here, have another drink of tea, dear, it will clear the pain."

The pain was already ebbing away as Edith was guided back to the sofa, where she sank down, picked up the tea and took another sip. There must have been some magic in this tea, because its ability to clear her head was nothing short of a miracle.

"Sorry," she said. "It just came on so suddenly. I wasn't expecting it."

Betty sat at her side and took her hand. Soon, Arnold had reappeared from his hiding place beneath the table and was resting his enormous head as if in sympathy, back on Edith's lap.

Looking at Betty's concerned face, Edith said, "I don't know how to explain it. The headaches ... sometimes they just come. It's like a buzzing behind my eyes and then these sudden sharp pains..." Edith tailed off, her eyes beginning to water. Her shoulders sagged and a sense of hopelessness washed over her.

Betty gave Edith's hand a little squeeze of reassurance. "Edie, my dear, we can deal with headaches in this house. Your uncle is quite versatile, you know." Betty paused and gave Edith a wink. "People are animals too. Given half a chance, your uncle will treat anything that moves. He loves projects, even when he shouldn't!" She gave Arnold a meaningful look, and the enormous hound wagged his tail in response. "Now, come on, I'll show you to your room. You can sleep off this episode of yours."

It had been a long day, the darkness was hardening all around the cottage, and Edith had no cause to complain. Bed beckoned, and she had never been more eager to climb underneath the covers.

Betty led her through the higgledy-piggledy house, up one set of crooked stairs, down another, up a third, and through all manner of hallways and rooms – until they stood in the doorway of a small room, big enough for a single bed, a wardrobe and a bookcase upon which were crammed many dozens of old books.

"There's a hot-water bottle already in the bed," Betty explained. "And water by the bedside. There are clean clothes in the wardrobe – they mightn't be to your liking, but I'm sure I can patch up anything you need! And, Edie. . ."

Edith had already ventured inside. Now, she looked back at Betty – who smiled at her from the door. This room, Edith decided, had a sort of circus show vibe. Its walls seemed at odds with each other, the angles all wrong. And yet, it was cosy and warm and, despite its awkwardness, it made her feel safe.

"Yes, Betty?"

"There are just a couple of house rules." Betty's tone, whilst still warm, had hardened as she paused for a moment, ensuring she had Edith's absolute attention. "The first is that you must promise me that you won't venture out into the forest alone, not without one of us with you and not without Arnold by your side. And Edie. . ."

Edith froze, for Betty's eyes had taken on a strange and forbidding air. She tried to meet her gaze.

"The second is that on no account must you go into your uncle's barn – not under any circumstances. Is that understood?"

There was something dangerous about the way Betty had said the words that unnerved Edith. Until this very moment, Edith could have sworn she was the kindliest, most warm-hearted woman in existence. But now. . .

Edith gave a solemn nod.

"I promise," she said.

Then she was left alone, listening to the patter of Betty's footsteps as she beat her way back through the topsy-turvy house, wondering at this strange, remote cottage she had been packaged off to, this strange family of which she was expected to become a part, this strange room with its crooked walls, ramshackle wardrobes and tumbledown bookcases.

In bed at last, she closed her eyes and thought about her parents. Wherever they were, she hoped they were with each other. Wherever they were, she hoped they were safe.

She snuggled down, eager for sleep to come and whisk her away and for nice, soothing dreams to draw her down.

At least the hot water bottle had made the bed toasty and warm – and, for now, this was enough.

CHAPTER FOUR

*In which Edith finally catches a glimpse
of a most unusual Doctor...*

A sudden clattering wrenched Edith from sleep and she remembered where she was: in a strange house, away from anything she had ever known. She looked around to try and locate the cause of the sound that had woken her.

Perhaps it was Arnold's snoring. Sometime in the night, the great big dog had wended his way upstairs and now lay, like a sleeping guardian, across the foot of her bed, his big chest rising and falling with every breath.

But no – there was something else. The clock on the bedside table read three a.m. *It was the dead of night.*

The witching hour. Edith remembered in fairy-tale folklore that this was when devils and monsters were supposed to be at their most powerful. She rolled on to her side in an effort to get back to sleep, pushing any scary thoughts from her mind and focusing on her pillow.

Then the noise came again. It sounded almost like *hoofbeats*.

Edith had always been a curious child. An ordinary child would have crawled deeper under the covers, found some comfort in Arnold's mountainous snores, and waited until morning. But, try as she might, Edith knew that sleep was not coming back to her tonight. For some reason, she suddenly felt very awake – as if her senses had begun to work overtime.

So she climbed up and out of bed and padded across to the window. Pushing aside the pale green curtain, she gazed out at the grounds of Forest Cottage.

The gardens, hemmed in on all sides by the first trees of the rolling New Forest, were bathed in an eerie moonlight. Beyond the lawns, the dark wall of foliage was impenetrably black. As Edith stared into its depths, she gave an involuntary shiver. There was nothing out there but the wilderness. The isolation of the cottage was absolute.

Then she heard the hoofbeats again. Her eye caught

movement in the trees – and, out of a portal of blackness, appeared a figure on the back of a white horse.

Cloaked as he was in the darkness, Edith could make out little other than the fact the horseman had a pointed cap perched jauntily on top of his head. As he moved into the clearing, she could see his body seemed small and round, a piggy barrel of a man sitting astride his huge mount. The cape he wore billowed behind him and was fastened by a single clasp about his neck. The horse came to a stop in the middle of the lawn, and the man dismounted clumsily but somehow landed on his feet. He stood straight, cap undisturbed and cape unruffled. Then he walked towards his horse's head.

Reaching up, he stroked the horse's ear, and Edith watched with mounting awe as the horse – apparently doing exactly as it was told – turned and trotted past the closed doors of the barn and back into the trees.

So, Edith thought, *this must be* him.

This was the Doctor.

Soon, she heard voices coming from below. Arnold woke at the sound of the Doctor's voice and bounded out of the room. Edith hesitated, but then she crept out on to the landing and tried to remember the way Betty had led her through the cottage.

At last, she reached the top of Forest Cottage's second staircase. This higgledy-piggledy house seemed to have been built upside down, so that its stairs criss-crossed in the middle, and hidden doors led either up into attics or down into the larders. From here she could peer through the rails and see all the way below, into the entrance of the house. Down there, trying to wriggle out of his black cape while Arnold bounced excitedly around, was the Doctor.

Edith caught her breath.

An explosion of wings sounded above her head. Gerry had appeared from wherever he'd been roosting and, in a ball of feathers and claws, he plummeted over the bannisters to flap wildly around the Doctor's head.

Betty was already at the Doctor's side. By the look

of her, with an apron wrapped around her midriff, she hadn't been to bed. But perhaps she'd been dozing in an armchair, because she was rubbing the sleep out of her eyes.

"How many, Doctor?"

"Three injured, but only one of them badly. I stitched her up and left her in the care of the herd."

"A wolf, do you think?"

"Arnold would tell us if a Dire wolf had come back to these woods. He'd feel a calling, wouldn't you, boy?" The Doctor dropped down to his knees and wrestled Arnold playfully to the ground. "Something else savaged those ponies. But what have I always said are the most dangerous hunters, Betty?"

Betty looked grave. "Human beings, Doctor."

"Yes!" the Doctor cried out. "Human beings, the most terrible hunters of all! There have been vandals in our woods, Betty. Those ponies need protecting."

"But why would a person savage a pony, Doctor? Are you quite certain?"

"Animals kill other animals for food, Betty. Only human beings –" He said the words like they were the worst insult he could muster – "Only human beings kill for sport."

The Doctor rose to his feet, sliding outside of Edith's

line of sight, and was clearly walking off when Betty said, "Doctor, there's something else."

"Oh yes?"

A new silence stretched on between them.

"She's here, isn't she?" the Doctor whispered.

"Yes," Betty said, and Edith was certain she could hear a new nervousness in her voice, "Edith arrived this afternoon."

Edith heard the Doctor mutter something under his breath, but she couldn't tell what.

"What does she know?"

"Well," Betty ventured, "she knows you're a veterinarian. And she's met Arnold, and Gerry, and. . ." She paused. "I told her to stay away from the barn, Doctor. Though she saw quite enough when she wandered up the path. Winged horses, indeed!"

"I don't mean about *that!*" the Doctor groaned, and Edith saw that he was holding his head in his hands. "I mean about her parents. Is there any news of them?"

"Only what the school sent us, Doctor. They're missing somewhere in the Amazon, and the floods have cut the search parties off."

"If only Scarlett was still here. I could send her searching."

"She only had one wing, Doctor."

"For a pigeon with one wing, she could fly like an angel with that prosthesis I made for her. Why, she could fly five hundred miles in a single stretch!"

Betty paused. "There is one more thing, Doctor."

The Doctor held up his hand in protest.

"It doesn't matter. We can't have a little girl here, Betty. We've too much going on. I need to give our patients the attention they deserve. And if I'm called away... No, it won't do! This is no place for a child! Keep her out of sight until her parents get back. If it had been a place for a child, I'd have had children myself, and then ... and then..."

Edith watched as Betty wrapped her arms around the Doctor.

"Doctor, there's another expedition in the same region as her parents."

"Oh yes?"

"It's the Syndicate."

The Doctor froze at the mention of the word. Arnold gave a single miserable howl – and this set off Gerry as well, whose squawking reached a different pitch.

The Doctor sighed. "Didn't I tell them there was always a chance the Syndicate would go after them? And now ... now *I'm* to be the one cleaning up their mess, is that it? Looking after a child they've abandoned.

When I've so much to do, Betty, so much to do!"

"Doctor," Betty said, both earnest and urgent. "Her name is Edie and I think she's delightful."

The Doctor drew back. Through the bannister rail, Edith fancied she could see the dark thoughts racing through his head.

"I can't do this, Betty. *I won't.*"

"Doctor, she's *family.*"

The Doctor, who until now had seemed so genial, roared out, "That's exactly *why* I can't take her in. They'll come for her. *You* know me, Betty. You know I'm a good man. You know why."

Betty rushed back to his side. At her touch, he seemed to calm down – and here, once again, was the good-natured, genial Doctor that Edith had first seen.

"Doctor, you take in every other waif and stray. Look at this place. We can protect her. Sheba's still in the den out back. You remember when she came to us – a wild boar without a friend in the world, until there was you. And Gabriel, up there in the Tallie's oak behind the barn. How many chicks has he raised this year? Gideon and Esther – the New Forest's only pair of Giant Barn Owls – brought together, and all because of you! That's not to mention what you've done for our other residents. You've never turned away a soul in need before, and I'll be signing my resignation letter this very evening if you turn that poor girl away now. That isn't *you*, Doctor. You help creatures. And your niece needs your help more than any other creature we have ever tried to rescue. Wilma would want you to do this!"

The Doctor remained silent. His face had taken on a somewhat tortured expression at the mention of the name Wilma.

"I'm going to see the King," he said, as if unable to continue discussing his new house guest any more. "Don't wait up, Betty. You should get some rest."

"Doctor, you've been out all day. You mustn't stay up all night; you need your wits sharp! No one can keep working so hard – you must get some rest!"

"I told you, Betty. I've got too much to do. Too much! The world's too full. Too many creatures need my help." He had already stomped his feet back into his boots, snatched up his cap and fastened the cape back around his neck, when something mellowed in the Doctor and, crouching to pet Arnold, he said, "I'd love some dinner, Betty, if I might. I know I've been a frightful bore, but. . ."

"Peanut butter sandwiches, Doctor? With raspberry jam?"

The Doctor nodded, glumly. "And marshmallows, if we have any."

"I made a fresh batch only last night."

The Doctor rose up and planted a kiss on Betty's cheek. "Look after the child whilst I'm gone. Perhaps I'll meet her tomorrow. I'll think on it. I couldn't do it without you, Lady Elizabeth."

"Be on with you." She grinned. "I want to see His Majesty flying through the skies before this summer's out."

Edith heard the door shut quietly behind the Doctor and she rushed back to her room to watch him stride across the lawn. Her heart was racing. Who were the Syndicate? Why might they be going after her parents – and why might they, one day, come after her? It didn't make any sense. What didn't she know?

And who was the King her uncle was going to help fly?

From the window, she watched the Doctor slip between the doors of the barn. The lawn was once again empty and the night swallowed up its secrets.

Edith flinched as an owl hooted loudly from somewhere in the garden. A faint buzzing pricked her senses and, before a headache could take hold of her, she quickly turned to climb back into bed. She closed her eyes, trying to calm her whirring mind. A large groan emanated from nearby. Edith sat bolt upright, a sense of panic flooding through her, before she realized the true source of the sound.

Arnold had snuck back upstairs and climbed on to the bed. Now he was pretending to be in a deep slumber, his eyes clamped shut and his body sprawled over the duvet. Despite her fears and the strange goings-on, it made Edith grin in the darkness. Arnold's great big tail gave a single large, solitary wag. Within moments, she felt snuggled and warm. There was something so reassuring about the companionship of the big dog that, before she had time to worry too much about the things she'd just seen and heard, Edith found herself drifting back to sleep.

CHAPTER FIVE

In which Edie explores a private woodland study, finds hints of the world's most mysterious creatures, and the magic of the New Forest first becomes apparent...

Edith awoke to the sensation of a slobbery tongue being dragged across her face, instantly followed by a familiar pain in her head.

"Argh! Get off, Arnold!"

The big dog whined in response and Edith felt a pang of guilt.

"Sorry, it's not your fault. I didn't mean that. It's just these headaches." It was the headache, Edith realized now, that had woken her. It was like a thousand tiny voices were all in her mind, each one of them clamouring to be heard. A little while later, the pain subsided and she managed a laugh.

She leaned over to give Arnold an apologetic rub.

Pushing back the covers and climbing out of bed, Edith took a deep breath. Today was her first full day at the cottage – her first full day of staying with an uncle she hadn't even known existed and who clearly wished that she had never been sent there.

As she hurried along the landing, the floorboards creaking underneath her feet, her eyes were drawn to a series of photographs along the wall that she hadn't noticed the night before. In one picture he was riding on the back of a great African elephant. In another, he had his arms around a baby giraffe. In yet another, he was with a train of camels, trekking across a desert. There was a picture of a much younger Doctor standing on the prow of a ship, with the great tentacles of some giant squid or octopus reaching up to take fish out of his hands. In the last, he was sitting on a mountaintop with what looked to be a baby crocodile in his arms.

At the top of the creaking old staircase, another headache began to wash over her. She looked down, and saw a pair of mice scurrying along the skirting board and vanishing into one of the walls. After they had gone, her headache seemed to go with them.

She moved down the stairs, wondering if the Doctor would be in the cottage. She desperately clung to the hope that she could win him round – that he wouldn't think of her as an intruder, or an annoyance. He was her uncle, after all. Surely that had to count for something.

As she pushed through the door into the huge kitchen, her heart bounded in her chest – but the room was completely empty.

Edith looked around. A tall thermos flask, a biscuit tin full of cookies, and a handwritten note sat on top of the kitchen table.

Morning, Edie!

Gone shopping with Francis.
Special tea in the flask, cookies in the tin.
Please feed the chickens behind the cottage.
Corn in the feed bin – Arnold will show you.
Back lunchtime

Love Betty x
P.S. Don't go in the barn!!!!!!!!!!

Edith heard the padding of giant paws around her and turned to see that Arnold had followed her into the room, his great tongue lolling.

"They've left me alone, Arnold," she said.

Arnold let out a single doleful bark.

"You're right; not *alone* exactly." She decided it was a good sign. It meant that they trusted her. It meant that, no matter how busy and fearful the Doctor had been last night – and what exactly *had* been savaging those ponies out in the woods? – the bonds of family held tight. The Doctor wasn't sending her away.

"Not yet, at least," said Edith aloud.

Arnold gave a little whine.

"What?"

The big dog moved his head slightly, with an unmistakable glance at the cookies, and then banged the wall with a quick beat of his tail.

"I think you're trying to take advantage because I'm new!"

Edith pulled out a cookie from the tin, broke it in half and tossed a piece to Arnold, who swallowed it in a single gulp.

With a bemused shake of her head, she poured herself a cup of the tea from the thermos and drank, admiring the strange swirls before swigging it down.

As she drank it, a warm feeling flooded her body and her head felt calmer, and she found herself feeling completely refreshed. All of those thousand voices, pulsing at her from the back of her brain, seemed to have been driven off too.

"Right," she said, "I'll give you another cookie, Arnold, but the deal is that you help me feed the chickens and show me where I'm supposed to go."

Arnold beat his tail twice and, in that moment, the deal was done.

Stepping out into the grounds of Forest Cottage in the daytime, Edith was filled with wonder. It was the height of summer and the smells of nature were in the air.

Edith would have liked to have pottered around, taking in the kitchen gardens and the little orchard where apple, pear and plum trees were in full blossom, but Arnold had other ideas As soon as they were out of the cottage, he was off.

"Arnold!" she called, as she watched him lolloping through the kitchen garden to the edge of the forest beyond. "Wait!"

Edith hurried after him as the big dog maintained a steady lope, making a beeline for the woods on the other side of the forbidden barn. As they passed behind it, Edith's eyes widened in amazement. Here, stretching into semi-circular glades infringing on the edge of the forest, were a series of paddocks and other enclosures. One contained a couple of pigs happily snuffling in a wallow; another a small herd of pygmy goats who watched with bemused expressions as they trotted past. Donkeys, cows, even a small herd of alpacas, all lived in the gardens – and, just when Edith thought there couldn't be any more farmyard animals squeezed into one place, a gaggle of geese waddled in front of Arnold. One of them gave a big hiss, causing the huge dog to pause – perhaps even a little nervously – as they passed by.

As they finally headed under the dappled mosaic of leaves, Edith could see they were following a well-trodden footpath that wove its way into the woodland, presumably down to the large hedge which bordered the property.

They hadn't gone far on this track before Arnold stopped and sniffed the ground. His tail wagged a few more times and then, with a quick glance back at Edith, he veered off the path, bounding through a dense clump of bushes.

Fighting the undergrowth, Edith wondered where on earth they were going and what she was doing. Then a small clearing appeared and Edith laughed as she spotted small russet brown creatures darting about amongst the trees.

"The chickens! You've taken me straight to the chickens!"

Arnold gave a bark and promptly flopped down in a patch of sunlight, watching as Edith walked towards them.

Chickens, as you may know, are curious creatures. They are amongst some of the most inquisitive animals you are ever likely to meet. Within moments, Edith was surrounded by their feathery little bodies. Some of the birds began harmlessly pecking at her shoes, their beaks darting against the sparkles. Before she knew it, about twenty chickens had appeared in the clearing, all happily clustering around her. The sound of contented squawks and clucks filled the clearing.

Edith spotted a big metallic bin, loosely attached to an oak sapling by a threadbare bit of old rope. Realizing it must be the chicken feed, she walked over to it, lifted the heavy lid and scooped out handfuls of bright yellow corn, scattering it liberally on the ground.

The chickens were delighted. The clucking increased to a frenzy as they scampered amongst the undergrowth, furiously pecking at the bits of yellow which Edith had spread around. Edith marvelled as the noise levels reached fever pitch.

Then an agonizing bolt of pain lanced through her head. Edith couldn't stop herself crying out and everything went black.

She wasn't sure when she came around. The chickens had gone and the clearing was empty, all except for Arnold who lay protectively beside her, his big amber eyes watching her.

As she lifted herself, Arnold gave a soft whine. The pain in Edith's head momentarily intensified again, but by the time she had raised herself to a sitting position, it was starting to fade.

"Thank you for not leaving me," she said quietly, reaching out to rest a hand on the dog's soft brown fur.

Arnold lowered his head and, using his nose, nudged the thermos flask which had fallen on to the ground.

"You want me to have a drink?" She shrugged. "Perhaps you're right. Let's see if Betty's tea can work its magic again."

Edith grasped at the flask groggily and managed to pour herself half a cup. As she drank, it was like a wet blanket had been lifted off her head and shoulders.

"Oh, Arnold, what am I going to do?" Edith said miserably.

"Drink more."

The voice seemed to explode in her head. Edith gave an involuntary gasp.

She looked around suddenly. *Where had that voice come from?*

"Who's there?"

Silence. Not even a rustle from the bushes.

"Drink mo. . ."

This time, the voice tailed off and Arnold whined.

Edith got to her feet and looked around. Peering through the bushes, she thought she could see movement.

Slowly, she edged in the direction of the disturbance.

"Hello?" she called again. "Hello?"

An explosion of wings sounded in the branches above her. Something of vibrant vermillion plumage – certainly no chicken, nor any other bird Edith might have expected to see in an English woodland – rocketed out of the branches and took to the skies. For a second, another headache flared; then, as quickly as it had appeared, it was gone.

For the first time, Edith saw another trail leading into the woodland beyond the clearing. There were other structures here – old coops and wooden houses, metal frames webbed with chicken wire, around which nettles and thistles had grown up. She was about to take a step closer when she heard Arnold whimpering behind her.

He seemed to want to go home.

"Come o. . ."

There was that voice again.

She turned on the spot and took three big strides under the trees, looking for a sign of someone nearby. Instead, she found a clearing. Three gigantic tree stumps remained in the middle of the clearing, and threaded through each were enormous metal chains, each with great iron collars at their ends.

Edith paused. What did the Doctor need big chains and collars like this for? They wouldn't have seemed out of place in some medieval dungeon. A terrible shiver moved up her spine.

She only stopped shivering when Arnold appeared at her side. The dog looked positively miserable to have followed Edith here, but his loyalty to her was obviously much greater than his fear. He rolled up against her, as if he might lead her back.

Edith dropped to her knees and cuddled him.

"What is this place, Arnold?"

He barked, only once.

Then she looked up and saw the hut through the trees.

Nestled amongst the trees on the far side of the clearing was a small stone building, with a roof of birch thatch and a stone table outside. Alone among all the enclosures in this part of the forest, the house looked as if it might still be in use. Purple curtains were hanging in the windows, and a teapot and cup were sitting on the stone table.

Edith picked her way, carefully, through the great metal chains and collars until she reached the stone building and could peer in at the windows.

She couldn't see much; the natural light of the woodland was so soft that all she could really see were motes of dust turning in the air.

Her eyes turned to the door.

Arnold had followed her and then lain down, his paws seemingly trying to cover his eyes, and set up a muted whimper.

Edith's hand hovered over the handle. She hesitated. Betty hadn't mentioned anything about not entering any other buildings.

Deciding to take one quick peek, Edith poked her head inside and gasped.

It was amazing. Floor to ceiling, books spilled out, many two deep on the shelves, jutting out into the room, pressing forward as if hungry to be pulled out and read. Edith couldn't help herself. Walking forward, with Arnold close behind, the door swung shut, and she turned to switch on the light.

It was a much larger space than it had looked from the outside, completely lined with shelves and crammed with books, except for one section of wall that held a gigantic map of the world. The map had different coloured flags stuck all over it. A cluster of black flags were ominously dotted around the north-west corner of Brazil, and Edith stepped closer to peer at the small, white label stuck on to each one. They each seemed to have a date written on them.

Edith's eyes roamed up and down the walls. Marvelling at the sheer number of leather-bound books, the first thing she noticed was their age. They were all seemingly ancient. Glancing at some of the titles, she realized that they were all books about veterinary medicine, covering every type of creature she could conceivably imagine.

Under a section entitled *Lagomorphs*, Edith could see books ranging from *Nutrition of the Colombian Basin Pygmy Rabbit* to *Behavioural traits of the Belgian Hare*. Moving over to a bookcase labelled *Equids*, Edith paused by a selection of papers kept in a Perspex box.

It had a label on it – the *Art of Horsemanship by Xenophon* ~*350BC*. The pages looked like they were made of a strange material and they were covered in symbols she didn't recognize. Edith froze as she worked out the date. Could they really be two thousand years old?

She scanned down the shelves. Texts on donkeys, zebras and even one on miniature Shetland ponies sat next to ones on creatures called "Protorohippus", "Hipparion", and creatures that – by the pictures on the book covers – looked even more outlandish than their names. The books on equids were extensive and filled about three entire bookcases. They also seemed dated throughout the centuries.

"You ... shouldn't ... be ... here!"

The voice was almost on top of her. She turned around on the spot, but couldn't see a thing. Unlike earlier, now she was so absorbed in the incredible books that filled the room, she barely paid the voice any attention.

"Arnold," she whispered, "look."

Her eyes had landed on one book, which seemed to stick out even more prominently than the others. As she reached for it, the voice that had sounded in her head came again – but this time, there weren't any words, only a long, exasperated sigh.

She lifted the book from the shelf:

A Natural History of the Pegasus

by Ted Fitzgibbon

The picture on the cover was beautiful: a magnificent white horse, with wings spread wide as it soared over a snow-encrusted mountaintop.

Edith read the back cover:

> Edmund "Ted" Fitzgibbon's travelogue is the classic text on the regal pegasi. Fitzgibbon devoted his life to the study of these rare and wonderful creatures in their natural habitat, spending three summers living with a herd in the French Dordogne, and developing the specialist veterinary knowledge on which the profession has since then relied.
>
> Fitzgibbon's other classic text on magical husbandry, One Year in the Forest, relates his seasons spent on the trail of the last English unicorn...

Edith looked up. Her eyes flashed up and down the shelves. There it was: *One Year in the Forest,* and on its cover a resplendent picture of the sort of unicorn she'd only ever seen in the pages of her children's books.

She spun around.

Now that she was looking for them, she spotted them everywhere. *Sea Serpents in the South Seas* by Apophis Weatherbottom. *The Medical History of the South Asian Wyvern* by Dr Thyrus Singh. *The Common Ailments of the Lesser Spotted Chinese Dragon* by Dr Xiùyīng Lóng.

"Arnold," she said, "this is the Doctor's study, isn't it? But these books, they're not. . ."

She was going to say "real" – but here they were, all around her. She was going to say "factual" – but then she remembered the barn, and the winged horse she'd seen when she stumbled in here last night. What if it wasn't really a hallucination after all? She scurried up and down the shelves, finding more books with outlandish titles. She'd heard of gryphons before – great big beasts, half lion and half eagle – but what a manticore was, what a hydra was, what a cockatrice or minotaur or roc was, she wasn't sure.

"Look, Arnold. Titiana de Forte's *Treatise on Fairies*. But there's no such thing as a fairy, is there?"

She came, at last, to a desk set against the bookshelves at the deep end of the study. There were yet more bookshelves, where titles ranged from a medical encyclopaedia on the common ailments of seahorses, to a big thick book with the word *Krakens* in gold thread on its leather cover. She took in the contents of her uncle's desk.

It had the feeling of a place of solitude, where someone could come and think in peace and quiet. Its surface was piled high with drawings and diagrams and, like a moth to flame, Edith found herself drawn towards them, unable to resist a quick look at the bright colours and intricate shapes that seemed to writhe on the paper as if alive. Snow dragons danced across one page, a mermaid adorned another. A large horn stored in a tall glass case was perched at the far end of the desk, and she tore her gaze away from the drawings to study it. It was almost like an elephant tusk – but upright and pointed, with spiral indents circling towards its tip. She bent down to look more closely, but as she did so, her arm brushed a stack of paper and, with a sudden thump, a large pile of documents spilled across the floor.

Quickly, Edith dropped to her knees and started to scoop them up, hurriedly trying to get them into some sort of orderly shape and stack them back on the table. It was then that her eyes landed on a map of South America. It had annotated markings along a thick line of blue. The Amazon. That was where her parents had gone missing. Had her uncle been there or was he keeping notes on their travels? She stared for a moment at the annotated markings, but she couldn't make any sense of them.

She paused as her hands felt a glossy texture. Photographs were mixed in between the pages. She didn't want to pry amongst her uncle's things but she couldn't help gazing at a picture of the same lady whose photo was framed above the mantelpiece in the kitchen.

Edith studied the face: blue eyes glimmering with intelligence, soft features and shoulder-length blonde hair. The woman appeared both pretty and interesting. There were more photos in the pile. The lady featured in nearly all of them. She was smiling in every single picture, radiating a warmth palpable even from a photograph. Some had been taken outdoors with spectacular scenery as a backdrop. Mountains, snow, crystal-clear sky. She looked like the sort of person who would be fun to be with. The sort of person who would have been a lovely aunt to have.

It was the last picture that held her attention. In this one, the woman was sitting at a table surrounded by people. It must have been someone's birthday party because a brightly decorated cake sat on the table with a large pink candle perched at a lopsided angle on its top, much to the evident amusement of all the people there. But it wasn't the candle nor the lady who drew Edith's attention. Her uncle was there, in his hat and his cloak, but so were her mother and father – only they looked so much younger. Another lady was there too – a bit older than the others. It was Betty.

Edith stared at the picture, searching for a date or some clue as to when and where it was taken. Nothing obvious jumped out at her. Betty looked as if the picture had been taken about ten years ago. She wasn't wearing glasses and her gaze wasn't square on with the camera; she was looking at something behind the lens, but Edith couldn't work out what. A small blue flower was tucked into her top pocket, bright against the pale yellow dress she was wearing.

Arnold's sudden bark made Edith jump. Pulling herself together, and knowing she shouldn't be poking around, she quickly stacked the papers back on to the desk. The photograph lay on top and, with a final look at it, she left the building.

"Sorry, Arnold," she said, as they reached the clearing with the giant chains. "Let's get back..."

CHAPTER SIX

*In which Edie breaks the rules and
finally ventures behind the big barn
doors, while the mystery of her headaches
takes an unexpected twist...*

The chair at the head of the table sat empty. Betty piled
Edith's plate high with pie and potatoes and then sat
down next to Francis. They faced Edith as they picked
up their cutlery, pointedly ignoring the absence of the
Doctor.

All day long, the things she'd seen in his woodland
study had been fizzing and buzzing around her head.
Unicorns and sea serpents, minotaur and gryphons –
she would have been able to ignore them all, if it wasn't

for that *thing* she'd seen in the barn when she had first arrived. She hadn't been supposed to see that. She was certain of it now. Betty had forbidden her from going anywhere near the barn. There were secrets at Forest Cottage with which she wasn't to be trusted.

Since Betty and Francis had returned from the village shops, she'd followed them up and down the grounds of Forest Cottage – but, of her uncle, there hadn't been a sign. Francis had let her feed Zoya, the old donkey who'd been rescued from a rural Eritrean village in the aftermath of a local war. He'd taken her to the aviaries set deep into the woodland, where the Doctor was rearing two baby bald eagles, Robyn and Damon, who'd each been abandoned by their mothers. She'd seen wild boar and lynxes, wild ponies and a warren of diseased rabbits that the Doctor was treating with specially medicated carrots. But now that she'd been inside her uncle's study, she got the feeling that their tour had been carefully orchestrated, so that she saw only what she was *permitted* to see.

And her uncle, it seemed, was as much of a secret as whatever was really living in that barn.

"Will I meet my uncle tonight?" Edith asked, for what must have been the seventeenth time.

"I don't know, my dear," Betty said. "He's a very busy man."

When Betty had returned from the shops and Edith had asked about her uncle, she'd said, "I believe he's running some errands." When Edith had come back from mucking out the donkey with Francis and asked again, Betty had said, "Gerry came in with an urgent message. He's had to go to one of the local farms." From then on, the explanations got even more outlandish. "A car hit a tree up the road somewhere. They're saying they saw wolves. Your uncle's gone to check it out." And, "He's gone out to the aviary to send a letter, my dear" – as if that made *any* sense at all.

Edith supposed she would find out soon enough. For now, with Arnold lying on her feet under the table, slobbering all over her trainers, she decided to play along.

"Does my uncle not like computers?" Edith asked, fishing for more information about her elusive relative.

Francis shook his head slowly, shrugging his massive shoulders with an exaggerated sigh.

"The Doctor doesn't trust anything that he can't treat," Francis said. "Give him a lapwing or a Bengal tiger any day. But a computer. . ."

It was on the tip of Edith's tongue to ask about what *other* kinds of animals the Doctor might have to treat – what was in the barn, what those enormous chains in the woodland might be used for, why her uncle had a collection of books about the most extraordinary things – things that weren't even *real* – but she heard Arnold give a whimper from under the table, as if he was reading her thoughts, and decided it was better to stay silent. She'd barely been in the house twenty-four hours. Betty hadn't said she couldn't explore that particular little building, but still, if they thought she'd *already* abused their trust by snooping around somewhere that was supposed to be private – well, she didn't like to think about what might happen next. The summer holidays were long, and St Margot Montefiore's was a very long way away.

A flash of pain coursed through the side of her head. She dropped her fork to rub at her temple and Betty reached for the teapot on the kitchen counter.

"Some more of my tea, I think."

"What *is* this tea, Betty?" Edith said gratefully. "When Arnold and I were out feeding the chickens today, I nearly fainted away. But one drink of this tea and I felt better."

"Oh," Betty said innocently. "I'm glad to hear that, dear." Her eyes were shining with a little twinkle of amusement as she spoke. "I've seen headaches like yours before."

There was another mystery in this, though what it

might be, Edith could not say. She shifted slightly in her seat, as the tea worked its miracles, restoring her to herself.

"There's something else, Betty," Edith ventured. She hadn't known she was going to say it but, now that the opportunity presented itself, she felt she had to. "When I drank the tea earlier, I started . . . imagining voices."

Francis banged his fist on the table, scattering peas. Gerry leapt down from his shoulder and, taking his chance, began gobbling up as many peas as he could find.

Betty fixed him with a stern glare and Francis said, "Excuse me, I do believe it's time to put Gerry to bed."

It took Francis a while to extricate himself from his seat, but once he had done so, he lifted his plate from the table with surprising gentleness and carried it over to the sink, before helping Gerry slip – with his belly now full of peas – into his bag. "It was nice to have dinner with you, Edie," he said, with a dainty little bow. Then, with a beam and a wave, he left.

"Did I say something wrong, Betty?" Edith ventured, once they were alone.

Arnold popped his head out from under the table and lapped at her hand in solidarity.

But, before Betty could answer, footsteps sounded loudly in the corridor outside the kitchen door. Arnold's tail started beating and he loped across the kitchen to greet the door as it opened.

There, silhouetted by the light in the hallway, and covered with grime from the woodland, loomed the Doctor. His face looked screwed-up this time, as if he'd spent the day engaged in a particularly thorny problem. His cape was pockmarked with leaves and catkins from his wandering in the forest – and, if Edith was not very much mistaken, his hands were still encrusted with the blood of whichever animal he'd been tending.

"I will be taking dinner in my study. Away from *prying* eyes." The words sounded short, each one clipped and succinct as he spoke. His voice was clear, quiet and controlled, but Edith couldn't make out his expression in the dark. "Francis may bring it."

"He's putting Gerry to bed," Betty replied, "but I'll be across shortly."

The door swung shut and the footsteps faded away as the Doctor headed back into the night.

In the kitchen, there was silence, until, finally, Edith asked, "Betty, why is my uncle upset that I'm here?"

Betty was busying herself, loading up a plate with pie and mash and covering it with tinfoil to keep warm. "It's not your fault, my dear. Your uncle is not always great with people he doesn't know."

"But he hasn't even met me."

"And when he does, he will like you very much. He just needs a little time to adjust. Well, my dear," she said, "I should really be taking the Doctor his dinner. And you've had a long day too. You could do with another good night's sleep."

A good night's sleep would have been a miracle. Even a bad night's sleep would have done. But, as soon as Edith's head hit the pillow, she knew it was going to be one of *those* nights.

A hundred thoughts from the day kept buzzing inside her head: there were so many new sounds and colours, new ideas and notions, that it was little wonder her headache kept coming back with a vengeance. Whenever she closed her eyes, she found herself back in the Doctor's woodland study, looking at the magnificent spiral horn that had stood, pride of place, upon his desk. Or she remembered the feeling that overcame her as she fainted clean away, the clucking of the chickens magnified in her mind. There was something else bothering her as well. It was the look on the Doctor's face as he stood in the kitchen doorway. And those four words: *away from prying eyes*. Was it possible, she wondered, that he'd *seen* her?

The old grandfather clock out on the landing tolled out the midnight hour, and still Edith couldn't get to sleep. She lay there a little longer, tossing and turning. Obviously, she was keeping Arnold awake too. He'd lumbered into the bedroom sometime after she'd turned out the lights and settled at the end of the bed. His head lifted every time she turned.

Perhaps, she thought, it was the summer heat. It was warm and sticky in the bedroom, so she went over to the window and opened it up – but the rush of sounds from the woodland at night just made her headache worse. Owls were hooting and foxes were rustling; bats were shrieking, somewhere up above. It only seemed to intensify the crackling sensation that ran across the sides of her head.

If only there was a television, she thought, something to distract her and lull her to sleep. A mobile phone would have been perfect, but she was about the only girl in her entire school not to own one, thanks to the headmistress declaring such a device could trigger one of her "episodes", and banning her from having one. A wireless radio, like her father liked to play. Or an old record player, like the one her mother used to play her favourite songs. She would have liked to listen to one of her mother's favourite singers right now.

Even a book would have done it. Edith had left most of her books at school – but, she remembered, now, there was a shelf in this room.

Finally, she reached out and pulled the cord for the light.

The naked bulb hanging from the ceiling flickered. A flurry of tiny silver moths lifted from the walls and began to circle it.

"Sorry, Arnold," she said, and swung her legs out of bed. She gripped her head by the temples and moaned.

"It's these headaches. I didn't think it was possible, but they're worse out here." She reached with trembling hand for the flask of tea by the bedside and took a sip; immediately, she felt the pressure recede. "But I can't drink this tea all my life, Arnold, can I?" she whispered, getting down on her hands and knees and crawling over to the bookcase by the furthest wall. Soon, Arnold had joined her there too, eager to be fussed. "I can't go through life with a flask of tea in one hand." She stood up and began to browse the shelves, but there was nothing quite as extraordinary as *The Natural History of the Pegasus*, or *Common Ailments of the Lesser Spotted Chinese Dragon* here. Just old adventure stories and travelogues – one explorer's journey into the Nepalese Himalayas, another's sojourn down the Ganges by coracle. There was a slim volume on early explorers to the Amazon, and Edith decided this would do. It would be good to learn a little about the place her parents were.

She had only just settled back on the bed, Arnold lifting himself up and flopping by her side with a contented grumble, when a crackle of pain sparked across her temples – and out of its echo, like a radio station being tuned in, came a tiny, squeaking voice.

"... *must get to the light ... the light ... come on everyone ... there's a light!*"

Edith's eyes darted around the room – but there was nobody there.

"Arnold?" she ventured. "Did you hear that?"

"... *almost there ... light ... gotta get to the light...*"

"... *ooh! That's some good light! I love this light!*"

"*Let me at it! Let me at it!*"

There was no doubt about it now. Those were distinct voices – at least three of them, maybe four. Edith dropped her book and put her arms around Arnold instead.

Suddenly, another voice joined the chorus:

"*Boys, boys, boys, calm down! You're acting like larvae! It's a LIGHT BULB!*"

Edith's eyes flashed to the light bulb dangling down from the old rafter. The little silver moths were still dancing around it, getting close, then fluttering away again, drawn by its light and repelled by its heat.

The most extraordinary idea entered her mind. But it *couldn't* be. It just *couldn't*. . .

It would be even more fanciful than those books in her uncle's study!

The voices continued to spill over each other, and then crashed together in an almighty blur of noise.

Suddenly, it was as if there were a thousand different voices at once. The chorus they made clouded Edith's every thought. It filled her mind. And now the pressure was back behind her eyes. The headache returning – more fiercely than ever before.

"What's going on?" Edith spoke aloud. She realized she'd been clinging on to Arnold too hard, and now she clambered backwards, cringing into the corner of the room.

Still, the moths danced up above.

On the bed, Arnold opened his droopy eyes.

The big dog raised his head looking at her expectantly.

"Drink more tea."

It was a different voice – deep and grumbly, but warm and familiar at the same time. Somehow, even though she knew she must be going mad, that voice steadied her.

She poured another cup of tea and lifted it to her lips.

As the headache faded, the deep, familiar voice returned:

"Not too much! There, there, there – that's it! That's perfect!"

Still shaking, Edith set down the flask. With her eyes wide, she scanned every inch of the bedroom.

On the bed, Arnold had stood up. His tail was wagging wildly and he had fixed her with his eyes.

"Arnold?" she stammered.

"Can you hear me?"

She could. Whoever it was, the voice was right there, in her head – as if it hadn't been spoken at all, but just plopped down into her consciousness. Her eyes roamed the room, searching out whoever it belonged to – but there was no denying it any longer; her eyes fell back upon Arnold.

Surely not.

Edith was about to raise the cup to her lips and take another sip, when one of the silver moths flickered past her eyeline, returning to the light bulb above.

"Light . . . lllliiiiiigggghhhhhtttttttt . . . ooowwww hottttt!!!!"

The words forced themselves into Edith's head and her mouth dropped open as she watched the moth bash against the light bulb.

"Arnold – what's going on?"

Edith looked at the dog.

"You can hear me, can't you?"

Edith shook herself then, and not trusting herself to speak, she nodded.

"*Well,*" the voice that was Arnold said, "*this will make things easier! Now, can you turn off the light so we can get some sleep? Those moths up there are driving me crackers.*"

Edith's eyes flashed back to the moths orbiting the light bulb. She tried to focus on the shrill little voices coming from up there.

"*Ooh, I do like this light!*"

"*Isn't it nice and yellow?*"

"*Lovely and bright!*"

"*I want to marry this light!*"

"*Marry it? No – you've got to share!*"

"*I don't care. I love this light and that's all there is. . .*"

Edith shook her head. "Arnold?" she dared to say. "C-can you u-understand me?"

Arnold's big jowly face cocked to one side, and his big shoulders shrugged.

"*Speak with your mind, Edie, not your voice. This skill you have, most humans won't understand it.*"

Edith's mind reeled. *Strange?* she thought. *It isn't just strange. It's mad. I'm mad!*

"*I heard that,*" came Arnold's voice, straight into her head. Then, with a consoling whimper, Arnold flopped off the bed and lapped at her hand.

"*You aren't mad, Edie. You're a polyglot.*"

"A polywhat?"

Arnold looked at her expectantly. This time, instead of saying the words out loud, Edith forced herself to *think* the question.

"*A polyglot,*" said Arnold. "*A telepathic polyglot, to be precise.*"

What does that even mean? Edith thought.

Moments later, Arnold's words popped into her mind. It was the most peculiar sensation, like bubbles bursting behind her eyes – and words pouring out of the soap suds left behind.

"*Polyglot. Poly Glot. It's one of those old human languages. Ancient Greek, I think. It means 'many tongues'.*"

Edith clapped her hands to her mouth.

"*Not like that!*" Arnold laughed. "*It means languages. You have a gift for them. You'll be able to speak to almost any animal, I should think – just using your mind. Not that you'll want to speak to most of them, I expect. Take those moths up there – chattering, chattering, chattering all night long! And have they anything interesting to say? NO! It's all 'ooh, I love this light' this, and 'I want to marry this light' that. And the houseflies . . . just don't go chin-wagging with a housefly, if you can help it. Or an ant! They're the most frightful bores.*"

"Arnold!"

"It's really not so bad. You don't have to be frightened."

"Don't I?" Edith thought, screwing her face up as she tried to make the words heard.

"Betty must have suspected it, at least. She has some experience in matters like this. And the Doctor. . ."

"My uncle?"

Arnold shook his big slobbery jowls. *"The Doctor has his own problems, I should think. Edie, don't look so sad! This is a gift! Something to treasure! And at least it explains those headaches of yours. That has to be a relief."*

Edith was getting used to the idea of speaking using her mind now, but the rest of it was still too discombobulating to be true. Arnold lay down, making a space on the bed as if she might want to sit down next to him. Cautiously, she did.

Arnold dropped his head in her lap once more. *"I'm still just Arnold,"* he said, *"only, now, I can tell you when I want an extra sausage."*

Edith looked at Arnold for a moment, her mind whirring.

"It was you who spoke to me when I came round after fainting with the chickens, wasn't it?"

Arnold didn't reply; he just gave a solid beat of his tail and lay his head back down on the bed.

"Light, oh lovely, lovely light! How I love you, lovely light! Love your lovelies, lovely light!"

Arnold rolled his eyes and put his paws over his eyes. Edith reached out and turned off the light.

"The light! The light!" a heartbroken moth exclaimed.

"It's the end of the world!" another one screamed.

"Save us!"

On the bed, Edith and Arnold sat in silence. As tempted as she was to drink more of the tea – knowing, now, that it might silence the voices for a little while – Edith resisted. Instead, she focused on her breathing, tried to calm herself, tried to understand what she had just been told.

"Arnold," she whispered, *"will I hear every animal?"*

"You'll need to train your mind," Arnold said. *"And do you know the best time to train your mind?"*

Edith shook her head.

"After a good night's sleep!" Arnold replied. *"And a nice big plate of sausages!"*

Arnold rolled over – but there was no way Edith was going to be able to sleep. Not now. She picked herself up, crossed back to the bookshelf and opened the window just above.

All the noises of night rushed in again. She heard an owl hooting, somewhere in the trees. She heard the rustling and crackling of branches on the forest floor. She narrowed her eyes, tried to focus – and then, instead of hooting and crackling, the whole of the New Forest night was filled with voices.

They came in a dozen different forms. Some were light and feathery. Others were whispers. Yet another was a kind of guttural growl.

"They always leave the bins out on a Sunday night at Forest Cottage," said a voice lurking in the shadows at the edge of the woodland. *"Come on, I'll show you!"*

"There's potato peelings in the compost heap!"

"I see you, little mouse," said a voice, soaring somewhere above. *"That's my dinner sorted, that is! The chicks are gonna be SO HAPPY!"*

Edith smiled, wider than ever. It was the most freeing sensation. With every single voice she picked out, the headache still buzzing behind her eyes faded a little further into the distance.

"An owl," she whispered in wonder. "I think I heard an owl. And foxes, right there! Coming to raid the cottage bins!"

She was so busy marvelling at the things she could hear that she didn't notice, at first, when the doors of the big barn opened, spilling bright yellow lamplight out on to the grassy expanse. She only looked that way when she saw movement.

Then her uncle came out of the big double doors, bounding across the grass to the kitchen and then moments later returned carrying two large jugs and disappeared through the entrance.

A tingling sensation spread over her body, almost as if some sort of electrical charge was pricking her senses. The hum in her head felt louder. It was strange.

"IT'S THE BASE OF MY WING! SURELY YOU CAN SEE THAT?" The voice was deafening. It had a regal air to it – like she imagined kings and queens spoke to their subjects. And the tone was certainly superior – this animal sounded as if it was completely exasperated with whoever it was speaking to. As Arnold had been with the dancing moths.

"HOW CAN YOU CALL YOURSELF A VET?" it was saying. *"BY THE WINGED KINGS OF OLD! STOP MESSING WITH MY FORELOCKS! IT'S THE BASE OF MY WING! AN INFECTION IS SETTING IN! IF YOU DON'T ACT FAST, I MIGHT NEVER FLY AGAIN!"*

Edith looked down. The voice was coming from the barn.

"LOOK UP, MY GOOD MAN! LOOK UP! OH, DOCTOR, YOU'VE BEEN SUCH A FRIEND IN THE PAST – A MOST LOYAL AND TRUSTED SERVANT

OF MY HERD! MY HERD NEED ME. DOCTOR, LOOK UP!"

Edith looked over her shoulder. *"Arnold, are you awake?"*

Nothing. The soft sound of Arnold snoring gently rose from the bed.

Edith thought hard about what to do. She had been told not to go into the barn under any circumstances. But someone, *something,* needed her help. She screwed her eyes up, debating her choices. Bed or barn...

On tiptoe, Edith moved over to her door and opened it. The hall was dark and deathly quiet. She squinted into the gloom. All along the hall, the pictures from the Doctor's various adventures gazed down at her. After midnight, having seen what she'd seen in the woodland study today, they seemed different somehow – as if they *meant* more. The eye of a giant eagle-like creature, with resplendent golden plumage, caught her eye. But the words of the beast in the barn were still buzzing in her mind. She hurried on. The stairs at the end of the hall creaked a little as she carefully walked down them. A light had been left on in the hallway below and she spotted a little mouse that poked its head out of the hall and said, *"Where are you off to? It's after your bedtime!"* then quickly scurried off.

Soon, Edith found herself outside the big back door. She'd come this far. With a gulp for courage, Edith swung it open and walked out into the garden.

So many voices in the night. She even heard one directly under her feet – *"Little human footprints, coming this way!"* – and wondered if it was some burrowing mole, or perhaps an earthworm. The shrieking, chittering voices of bats turned overhead. The tiny, snuffling voice of a hedgehog – *"Quick, here one comes, get into a ball!"* – came from somewhere in the darkness.

Edith stood alone, in the middle of the grassy expanse, with the stars wheeling overhead, and took a deep breath. She'd only been here two nights. By rights, she ought to be keeping herself to herself, doing everything she could to make sure they didn't send her packing. But she could still hear that big, regal voice from behind the barn doors.

"OH, HEAVEN FORFEND, GOOD DOCTOR, STOP LISTENING TO MY BREATHING! IT'S THE BASE OF MY WING! CAN'T YOU SEE?"

The moment she crossed the lawn and went into the barn, there would be no hiding, no pretending she had just wandered in by accident. She would come face to face with her uncle . . . and whatever creature was talking to her in her head.

It was the desperation in the animal's voice that made up her mind. There was such urgency, and such pain as well. And if her uncle sent her away, well, she would rather that than leave this animal to suffer.

"IT WON'T HEAL IF YOU DON'T TREAT THE WOUND AND BANDAGE MY WING IN THE CORRECT POSITION! THE INFECTION WILL SPREAD! I MIGHT NEVER FLY AGAIN! DOCTOR, YOU'RE TAKING ON TOO MUCH! YOU SHOULD BE ABLE TO SEE THIS FOR WHAT IT IS. HELP ME, DOCTOR. HELP ME, PLEASE!"

Edith stole across the grass and opened the doors.

CHAPTER SEVEN

*In which Edith gets her very first audience
with the Doctor and meets an aged, unruly
old King – who just might need her help...*

Edith had imagined that, upon opening the doors, she
would come face to face with the Doctor himself – but
there, standing before her, were none other than Francis
and Betty. When they saw Edith, Betty's eyes almost
popped and Francis's face was etched with concern.

"Edie, my dear, what are you..."

They were standing in a kind of reception hall, with
wood-panelled passages branching off into different
enclosures of the enormous barn. From one of them,
there came the Doctor's booming voice.

"THIS BARN IS SECRET! It is where my very sick and special patients stay. It's where they receive their treatment and have a chance to rest and recover. They must have peace and *sanctuary*. Was it not made explicitly clear that you were NOT TO COME INTO MY BARN?"

The Doctor came barrelling towards her from out of a stall, his eyes flashing.

"I knew it! I knew she couldn't be trusted, Betty. I said as much. She is too curious! This is why visitors are forbidden. They simply cannot be trusted!"

Edith's eyes welled with tears. She couldn't help it. Everything seemed to come crashing down on her shoulders. Her parents missing, the strangeness of her headaches, the loneliness of not having any friends or family to turn to, no one to guide her through this dark time. And now her worst fears had been realized. Her uncle was going to throw her out.

"She'll have to go, Betty! Take her back to the house. We'll need to find another solution. She cannot be allowed to enter the barn. She's brought it on herself – she knew it was forbidden!"

The Doctor reached them, his face flushed and red. "Haven't I enough on my plate tonight, without our guest breaking the one and only rule of our house? Call her a taxi, this instant! I order it!"

Evidently, Betty knew better than to argue with the Doctor. "Francis, dear," Betty said. "Perhaps you might take Edie back to the house?"

Francis said, "Yes, Mother," and laid his enormous arm around Edith's shoulders. "I know where there's a special midnight cake," he whispered. "Just the ticket for a night like this."

Francis had already started ushering Edith out of the barn when, all of a sudden, she dug her heels into the earth and turned back to face the Doctor.

"I'm sorry, Doctor," she ventured. "I know I wasn't supposed to come through here. And I'm sorry, too, that I had to come here at all. But if you're going to throw me out, if this is really my last night at Forest Cottage, well, you should know something." She paused to take breath. The three adults were staring at her with the most perplexed looks. "It's the base of his wing. He wants you to treat the wound that's there, stop the infection spreading and then bandage his wing in a flexed position so it will heal correctly. I had to come and tell you. He's shouting and shouting for you to understand, but you don't seem to hear him. He said it was extremely important. If his wing isn't bandaged when it is flexed, the tendons could be damaged and he might never fly again."

The Doctor staggered backwards, knocking over a bucket. It rolled on the floor. His face, red just a moment ago, now had gone as white as a sheet.

"W-what are you talking about, girl?"

"You're in there listening to his breathing and checking his feet, but it's his wing. That's what's injured."

There was a silence. Edith turned on her heel, tucking herself back into Francis's arm.

"What's a midnight cake, Francis?" she asked, as they started to walk back over the lawn.

In the kitchen, Arnold was already awake. He leapt up at Edith as she followed Francis in. Then, together, they sat at the kitchen table while Francis lifted out a tin with a big slab of fruit cake in it, slathered with marzipan and rich, buttery icing.

The headache was slowly returning – but at least Edith knew what to do with it now. She was busily fixing a pot of tea to go with the cake when Betty burst through the doors. As she took her first sip and sat down, Arnold's voice came back out of the background noise.

"What happened, Edie? What did you do?"

"I'm sorry, Betty," Edith burst out, seeing the flabbergasted look on Betty's face. "I had to. That animal was in such pain..." She paused. "Did the Doctor manage to help him, Betty? The winged horse, I mean."

"Don't you worry about that, my dear," Betty said. "What about you? I feel that we've done you a disservice. I suspected what those headaches meant the moment you arrived, but I just didn't know what to do! Or how to speak to the Doctor about it. You see, you aren't the first to have this gift, my dear. There was someone very close to the Doctor who was gifted in exactly the same way, and she..." Betty caught herself before she said too much. "Well, that's all ancient history."

"It was Arnold who explained what was happening to me."

Betty's eyes flashed at the big, lumbering dog, whose tongue lolled out happily.

"Oh, Arnold!" she beamed. "What I wouldn't have given to be able to speak to you myself over the years!" She bent down and gave him an enormous cuddle. "You're a good dog."

"I can hear the voices now, but I'm still getting the headaches. I wish I could get rid of them once and for all!" Edie realized, as she spoke, just how exhausted she felt by everything that had happened since she had arrived at Forest Cottage. It had been both the most incredible but also the most terrifying day of her life. She took a deep breath. "Can you teach me to control it?"

Betty slowly shook her head. "There's only one person I know of who will be able to guide you and help you learn how to adapt. He's done it before. Trained someone in the arts of the mind."

"My uncle?" Edith said quietly, knowing the answer.

"But now he's sending you away," boomed Francis, and a tear rolled down his cheek, while – if only to feel a little better – he shovelled an entire piece of midnight cake into his mouth.

Betty was about to say more when the kitchen door opened and the Doctor came bustling in.

"I need her," he said, through gritted teeth.

Edith said, "Me?"

"Yes," the Doctor said gruffly – but he would not look at her with his eyes. "Come."

Betty said, "Come on, Edie, I'll be with you. So will Arnold. And . . . Francis?"

Francis, who had just polished off the rest of the cake, gave a salute and got back to his feet.

The Doctor strode out of the house and ahead of them, back across the grassy expanse – where a darting field vole shrieked out, *"Big clumsy man foot! He nearly trod on me tail, he did!"*– and through the barn doors.

Edith had to hurry to catch up. When she got to the place where the Doctor had nearly trodden on the foraging vole, she closed her eyes and scrunched out an *I'm sorry! He didn't mean to!* before following through the barn doors.

The Doctor had already headed down the central archway to the enclosure at the end. Edith looked up at Betty, who gave the faintest of smiles and gently steered her after him.

The barn had a thick air of mystery that enveloped Edith as she walked on. It was bigger on the inside than she'd expected. From the garden it looked like it would be a simple rectangular building about the size of a tennis court – but inside the space felt vast. Once through the cavernous entrance, the walls stretched into the distance. Edith wondered if it was some sort of optical illusion, or a special design that made it seem so big.

She turned to see Francis sliding a bolt across the doors they had just passed through, then adding a thick wooden bar to secure the entrance.

Francis waved in her direction. "Go on, Edie, make some new friends."

As Edith followed the Doctor, she looked around. There were pens on both sides but no single one was the same as the one next to it. Instead, each was individually customized to specifically suit the occupant. Signs adorned the front of each door and she read them with wide eyes as she went.

In the first pen, a drove of brown hares sat calmly grazing a miniature field of long grass, their long, black-tipped ears twitching in contentment. In the next pen, the sign said "Hedgehogs" but Edith couldn't see them – their pen was kitted out like a tiny woodland with thick undergrowth thick underfoot. They were completely camouflaged, except for one who sat brazenly on top of a log, watching her with fearless little black eyes.

Two large donkeys with shaggy coats both walked over as soon as they saw her, forcing her to stop and give them a stroke. Edith marvelled at their size – they were much bigger than she had expected donkeys to be. Their sign said:

> **NOAH AND PIERRE**
> POITOU DONKEYS

"They're a particularly large and strong breed of donkey which are used for breeding mules," Francis explained. He had been walking behind her. "Noah and Pierre were rescued from a mule breeding farm in Northern France. They've been with us three weeks. They'll go out into the field as soon as their quarantine is over."

Francis reached into a deep pocket and handed her a fistful of sugar cubes, before reaching over to give the two animals a gentle rub on their foreheads.

"They seemed pleased to see you," he said – but Edith already knew it. As she opened her palm to feed them the sugar lumps, she could hear them talking.

"Anyone with a sugar lump's got to have a good soul, Noah."

"Yes, Pierre. Anyone with a sugar lump's fine by me."

"Nice and sugary, Noah."

"Sugary and nice, Pierre."

They walked on. Edith found herself turning sharply left to avoid a spreading puddle that was leaking from a makeshift wetland feature housing a raft of baby ducks.

"Like a duck to water!" their mother was calling out. *"But up after midnight again – you ducklings will be the death of me!"*

"You have so many animals," said Edith. "It seems to go on for ever."

"We are not there yet," the Doctor replied from up ahead, tersely gesturing for her to walk on.

Edith suddenly gave a yelp of surprise. A zebra was staring back at her from one pen and an ostrich from another. She spun on her heel.

"We take in animals from all over the world," Betty said. "But some are rarer and more exotic than others..."

They had come, at last, to the enclosure at the end of the passage.

Edith felt all the tiny hairs on her arms, legs and neck tingle. She stopped. The Doctor had already gone on ahead, ducking underneath a single metal bar to enter a bigger enclosure, like a stable, liberally covered with a carpet of straw. Behind her, Francis and Betty stood watching her closely.

"Go on, Edie, he's expecting you," Francis said, softly.

"I . . . I feel funny," Edith said, running her hand over the back of her neck.

"They'll do that to you, the first time you see them," Betty said. "Just take a few deep breaths, my dear."

Edith gave a small nod and started forwards again. Everything seemed strangely quiet, considering the huge number of animals. Up ahead, Edith saw a pen much larger than the others, hexagonal in shape, filling up a large section of the barn. Slowly, she walked towards it.

The entrance to the pen didn't have a door. Instead, a single low bar – low enough that any animal could step over it with ease should it choose – rested lightly on stirrups either side of the opening.

Time seemed to stand still as Edith approached. She looked inside.

There the Doctor stood, beside a gleaming white horse. Folded flat back against its body on either side were two magnificent wings. They flowed from the top of its shoulders, almost glowing with a brilliant white as their feathers tapered to delicate points, perfectly symmetrical and travelling the entire length of its body.

"Well, Edie, you wanted to see what's in my barn," said the Doctor. "And here he is. A winged stallion. The king of his herd. The first pegasus you'll ever have seen, I shouldn't wonder."

The Doctor fixed her with a look. "Are you going to come and say hello?"

The Doctor seemed to be challenging her. But he obviously needed her help. She knew there must be a reason that he'd changed his mind and instructed her to follow him into his secret barn. Edith took a few faltering steps, and the pegasus fixed her with its gaze.

"It's real," she whispered.

"Why, of course it's real," the Doctor huffed.

Edith thought, suddenly, of all the books in his woodland study and stifled the thousand questions she wanted to ask.

"Pegasi like this are very wild creatures, Edie. Far more dangerous than any lion or tiger. This old king is lame. He's been faltering for weeks. I've had him in this enclosure three times already, patched him up and sent him back to his herd – but every time he comes back." There was a pause. It clearly pained the Doctor to say what he said next. He fixed his collar and looked a little shamefaced. "He's clearly in pain, but he won't let me touch the wing. I think . . . I think he wants you to take a look."

The pegasus, watching Edith, snorted and pawed the ground. The slight motion sent a wave of trepidation through her body. He gave another snort then, much gentler than the previous one. The pegasus looked at the girl, his deep brown eyes locking on to Edith's blue ones.

"I heard you, from my bedroom window. You're in pain."

The pegasus whickered anxiously, and the Doctor staggered back and called out, "Your Majesty!" – but the creature was far more interested in Edith.

"DID YOU . . . SPEAK?"

"I did," Edith ventured.

She became aware that the Doctor and Betty were staring at each other. Betty gave a shrug.

"BUT HOW IS THAT POSSIBLE?" the pegasus asked.

"Believe me," said Edith, *"it came as rather a surprise to me as well."*

"I HAVE NEVER SPOKEN WITH A MONKEY BEFORE."

"A monkey? But I'm not a monkey! I'm a girl!"

"A GIRL MONKEY OR A BOY MONKEY, HAIRLESS MONKEY OR TREE MONKEY, IT MAKES NO DIFFERENCE TO ME!"

"Well," she said, out loud, "I've never spoken to a horse either!"

The pegasus's nostrils flared. In a second, he had spread his magnificent wings and risen on to his hind legs.

"A HORSE!?"

The Doctor's face turned bright purple. "Don't call him a horse!" he gasped. "Down on your knees, Edie! Quickly!"

"I'm sorry," said Edith, quickly bowing down. *"I didn't know. . ."*

"IGNORANT MONKEY GIRL! HAS A SIMPLE HORSE EVER SOARED THROUGH THE HEAVENS? HAS A SIMPLE STABLE HORSE EVER SPREAD ITS WINGS AND. . ."

The King said no more. When he'd spread his wings,

it had obviously pained him greatly. Now he sank back to the enclosure floor, folded his wings, and shook his head angrily, as if that might drive away the pain.

"*It's the base of your wing – it needs to stay flexed,*" said Edith.

"*I KNOW THAT, MONKEY GIRL. IT'S HIM WHO DOESN'T.*"

Was Edith mistaken, or was there something petulant – something almost *bratty* – about the King's demeanour? Well, she thought, human kings and queens could be spoiled too. Perhaps it wasn't only a human – or even a "monkey" – trait.

On impulse, with everybody else still kneeling down, Edith stood up and stepped over the low bar to enter the pen. It was as if she was being drawn by an invisible force that was pulling her towards the magnificent creature.

"No, Edie!" the Doctor was calling out. "Betty, stop her! The child has a habit of not doing what she's told!"

"*Show him,*" Edith said to the winged stallion. "*He can't hear you like I can.*"

"*THAT MUCH IS OBVIOUS! TELL HIM TO COME AND LOOK, GIRL. I CAN'T RAISE IT HIGH ENOUGH. THE WOUND IS UNDERNEATH!*"

The pegasus whickered as Edith got nearer. It was a strange sound to hear, almost welcoming in tone, and in sharp contrast to his normal snorts and protests. His huge wings remained folded close to his body, flexing slightly as she approached, almost beckoning her forward.

She turned back to her uncle. "He says you should go and take a look."

The Doctor looked at her and gave a deep sigh. "Did he just say that to you . . . in your mind?"

Edith nodded. "He says you haven't been listening. He's been trying to tell you."

Her uncle's mouth was working a little like that of a fish. His head darted from Edith to Betty and back again repeatedly. Finally, he found his voice.

"She wasn't putting it on then. It wasn't all a big joke." He sighed deeply. "I can't do this again, Betty," the Doctor said. "She's too young. The timing is *terrible*! We can't do this again. . ."

"One problem at a time, Doctor," Betty called out across the enclosure. "And it does look as if this rare gift might, on this occasion, benefit your patient."

The pegasus stamped his foot angrily.

"HE KNOWS IT'S TRUE. HE JUST DOESN'T WANT TO ADMIT IT."

Edith moved forward again, her hand reaching into her pocket and pulling out the last of the sugar lumps.

Holding it out in her hand, she offered it to the most beautiful animal she had ever seen.

"Right," muttered the Doctor, shaking his head. "He said it's the base of his wing, did he?"

"Yes. And he says after you treat the wound to ensure you bandage the wing flexed."

The pegasus took a small step forward, stretched out his gleaming white neck and gently took the sugar lump from Edith's hand. He dwarfed Edith, her head barely reaching the top of his leg as he approached. When close enough, the King carefully sniffed Edith's hair. Seemingly satisfied, the magnificent animal lowered his great head so it pointed downwards, exposing his neck for her to reach up and stroke.

Edith reacted on instinct. She wrapped her arms around his neck, her face melting into the smooth warmth of his coat.

"You're so beautiful. I do hope you're feeling better," she found herself murmuring, giving him a little kiss on his neck as she did so.

"THANK YOU, LITTLE MONKEY."

"Can we try to show him your wing stump now? So he can help you?"

Very slowly, the King lifted his magnificent wing and held it out.

Moving haltingly, the Doctor, Betty and Francis all came forward and peered under the wing. A large gash, inflamed and sore, was clearly visible.

"By all the Seven Corners of the Earth!" the Doctor gasped. Then he looked back at Edith. "You were right."

"MONKEYS NEVER LISTEN," the King said. *"BUT LITTLE MONKEYS SOMETIMES LEARN."*

Edith smiled, enjoying for the first time the knowledge that she and she alone could understand the King's words. Maybe this skill was something she would come to love after all.

"Right," the Doctor proclaimed, "we need to get to work. Francis, we'll have to put a salve on that wound and bind the wing ... flexed. Betty, please take Edith to the kitchen. We'll be joining you shortly."

Betty came to her side, beaming from ear to ear, and put her arms around Edith. Then, when they were almost at the edge of the enclosure again, she turned back and said, "What about the taxi, Doctor?"

"Taxi?" the Doctor asked. His mind was obviously in another place altogether.

"You asked me to call a taxi, Doctor. To take our Edie away."

The Doctor looked up, while Francis began to lay out instruments from a bag, ready for them to get to work.

"No," he said, "no taxis tonight, Betty. I was, perhaps, a little hasty. I fear my heart and mind were rather bound up with this poor pegasus." He paused. "No taxis," he said, "but perhaps you could put a pot of tea on the stove? And I should think, after our work is done here, we might need a couple of currant buns as well. Edie, we have much, much talking to do."

CHAPTER EIGHT

*In which Edith begins her apprenticeship
with the Doctor and begins to understand the
mysterious Syndicate in a different light...*

Edith was sitting at the kitchen table, listening to Arnold pleading with Betty for some midnight sausages – even though Betty couldn't understand a word – when the door flew open and the Doctor appeared at last.

Francis was looming behind him. Both of them had their sleeves rolled up, both of them had their hands slathered in some antibiotic ointment they'd been applying to the pegasus's wound – and both of them had barely controlled smiles on their faces.

"*Oh!*" lamented Arnold, who came to flop his head in

Edith's lap. *"I'll never get a sausage now! Not even a little chipolata. Not even a cocktail sausage."*

Edith tousled the fur on the top of his head.

"I'd give anything for a Cumberland swirl," he grumbled.

"Is everything going to be all right, Doctor?" asked Betty, who was taking currant buns out of the warming oven.

The Doctor nodded. "He'll be in flight by August. And it's all down to. . ."

His eyes fell on Edith, who looked away uncertainly. She didn't know whether to feel proud or humble or what exactly.

"Don't let him frighten you," said Arnold. *"He's a big softie at heart."*

A wild screeching sounded, just outside the kitchen door – and the next moment, Gerry appeared in a thunderbolt of black and white feathers, his orange bill like a dagger as it collided with Francis's shoulder.

"It's not morning!" he squawked. *"All the human beans are having a feast and it's not even morning!"*

Edith's eyes turned as wide as saucers. Until this moment, she hadn't heard Gerry's voice, but it was exactly as she'd expected – a kind of screech that, somehow, transformed into words.

She focused.

"*Hello, Gerry,*" she said.

Gerry had lifted himself from Francis's shoulder but, upon hearing these words, was so startled that he dropped straight out of the air, upsetting the sugar bowl on the table. Then, encrusted with crystals of sugar, he hopped across the tabletop to look Edith square in the eye.

Arnold lifted his head from Edith's lap and balanced it on the table edge.

"*Yeah, Edie can talk now.*"

"*This . . . human bean . . . can talk?*" Gerry gasped.

"*It's going to make things much easier round here. We can ask for sausages whenever we want them.*" Arnold turned his doleful eyes on Edith. "*We won't always get them, of course.*"

Arnold's head disappeared from view, but Gerry was still considering her with a quizzical eye.

"*Say something,*" he screeched.

"*Say what?*"

Gerry staggered back. "*Well, I never! Another human bean who can TALK! Human beans just walk around moaning. Human beans just groan and groan and groan. But . . . to find another human bean who can TALK? What are the odds of that?*"

Edith, who still didn't understand it herself, remembered how Arnold had explained it and said, "*I'm a telepathic polyglot.*"

Gerry hopped back, dramatically. "*Well . . . quite. You're just like. . .*"

The Doctor cleared his throat, straightened his cape and looked at Edith. "You must have an inkling, now," the Doctor began, spreading butter on his currant bun, "why Forest Cottage is such a private place, why Pilgrims Veterinary Practice has such a remote and – dare I say it – *unhelpful* location. We are veterinarians here. My father used to own Forest Cottage, and his father before him – and his father, and his father (then his mother – that was a different time and a most unusual circumstance), and her father, and his grandfather (her own father was a lazy man, too idle to ever work!), and his father, and so on and so forth. All the way back to the days of Edward the Confessor. That's nearly a thousand years, Edie. Now, of course, the world was different back then – and what we do here, in the utmost secrecy, was not quite as rare as it is today."

The Doctor glanced down at his currant bun and, clearly deciding it didn't have enough butter on it, paused to lather on another dollop.

"In those days," he continued, "there were all sorts of creatures roaming the land. Edward the Confessor himself had a stable of hippogriffs – not that it did him much good when William the Conqueror came barging in – and there were more than ten different types of wyvern known to be roosting in the Scottish Highlands. In those days, the New Forest extended much further than it does today – half of England was forested, except where the woodsmen had chopped out clearings for their smallholdings. And those woods were the homes of unicorns and gryphons, brownies and kobolds, satyrs and fawns – and pegasi, like the King you met tonight!"

The Doctor was in full flow now and he wildly gesticulated with his half-eaten currant bun as he continued. Edith marvelled at his passion for his work. He seemed quite a different person to the glowering figure who had refused to even speak to her just hours earlier.

"Did you know there were sea serpents in the English Channel? A kraken, no less, or so they said in 1566! – and Sir Francis Drake brought back England's first roc for Queen Elizabeth herself. Well, extraordinary animals like those required extraordinary veterinarians. And that, Edie, is where my family came in.

"We were veterinarians to kings and queens – human ones, I mean. It was my family who were called when the king's prized gryphon got a canker, or when the dire wolves in the national forest contracted distemper. It was my family who were called if a dragon hurt its wing and took its pain and anger out on a local village. My family who had to help when a werewolf got injured." The Doctor stopped, flushed with pride at his family's accomplishments. "We've been doing it ever since."

Edith flashed a look around the kitchen. "But there aren't dragons here, are there?" Edie asked, trying not to let concern show on her face. "And the woods – they can't be full of . . . of . . . werewolves!"

The Doctor shook his head ruefully and sat down for the first time, manfully trying to keep Gerry away from his currant bun as he continued to explain. "Alas, we only see them very rarely nowadays. Yasmin, the baby snow dragon, is our only resident dragon. She has been with us two years, tucked up in the rafters of the barn. The world is a different place to the way it was when my ancestors first took up this noble profession. You'll know all about extinctions, a bright young thing like you. How there used to be woolly mammoths. How there used to be sabre-toothed tigers and giant armadillos the size of a car, just happily wandering around this planet. That is, until *human beings* started to get their wicked way."

The way the Doctor had said "human beings" made it sound like the most horrible, unutterable, nasty thing on Earth. His words were quickly echoed by Gerry, who took off with a currant in his bright orange bill and shrieked out, *"Human beans! Human beans!"* in a voice only Edith could hear.

"Ask him about dinosaurs," mumbled Arnold.

"But dinosaurs are extinct!" Edith said, out loud.

"Not all of them," said the Doctor. "There's a certain place, in Tierra del Fuego – a lost valley, you might say – where some dinosaurs still survive. I, myself, have cured the acne of a Diplodocus – and that, I might add, is quite a bit more spectacular than it might sound. Imagine pimples the size of ponds! Blackheads the size of buses!" The Doctor was silent, and his voice took on a more sombre tone. "How long have you known?"

"Known?" Edith whispered.

"That you're a telepathic polyglot."

"Only a few hours," Edith said.

"Before now, she's been having to deal with these headaches, poor dear," said Betty, presenting Edith with a mug of tea. "You'll remember what that was like, Doctor."

A look of deep sadness ghosted across his face, but it was gone in an instant. Then he continued. "I may regret what I'm about to say, Edie. But I think a mind like yours could help a great deal at Forest Cottage this summer. And the bonds of family, of course, are not to be taken lightly."

Edith felt herself tensing. Arnold lifted his head.

"What are you thinking?" he asked.

Edith answered, *"Bonds of family? They didn't seem so important a few hours ago. He was ready to call me a taxi."*

"Give him a chance, Edie. If he says..."

"Sorry," said the Doctor, finishing the sentence as if he too could read minds. "I'm very, very sorry, Edie. You see, we've had to get used to keeping secrets at this cottage. It isn't without reason. The animals we look after here – why, if the world was to know... There is a reason so few fantastical animals are left in this world. The world is full of people who would have it otherwise. Consider what *human beings*..." He said it with venom again, as if he could think of no worse thing in the world. ". . . have done to nature's other wonders. Elephants and rhinoceroses, tigers and panda bears. All of them hunted and decimated, and for what? The animals I treat have powers so magnificent that, if mankind knew of them, they would not stay safe for long. Take the King, whose life you've just saved."

Betty said, "It's late, Doctor. Perhaps this can wait for the morning."

But Edith did not feel tired at all – her mind was whirring with everything the Doctor was telling her and she wanted to more. "Doctor, are you the *only* one who knows about pegasi and unicorns and hippogriffs and baby snow dragons and sea serpents and rocs and dinosaurs in Tierra del Fuego?"

Around the kitchen table, all were silent. The Doctor was silent. Betty was silent. Francis was silent. Even Gerry, who had finished clearing up the spilled sugar but still hopped from one side of the table to the other, was silent.

"You're not, are you?" Edith whispered. "My parents. . ."

"The cloak of secrecy is everything," the Doctor announced. "The work your parents do is more dangerous – but also more important – than anyone could ever know. If the world knew I had a pegasus here, the King no less, descended from the most ancient line – traced all the way back to the pegasus the great Mongolian emperor Genghis Khan tried and failed to tame! – it wouldn't just be journalists and photographers who mobbed Forest Cottage. It would be people with guns and cages and traps and knives!" He took a deep breath. "Specifically, the Syndicate."

There was a barely concealed fury in the Doctor's voice.

At the mention of the name, Arnold lifted his head from below the table, moaned, *"Sausages!"* and promptly disappeared again.

"Who are this Syndicate?" Edith asked nervously. As she asked, she thought desperately of her parents, and shuddered.

"You deserve to know the truth, Edie. I won't hide it from you. The Syndicate are the most cruel and ruthless hunting collective in the world. A collective that is responsible for the deaths of almost a third of all the world's African elephants and the harvest of their ivory. Were they ever to find out where Forest Cottage hides, they would seek out and hunt the pegasus in a heartbeat. Had I a unicorn in my stable, they would move heaven and earth to take it. If I was curing a baby sea serpent of its seasickness – it happens! – in my pond, they would do whatever it took to wrestle it into a tank and cut it up for its precious scales."

"Do they know, then, the kinds of animals you look after?"

"My patients have fallen prey to the Syndicate before, yes."

"It's not all doom and gloom though, my dear," Betty chipped in. "People like the Syndicate also want to keep their activities secret – the more people who know that mythical creatures actually exist, the more competition they would have. It's in their interests to keep these animals secret."

"A fly that dances in front of a spider's web always risks the wrath of the spider's teeth."

Francis's voice made Edith jump. Both Betty and the Doctor flashed him a reprimanding glance.

"What he means, is that we have to keep hidden from the Spearstrikes, and their ... Syndicate." Betty said, faltering slightly on the last word. As though, Edith thought, she had wanted to say something else.

"And now that you know our precious secret, the Doctor said, "it's down to you, as well, to guard it with everything you have."

Edith sat there for a moment, seemingly paralysed

with shock. The night had been almost too overwhelming.

The Doctor stood up abruptly. "Sleep, Edie. To bed! Because, if you'll have us, if we haven't already frightened you off, tomorrow's going to be a busy day. Edie, I should like you to be my apprentice."

The next morning, Edith was standing, again, in front of the King, while the Doctor checked the dressing on his wing stump and pronounced himself happy with the way it had started to heal.

"The King of a herd has an incredible capacity to heal himself – and others," he said. "The trouble is, they can only do so much healing before they have to recharge their strength to be able to do it again. He must have been exhausted and he had no power left to heal himself. I'm guessing he'd used it on other pegasi who must have been injured in his herd."

"But what happened?" asked Edith. "Are the others OK?"

The Doctor stood back and looked the magnificent white stallion up and down. "The same thing that happened to the ponies in these woods, I shouldn't wonder. But perhaps you can ask him?"

Edith focused her mind. *"Hello, Your Majesty."*

The King inclined his head in a gracious bow. *"HELLO, LITTLE MONKEY GIRL. You saved my life. I know it was the Doctor and his big friend Francis who applied my ointments – but that honour is yours. Perhaps, one day, I might repay the favour."*

"How were you injured?" Edith asked. *"The Doctor said you can heal yourself. . ."*

The pegasus whinnied sadly. *"One of the mares in my herd gave birth to a foal. The little thing was born weak and limp and needed a touch of my magic to survive. I was exhausted from it and. . ."*

"Something attacked you?" Edith asked.

"THERE WERE POACHERS IN THE FOREST, ALWAYS KEEN TO SNAFFLE A FOAL IF THEY CAN – BUT, TRUTH BE TOLD, IT WAS A . . . bramble bush!" the King announced, lifting himself to his full height. *"I'm rather partial to blackberries – the green ones, before they start ripening. I was grazing on some and I tripped."*

Edith couldn't help but giggle.

"What is it?" the Doctor asked, his eyes wide in concern.

"Don't tell the Doctor, MONKEY GIRL. It isn't befitting of a king."

Edith looked at her uncle. "Oh, nothing," she said. "It

was an accident, not an attack, that's all. The herd are safe and no one is hunting them."

The Doctor looked at her curiously, then led her into the barn's outermost reaches. "I had a hippogriff chick in there last year. I could have used your help then, Edie. Now, your average winged stallion – they're proud and noble creatures, but at least they understand that sometimes they need a little help. But your average hippogriff – well, they'd as likely nip off your arm as accept treatment. Poor Francis had his arm in a sling for a week!"

"Will the King be OK?" asked Edith.

The Doctor nodded. "I'm certain of it. He's very ancient from our perspective, but still in his prime for a pegasus. He leads the herd we have here in the New Forest. Won his place in combat long before even I was born. You see, Edie – pegasi are a bit like wolves, they lead until they're challenged and beaten. The loser can remain with the herd – but they rarely do. Those hooves and teeth aren't especially forgiving."

They had reached the donkey enclosure, where Noah and Pierre were bickering over who got to eat the freshest of the carrots Francis had brought out. Edith tried to tune out their arguing while the Doctor continued.

"There are only a few hundred pegasi remaining

in the world. Only a king can lead a herd and only the rarest of foals ever becomes one. They are so vulnerable when they are young, and it takes them so many years to learn how to fly. I've often wondered if there was more I could do to help them, but. . ." He stopped. "Maybe it will be different with you here, my girl. Maybe they'll start to listen; we can keep them hidden in the Forest. The King likes you! The honour he gave you last night is almost untold, Edith. To speak with a pegasus! Why, you are gifted beyond imagination!" He paused. "But don't be deceived. They are creatures of free choice. If the King hadn't seen into your heart, trusted you to be good and true, he wouldn't have answered you. I doubt more than five or six human beings have ever got within a few metres of him. They can be a handful – or a wingful, I should say! Fearsome creatures when angered. A few beats of those wings could blow this old barn down."

"And they live in the New Forest? How many are there?"

"Seventy in this herd," replied the Doctor. "There's a smaller herd in the Dordogne. And a much smaller relic of a herd in the mountains above Kathmandu. They're as rare as the giant panda – and without a conservationist in the world to help them."

"But what if they came out of the dark?" asked Edith.

"What if they gave up their secret and let the world know they were here? There could be a nature reserve. Surely people would help them."

The Doctor shook his head sadly. "The best protection is ignorance. There's a reason there are only so few of them left. Feathers from those magnificent wings are some of the most prized and fabled treasures in the world. Hunters would cross the ends of the earth if they knew there was a living herd of pegasus they could kill. Just think of the magic in a beautiful beast like the King. The bounty on each pair of wings would be vast."

Once the Doctor had checked on the two donkeys, momentarily interrupting their battle for carrots, he whisked Edith on.

"I've had all sorts in here. There are times when the animals who need me can't come to Forest Cottage – I have to go to them. But stick around this summer and you never know what you might see. One summer, we hatched a roc chick, right here in the barn. His mother didn't make it, alas, but we looked after that egg until it cracked open – and Francis kept the chick fed all summer long. A roc, Edie – an eagle with a wingspan bigger than the length of a bus! Yes, you might see some things this summer. . ."

He stopped and pointed up at the rafters. Peering in

the direction of his pointed finger, Edith could make out something white, curled amongst the beams. It seemed somehow moulded into the roof space and, as she stared, she could see it was alive.

"Yasmin," said the Doctor proudly. "The baby snow dragon from Mount Denali! Did you know it once reached −73°C on that wild Alaskan peak? I bet you thought grizzly bears didn't have any predators! Looks can be deceiving; never upset a snow dragon, Edie, that's a tip for you. Even a baby. Yasmin was in a dreadful state when she was brought to me – but she's doing much better and, after another three years of sleep, I think she'll be back to full strength."

Edith jumped as she suddenly realized the baby dragon was watching her with unblinking calmness.

"Yasmin has her eyes open, Uncle," Edith said nervously.

"All dragons sleep with their eyes open. There is a difference between the passing of time and time passing, after all. Dragons are just those kinds of creatures, you see."

Edith didn't see at all, but the Doctor was leading her on again. "Anyway, there's a patient I need some help with," he said. "I haven't been able to work out what's wrong. But perhaps, now you're here. . ."

"Who brings the animals here, Doctor?"

As they walked, the Doctor said, "A lot of the time, they'll bring themselves. Over the years, we've built up a modicum of trust. The King, here, limped in with his infected wing a week ago. But there are always good souls out there, in every one of the Seven Corners of the Earth, who know where to find me when I'm needed." He paused. "I'm not the only one in the world who knows these animals."

Edith wanted to ask about the Syndicate, and might even have found the courage to do so, but the Doctor quickly went on.

"There's a wonderful lady, a striking octogenarian named Dr Ruth Bagshot, who has devoted her life to the Bigfoots of North America. She's been living with them since she was scarcely older than you. She has a satellite phone and calls me when I'm needed. She brought Yasmin to me, in fact. And my old partner, Professor Briar – living on the shores of Loch Ness, enjoying a fine retirement, and keeping an eye out, just in case that ol' monster needs a tooth extracting. Aha, here we are!"

They had arrived at the very back of the barn, where a small porthole door opened out on to the forest. In one straw-strewn enclosure, hutches housed rabbits in various states of disarray – "I'm afraid the foxes, and even Arnold, terrorize the bunnies around here, so they need a readily accessible escape route." He then turned, pointing towards the corner where a hedgehog sat grumpily over a dish of doggie treats in front of a shelter made from old shoeboxes.

The Doctor nodded at the hedgehog. "This is the patient I was wondering about. We came out one morning, and he was just sitting on the doorstep. Ordinarily, I leave Francis to deal with the woodland critters. You've never seen a man as in tune with the rabbits and water voles of this forest as Francis! I've seen him sitting cross-legged, out there in the grass, with wild bunnies hopping in and out of his lap. Francis ought to have got this little man back in the hedgerow by evening. But it's been ten days. He hardly eats, he hardly drinks. There's not a thing I can find wrong with him. Not a scratch on him."

Edith stepped into the enclosure, sending lame bunnies darting to their hutches, and crouched in the straw beside the hedgehog's makeshift house.

"Hello?" she thought.

The hedgehog shifted. *"Who said that?"* he called out.

"Hey, it's me," said Edith, *"up here."*

The hedgehog turned its snout plaintively upwards.

"The Doctor's worried about you," Edith began, while the hedgehog came to terms with this strange new experience. *"He says you haven't been eating. You haven't*

131

been drinking. You just turned up, looking for help, but the Doctor doesn't know how to help you."

"I'm sad," the little hedgehog said.

"Sad?" Edith gasped. *"But why?"*

"My girlfriend left me!" the hedgehog wailed. *"She said I was too prickly with her. She wanted somebody calmer. Somebody less pointed. Well, what's the point of me now? All alone in the world! She's got a new boyfriend now. A real smooth customer. Took her out looking for nice juicy earthworms last night."*

"You're the most handsome hedgehog I've ever met," Edith said.

"Really?" The hedgehog raised his snout. *"You're not just saying that?"*

"Absolutely not. You mustn't waste away, it would be terrible."

"But the love of my life has gone off!"

"No she hasn't; you haven't met her yet. You need someone who appreciates proper spikes. You are strong and powerful. But you need to keep eating. The real love of your life might just come along before you know it, so you'll need your strength!"

Edith looked up at the Doctor, who was standing patiently at her side.

"Well?" the Doctor asked.

"It's . . . personal," Edith said, and gave the hedgehog a friendly grin. "He'll get over it."

The two of them looked on as the hedgehog stood up, shuffled forward and then plunged his nose into a saucer of wet cat food.

"Well, I never," said the Doctor, lifting his cap to give his head a quick scratch.

The next two weeks passed in a happy but exhausting blur. The Doctor, having decided Edith could stay, had gone from one extreme to the other. Far from being elusive, she simply couldn't escape him. Edith quickly realized that her uncle's whole existence was focused on the animals that needed his help.

She was busy from dawn to dusk with endless tasks and chores about Forest Cottage. Cleaning veterinary equipment, mucking out stables, and feeding an increasing variety of animals were now all part of her routine – and she took on the challenge with an eagerness to learn and spend as much time as possible with as many animals as she could. For someone who had never spent any time with animals before arriving at Forest Cottage, she marvelled at how she had taken to the role as if it were what she had always been meant for.

By the start of the second week, she had – so Betty said – already proven herself invaluable to the daily operations at Forest Cottage. She had accompanied the Doctor to one of the local farms to deal with a truculent cow (*"It's something I've eaten!"* the poor cow lowed at her – and the Doctor had discovered twists of bail twine in her stomach, knotting up her insides). She had helped him diagnose a nasty case of food poisoning among the squirrels in the forest (*"It's the nuts, they're driving us nuts!"*) and persuaded a lame deer to come into the barn for recuperation (*"Oh dear, my dear, I'm just a fallow deer!"*). She had even, much to Francis's delight, convinced the family of moles who kept building their hills on the front lawn, to move to the back of the cottage, where they could dig burrows and upend earth to their hearts' content.

As one week turned into the next, Edith even thought she was getting the hang of managing the voices in her head without having to resort, every time, to a flask of Betty's tea. Every evening before dinner, she sat in the garden and practised. Arnold invariably joined her to impart a running commentary of what the animals around the garden were getting up to. She was getting stronger. She could feel it.

Her uncle, for his part, flitted around. Darting from pen to pen, disappearing for an hour or two here and there, only to reappear in the most unexpected corners of a field or a stable. Edith quickly realized that her uncle's energy was inexhaustible and his whole existence was focused on the animals that needed his help.

The best time of the day was between three and five p.m. It was the period when the Doctor insisted she take notes as he dictated his assessment of the animals on his rounds. There hadn't, yet, been anything as magnificent as the pegasus to study, but Arnold told her it was only a matter of time. *"You'll see. Just pray it isn't a basilisk next time. If you look them in the eye, you'll turn to stone – and then who will talk to me? Who will fetch me my sausages?"*

Hastily, Edith would try to keep up with the Doctor's words as they raced from his lips. Comments about the state of a donkey's coat or the degree of inflammation in a pig's snout would all get noted down with a date and time. Edith wasn't sure how legible her handwriting was at times, scrawled in a small blue notebook, but she also knew that this was her best chance to learn from the Doctor, so she diligently wrote down as much as she could.

Sometimes there were books to study. The Doctor gave her a treatise on the Canadian Sasquatch, a seven-foot ape-man, and she stayed up late at night devouring the tales of the first explorers to make contact with them.

He gave her the journals of one of the first Polynesian explorers, who'd brought a mermaid to London to present to Queen Victoria in the year 1856 – and came back from his voyage, too, with the scaly skin of a sea serpent in the hold of his ship. She read, with great delight, Ted Fitzgibbon's *Natural History of the Pegasus* – and, in the second week, gathered after midnight with the Doctor, Francis, Betty and Arnold (with Gerry happily sleeping in his bag), as the King returned to the skies that were his home, and soared away to rejoin his herd.

"All thanks to you, Edie," the Doctor said, with a warm smile.

Every morning, Edith woke early and, after completing her rounds with Arnold – feeding the chickens, cheering up the love-sick hedgehog, catching up with a brave little muntjac deer who, after a chance encounter by the Doctor's woodland study, had promised to provide information about animals deeper in the woodland – she would follow the overgrown, brambled trail to the roadside to collect the post from a small letterbox by the track where the taxicab had left her. The gate had been taken away by Francis, so she would squeeze through the hedge.

The postman, an elderly chap named Fred, knew not to go on to the grounds of Forest Cottage – "just too brambly," they'd told him, "so please leave our letters in a box down on the edge of the road".

Fred was happy to oblige. He was eighty-two years old and had been delivering mail by bicycle across the New Forest for sixty-five years; anything that saved his old legs and got him back to the fireside and a nice cup of tea was very welcome indeed.

But today, though Edith waited as the sun rose high over the forest, Fred did not appear.

"No mail today," said Arnold, who was luxuriating in a bed of bracken and leaves by the edge of the track. *"Not a single one. Lucky old Fred! Should we go back, Edie?"*

Just then, Edith heard her voice being called, sailing up and over the outermost hedges of Forest Cottage.

"It's Francis," she said. "Come on, Arnold."

Francis was waiting on the lawn, with a bucket full of nuts and seeds in his enormous hands. "There you are, Edie! The Doc's had to rush off to Staghill Farm. Two of ol' Jonesy's rams got their horns locked together, so now there's a two-headed ram bouldering all over the place. He wanted you to go and check on the squirrels. See if that stomach flu has passed."

Edith nodded. She'd been eager for an excuse to go back and see the squirrels. *"Are you coming, Arnold?"*

The smell of sausages wafting out from the kitchen window was too much for the great dog. *"I'm sorry, Edie. Squirrels can't compare with sausages."*

Soon, Edith had ventured past the woodland study, along a narrow trail between stands of beautiful alders, and reached the hazelnut trees where the squirrels made their homes. It didn't take long before she started to see them, darting hither and thither in the branches above. It was birthing season for the red squirrels in the woodland, and a mother looked warily down from her nest up above. Then, upon seeing Edith, she slowly zigged and zagged her way to the forest floor.

"Hello," said Edie, *"the Doctor sent me. How are you all feeling?"*

The squirrel scampered around nervously.

"Better. It was those nuts. Far too nutty."

"The Doctor thinks it was a stomach flu."

"Pah! In the middle of summer? No, it was nuts gone bad, you can count on it."

"But everyone's well now?"

"I should say so. I have four kits! Want to see them?"

Edith had never seen a squirrel kit before and felt honoured at being asked. *"Oh, yes, please!"* she said.

The squirrel scurried back to its tree. *"Come on then. Follow me!"*

The squirrel was at the second branch, already above Edith's head, when she called out, *"But I can't climb a tree!"*

"Can't climb a tree?" the squirrel gasped, as if such a thing was impossible. *"Funny joke! Come on, lazybones! My drey isn't far. Three branches down from the top, to the left, two down, six back up, and one forward round. You've just got to go top-wise. Couldn't be simpler."*

With that, the squirrel vanished between the emerald leaves.

Edith was about to turn around when, with a quizzical expression, the squirrel reappeared. *"You weren't joking, were you?"*

"No," said Edith, sadly. She would have enjoyed meeting the kits. *"Maybe when they're a little older, and out in the trees, I can come back?"*

The squirrel laughed. *"You monkeys have forgotten trees!"*

Edith was thinking of what she could possibly reply when she heard the scream.

It was coming from the other side of the woodland study, the other side of Forest Cottage, way beyond the chickens and the barn. Not a voice she had ever heard before. Not Betty. Not Francis. Certainly not the Doctor. And there was no doubting it was a human voice. This wasn't one of those unusual, extravagant, unearthly voices she heard in her head when an animal was projecting its language into her. This was the scream of a fully grown human man – and, by the sounds of it, he was terrified.

Edith started to run.

By the time she reached the woodland study, the scream was getting louder. By the time she'd come past the chicken coops, it was louder still. She still didn't know where it was coming from, but by the time she reached the barn and the scream sounded again, she thought she could pinpoint its direction.

"Francis!" she called out. "Betty!"

But nobody came, so she bolted around the back of the cottage, over the kitchen garden, through the next line of trees – and there, beside the great forest lake where the Doctor said he had once nursed a baby sea serpent back to good health, stood a gangly young man with a scarlet mailbag slung over one shoulder – and a huge, ferocious, wild creature growling at him, forcing him back to the water's edge.

It took Edith a wild-eyed moment to realize who that creature was.

"Arnold!" she called out.

Arnold turned. She had never seen him like this before. His teeth were bared and his hackles raised – and, to the poor postman, gibbering on top of the big boulder he'd climbed upon to try and keep out of trouble, he must have seemed the most fearsome brute in the world.

"Stop, Arnold! He's not bad. He's a postman!"

Arnold had turned his eyes back to the man, but Edith could tell the ferocity was slowly leaching out of his growl.

She hurried forward. "Hello?" she called out. "Are you lost?"

The panicking postman looked from Edith to the huge, wolf-like dog and back again. He nodded vigorously.

"Can you call him off?"

"He won't attack you," Edith said – but, as if to prove her wrong, Arnold let out a ripping bark again. *"What's wrong with you?"* she demanded, sending her thoughts down to the water's edge. *"Arnold, what's got into you!"*

"I'm used to dogs not liking me – it goes with the territory! But normally they're little spaniels, or cute pugs. This takes the biscuit!"

Arnold's face transformed and he flicked a glance to Edith. *"Did he say biscuit?"*

The thought of a simple digestive had stopped Arnold

growling, and everybody took their chance. Edith hurried down to the water's edge to put herself between the dog and the postman. The postman – thinking that he might even live to see his birthday next week – scrambled off the boulder and up the shingle.

"Arnold, stay where you are!" Edith insisted.

"It's my first day," the postman stuttered, through tears of relief. "Fred got himself a sprained ankle, so they put me on his rounds. It was a devil to find you. Not even a signpost! I ended up going all the way round the back, getting in by the woodland trail. Then this wolf-like creature just set on me! I haven't been that frightened since the day I got my first bunk bed and my mum said I had to sleep up top."

As he dug into his satchel, Edith said, "Fred always leaves the mail in a box down by the road."

"They didn't tell *me* about any box," the postman sniffled. "If they'd told me about a box, that wolf wouldn't have tried to kill me. I'd have known not to come in."

Suddenly, Edith understood. She looked again at Arnold, who looked back with guilty, shame-filled eyes. *"He mustn't get near the barn. It's the Doctor's orders. Or down near the woodland study, and those big chains from when the Doctor last had a dragon in here. I'm sorry, Edie. I don't like being a big, bad dog. But it's part of my job. Francis says."*

"He was scared witless, Arnold."

"I know," the big dog grumbled. "I can smell his pants."

Edith spluttered suddenly, with great gales of laughter. The poor postman looked bewildered.

"Here," he said, brandishing a letter.

She took the envelope. A pale eggshell blue, it was covered in a curly script she could hardly read – she could just make out the Doctor's name and, in its corner, a deep purple stamp showed tall, jagged mountains. Various different postal services had stamped it on its long journey to Forest Cottage, so many times that the envelope was a patchwork of black.

"That's come from the other side of the world, that has," said the postman, "but don't mind me, I'd better be. . ."

He took a stride in the direction of the barn – but Arnold let out another terrible growl. Then he said to Edith, "I'm sorry! I am! It's my job. I get paid in sausages."

Edith and Arnold showed the postman back to the woodland trail, and accompanied him a full mile through the brambles and bracken of the forest paths, back to where his bicycle was waiting. Then, as they watched him cycle furiously away, Edith turned to the letter at last.

"This could be it, Arnold!" she whispered. "News of my parents at last."

There was only one way to find out.

So, whilst opening someone else's mail wasn't something Edith would ever normally consider, she just had to know and found herself ripping it open in desperation.

Dear Doctor,
My old friend, we need your help...

CHAPTER NINE

In which an urgent request for the Doctor's help
opens the door to an extraordinary expedition...

The letter wasn't news of her parents at all.

Far from it.

Edith put the letter down on the kitchen table and Betty, who had been busily chipping potatoes at the sink, wrung her hands dry before picking it up.

A strange look flickered across her face when she realized the letter had already been opened. She peeked inside and hers widened as she caught a glimpse of the writing within.

"Edie," she said, pushing down the flap on the envelope to reseal it "did you read this letter?"

"Better tell her the truth," whispered Arnold from under the table, where he was merrily gnawing on a bone, *"Betty knows everything."*

"Not all of it," Edith admitted. "The writing, it's so . . . curly. I'm sorry, Betty. I thought it might have been news about my parents. I've been waiting every day for some news. . . I just couldn't help myself."

Betty nodded, then turned on her heel and shook open the laundry bag, revealing a sleepy Gerry. "The silly bird was up all night, following the Doctor. Gerry," she said, "fetch the Doctor. Now."

Gerry must have thought he was dreaming because, rather than take to the wing, he turned around to wriggle back into his bag.

"The Doctor, Gerry," Betty said, more sternly now. "Oh, hang it – Edie, perhaps you might. . ."

"Gerry," Edith said, *"Betty needs the Doctor."*

"Why? What's wrong with her?"

The toucan bobbed up and down, appraising Betty with a concerned eye.

"She does look a bit peaky, don't she?" Gerry said. *"I'll fetch the Doctor straight away!"*

It took Gerry three false starts, one head-first crash into the kitchen window, and half a minute being entangled in an old feather duster hanging out to dry, but finally he was off, soaring out of the kitchen window and through the skies.

It was another hour before the Doctor arrived back from checking on the forest ponies. In all that time, not once did Betty speak of the letter. She asked Edith to help her with chipping the potatoes for dinner, then scrubbing down the carrots Francis had pulled up from the kitchen garden. Francis himself, who arrived with a couple of baby bunnies snuggled in each pocket for safekeeping – "A fox got into the warren again" – read the letter, his eyes goggling as he took in the words. But he didn't say a word either. Edith was beginning to think it unjust and unfair when the Doctor appeared, an exhausted Gerry snoozing on his shoulder.

"Doctor, it's urgent," Betty began, and handed him the letter.

Pulling the letter out and unfolding it with a dramatic flourish, the Doctor bent his head to read. The writing looked like a work of art in dazzling blue calligraphy.

"It's so beautiful," said Edith. "It must have taken ages to write."

Betty was watching the Doctor, concern crinkling the corners of her eyes. "They are very rare letters, Edie. Never rushed. Always important."

"The ink is matched to the colour of the Himalayan

blue poppies, *Meconopsis betonicifolia*," her uncle intoned as he studied the lettering.

Suddenly, the Doctor's face paled. As he got to the end of the page, he shifted unevenly on his feet. Gerry, noticing the sudden imbalance, awoke with a start, shouted *"Danger! Danger!"* and promptly cast himself, face first, into the kitchen window again.

Clearly shaken, the Doctor quickly read the letter a second time, his mouth moving soundlessly as he did so.

Betty, Edith and Francis all waited expectantly. When he raised his head, his expression had altered. He looked directly at Edith.

"I'm afraid circumstances have changed, Edie. Your training must be delayed a little. Please retire to your room."

"But..." Edith protested, then stopped herself as she saw a flash of steel in the Doctor's expression and Betty glanced at her sternly. "No one is cross with you, dear, but please do as you have been asked."

Arnold gave a whine, sensing her distress, but Edith steeled her mind, blocking any communication. Determined not to look silly by showing she was upset, she pushed back her chair and marched out of the kitchen. Out in the hall she sank on to the bottom stair. Arnold had followed her and the big hound whimpered sadly, resting his head in her lap.

"You're really sad," Arnold's voice echoed in her mind.

"He still doesn't trust me, does he? I helped him with the pegasus. I've been doing jobs for him for weeks. And he still doesn't. . ." Just then, Arnold leaned forward and gave her a great big lick with his wet, leathery tongue.

"Arnold!" she groaned – but she couldn't help but laugh.

"He does trust you," Arnold insisted. *"It's not that at all."*

"He sent me away as soon as he saw what was in that letter."

Arnold shuffled back, fixing her with his eyes. *"Don't you see it yet?"* he whispered. *"He's frightened."*

Edith blinked. She hadn't expected an answer like that. *"Frightened? Why?"*

"Come on," said Arnold. *"If they won't tell you, I will."*

"The postman was lucky Geoffrey wasn't out," Francis was booming, his voice rising through the floorboards.

"Who's Geoffrey?" Edith asked as they stole along the landing.

"Oh," said Arnold, *"he's the crocodile who lives down in the lake. A terrible grouch he is too!"*

"A crocodile?"' Edith said. *"But we were right by the water's edge!"*

"He wouldn't hurt us. Not Geoffrey! The Doctor took

him in – *somebody thought it was a smart idea to buy a baby crocodile as a pet. But you can't keep a croc in a bathtub for ever! So he came to Forest Cottage. Never wanted to leave. Look, here we are."*

They had stopped beneath a clutch of pictures: the Doctor in times gone by; the Doctor, in exotic climes. In some of the pictures, there stood Betty. In others, was the same pretty woman she'd seen before, with her hair the colour of gold and her button nose exactly the same as Edith's.

"She's beautiful," Edith finally said.

"She was talented too. Talented, just like you, Edie."

Edith stared long and hard at a picture of the Doctor and the beautiful lady standing around a bonfire. Only, when she looked closer, she realized it wasn't a bonfire at all. She recognized the location too. There, in the background, was Forest Cottage itself; and there, looming over it all, the big barn where she'd met the pegasus King. The bonfire itself sat in the middle of the lawn – only it wasn't a bonfire, not really. It was a giant nest, with flames crackling underneath – and, in its basin, sat an enormous golden egg, with cracks splintering around its outside and a tiny, reptilian beak just poking out.

Edith was spellbound.

"What do you mean, Arnold, that she was talented like me?"

"She's the last human being I spoke to, before you came along. The only other human being, as a matter of fact. Wilma used to give me sausage rolls under the table, when I was only a pup. She used to keep me bits of bacon from breakfast, and dig out the insides of a chicken pie. Oh, everything was so much tastier when it was from Wilma's hands."

"Wilma?" thought Edith.

"BECAUSE OF WILMA!" shouted the Doctor's voice from the kitchen.

Edith gave a jump.

"The very suggestion is absurd!" thundered the Doctor – and Edith remembered, suddenly, the cold and aloof man she'd first encountered on arriving at Forest Cottage, not the avuncular old gent she'd been working with since. "Take her with me? To Nepal? Lady Elizabeth Beatrice Violet Thornfrulnaught. . ."

"Please don't use my full name, Doctor. You only use it when you're cross with me, and it just won't do. What happened to Wilma was a tragedy, pure and simple. You lost the light in your life, Doctor. But it doesn't mean. . ."

"The girl's not ready." There was a loud bang, as the Doctor slammed his hand upon the kitchen table. It echoed all the way up the stairs. "She can't get drawn into this world – not yet. Why on earth did you think I agreed to let her stay at Forest Cottage? I've been tending to these animals alone for most of my life, Betty. I don't *need* an apprentice. No, she's here so that she's safe. She's here so that the Syndicate never discover there's somebody else in the world who can speak with animals. The girl is safe here, Betty. If I took her to Nepal . . . imagine the danger."

Edith looked sidelong at Arnold. *"The Syndicate,"* she whispered.

"Now do you see why he's frightened?"

Betty's voice came then. "What if you can't help them, Doctor? What then?"

"Betty's right, Doc," boomed Francis.

"And you *do* need an apprentice. Doctor, please. We are none of us getting any younger. These animals will outlast each one of us in this room, and that's how it should be. But there needs to be someone to look after them when we're gone."

"She's a child."

Betty drew a deep breath.

"A very capable child, and you know it."

"I won't risk it. Never again! Not to Nepal, Betty." His voice had become suddenly frail. "Why did it have to be Nepal?"

"No one can change history – even if we wish it were so," said Betty. "Wilma was her own woman. She wanted to go. She wanted to be with you – she loved you and you loved her. There's no crime in that. But we mustn't relive what happened any more. We have to help those in need. Edie could help you. Don't deny her a destiny, Doctor. That little girl could be the future of everything we do!"

There was silence, thick and long, until at last the Doctor said:

"Betty, dearest. I am going to my study. Please don't disturb me. I have to prepare."

Edith hurried up the stairs so he wouldn't see her as he emerged from the kitchen, and peered through the bannister to see his ruddy face checked with tears.

"I'm going after him," said Edith.

As she took the first stair, Arnold snagged her shoelace in his teeth, pulling her back.

"You can't."

"I have to!"

There was no stopping her this time. Arnold sank on to the top of the stairs and watched as Edith followed her uncle out of the front door.

* * *

Edith faltered only when she was stepping through the great chains and hoops, on the way to the woodland study. She could see her uncle already, moving in silhouette against the study windows. She could almost hear him pacing.

A headache crackled across her temples. It was the first one she'd had in days. It was only because she was so emotional, she told herself. Only because she'd lost focus. She breathed deeply, found her focus again, listened to the voices all around her. One particular voice stood out.

"Help!" it was saying. *"Mama, help!"*

She cast her eyes around. There, at the bottom of one of the trees, lay the ragged remains of a blackbird nest – and, among its tangle of twigs and grasses, a featherless chick. She hurried over, cupped the tiny thing in her hands, and dared to whisper, *"You're going to be OK."*

And he really was, she thought – because there was the Doctor, framed in the study's open door.

"Doctor," she said, as he turned to disappear within.

"I'm sorry, Edie. I've been called away. I need to prepare."

She rushed to the study door, followed him into its shadowy interior. "Doctor. . ."

"NOT NOW, EDIE."

His voice shook her. She took in the room. He'd already filled one suitcase with various texts and medical equipment. The trunk where he kept phials of his most important tinctures and medicines was open on the desk – and there, spread all around it, were pictures of the beautiful blonde lady. Wilma.

"Doctor, he fell out of his nest."

He can't send me away now, she thought. *He has to let me stay.* She could feel the baby bird's heart beating in her hands. *"Mama?"* it kept twittering.

"Bring him to me," said the Doctor. "Quickly, now."

With a sweep of his arm, he cleared a space on the desk, saving only the photographs of Wilma from tumbling to the floor. When he caught Edith staring at them, he hid them swiftly beneath another stack of books: *The Guardians of Everest: An Explorer's Guide to the Mountainous Himalayas.*

The Doctor worked quickly, unearthing a little incubator, lining it with cotton wadding and bits of dry leaf and twigs from outside the study door. Then, taking the baby chick from Edith's cupped hands, he slid it within.

"This is a job for Francis," the Doctor said. "Quickly, now. The poor thing's in shock, but he can be saved.

He'll be back in the wild by the end of the summer. Go, Edie. On with you, now."

Her chance was slipping through her fingers. She felt the incubator, with its resident, pressed into her hands. She said, "Doctor, I can help."

"You're helping right now," he said, hurrying back to his case. Edith watched as he put a framed photograph of Wilma inside. Evidently, wherever he travelled, Wilma went with him.

"I mean – I can help in Nepal."

The Doctor stilled. "You were eavesdropping." He snapped his suitcase shut, rose to his feet. "You're a child, Edie. Your parents. . ."

"I helped with the King, didn't I? If I hadn't been here to listen to him, you would never have fixed his wing. The infection would have spread. His wings would have fallen off, and he'd have died. Four hundred years old, you told me he was. All of those centuries, wasted, because you wouldn't listen."

The Doctor had become ashen-faced. He said nothing. He folded his hands in front of him and remained still.

"Betty and Francis think you should listen now. Arnold thinks you should listen. Even Gerry, if he'd climb out of his bag, would say the same. I only want to help, Doctor."

The Doctor whispered, "You don't understand the dangers."

"Then tell me. Whoever it is you're going out there to help, they need you desperately. But perhaps they need me too."

But the Doctor only glared. "That chick needs feeding, Edie. Francis can show you how. That's the kind of work you're ready for. I'm sorry, my girl."

With her heart sinking, Edith returned to the study door. It was still the bright of summer outside. She didn't know how it could feel so cold and lonely within.

She was almost gone when she heard a voice – *"Stop! No! Your boot!"* – and turned quickly to see the Doctor about to take a step.

"Doctor, no!" she called out – and, hurrying over, she reached under the Doctor's hovering boot, where a big black spider scurried off to the safety of a crack between the floorboards. "You were about to squash him."

"See you later, suckers!" called the spider, as it slipped into the darkness underneath.

Edith picked up the chick and went back into the woodland. She was tramping back through the great chains and metal hoops when the Doctor called out, "You're getting better, Edie. Three weeks ago, you wouldn't have heard a thing. Three days ago, that spider might have been trampled."

But Edith did not stop. She'd been told what her place was. At least, now, she understood.

Late that night, with her tummy full of Betty's wild mushroom pie, Edith sat up listening to the bats in the attic. Every animal had a distinct voice. The bats were soft and whispery, the mice in the walls fast and anxious. Arnold, who – judging by the way he was drooling – was hunting sausages in his dreams, had the most comforting voice of all. She wished he was awake now. Or she wished dreams would come to whisk her away.

Downstairs, the baby blackbird – its belly full of egg from a little pipette – sat snug and warm inside the incubator. Edith had heard his teary cries for his mother fade away across the day, but Francis said he was going to be all right. They'd looked after countless orphaned chicks and fox cubs at Forest Cottage over the years.

The moths were buzzing again. There were more of them tonight, all congregating around the light bulb. She'd learned to tune out the voices, but occasionally, when her mind drifted, they crept back in.

"*I'm sorry, chaps,*" she thought. "*That's enough for tonight. It's lights out time.*"

"*No!*" they all screamed in chorus. "*Please, for the love of all that's holy and light, NO!*"

She reached out for the light cord.

There came a knock at the door.

Edith scrambled up. The light remained on and in one great burst, twenty moths screamed in delight, and started feverishly beating their wings around the light.

"Hello?"

"Edie?" came the voice of the Doctor.

Inch by inch, the door opened up. The Doctor, when he appeared, was in his usual cape and cap, but he clutched a thick woollen scarf and a pair of fur-lined gloves. In one hand, he carried a suitcase, as battered and old as (or so it seemed) Forest Cottage itself; in the other was a dog-eared old tome. He handed it to her.

ABOMINABLES

by Ellen Bellamy

A LIFETIME'S STUDY IN THE
NATURAL HABITAT OF THE
HIMALAYAN YETI

"Doctor?" she said.

The Doctor was wearing a strange expression. Regret and embarrassment, but fear as well.

"I've been hasty," he uttered, seeming like a small boy sent before his school teacher to make amends. "I've had much on my mind – and this expedition. . . You must understand, Edie. I haven't been to the Himalayas in many years. When I was last there, I. . ." Here he faltered, and said no more – but, in her heart, Edith already knew it had something to do with Wilma, with the aunt she never knew.

At the bottom of the bed, Arnold started to stir. He beat his tail, happily.

The Doctor cleared his throat. "If I take you on this journey, if I ask you to use your precious skills to assist me, you will do what I ask, when I ask it, won't you?"

Edith could hardly believe what her uncle was saying. She nodded.

"Well then, you'll have to change out of your pyjamas, and grab a jumper," said the Doctor. "We must set off at once. There's a family of very special animals that need my help and there isn't a moment to lose. Your budding talents are going to prove invaluable, I'm sure."

Edith reached for the book and looked at the raggedy old cover: a painting, in oils, of a hairy ape, as white as the snow, knuckling up some mountain ravine, its younglings following after.

"Yetis, Doctor?"

"Indeed. The so-called 'Abominable Snowman' – though you'll soon discover that the legends don't always get everything right. Well, they never do." For the first time since the letter had arrived, the Doctor's eyes lit up. Gone was the melancholy of earlier today. Gone was the frustration and fear – and, in its place, the twinkling mischief of old. "Pack a bag. We're going to the Himalayas!"

CHAPTER TEN

*In which Edith embarks on a quest with
the Doctor – and has her first glimpse of
the wonders of the big wild world...*

A jagged line of snow-capped mountains marched underneath them.

Edith looked down through the windows of the rickety old aircraft as the wild, unforgiving terrain of the Himalayan mountains stretched out in every direction.

The Doctor was sitting next to her, fast asleep. His mouth was slightly open and he was snoring softly. She couldn't help but smile. The looks they had got in the airport as they had walked through, the Doctor in his cape and cap, had been extraordinary. She had had to

stifle a giggle; she had overheard one family wondering if they were in fancy dress.

After that, things got even stranger. The flight attendant on the first plane (there had been three so far, and the Doctor assured her there were going to be more – where they were going was one of the most remote places on earth) had asked the Doctor if he was, perhaps, travelling to the International Confederation of Magicians. The Doctor seemed to take it all in good humour, tipping a wink at Edith every time somebody made one of these jokes. "After all," he said, "the real reason we're on this plane is even more extraordinary!"

Before the Doctor fell asleep, he had reached into his case and handed Edith another book. "This will get you started. The rest you'll just have to learn on the job – just like I did, back in the day! Wake me up when we reach Kathmandu, won't you?"

In seconds, he was snoring. But Edith – who had been awake all night long, and watched the new morning spilling its sunshine on the plateaus of ice and snow underneath – hadn't been able to sleep a wink.

She turned to the cover of the book and started to read. The book was called *So You Want to be a Vet: Ten Principles for the Budding Veterinarian*. The cover also promised "added pictures – not suitable for readers of a nervous disposition!". Edith had always enjoyed science at school, but on these pages science really was brought to life. It was all about diagnosing disease and, within the next hour, she had devoured each page with a hunger to learn more. She'd never read a textbook like it in her life; every passage seemed to teach her some fascinating fact about how bodies worked and the simple approaches to find out what was going wrong. From a bat to a buffalo, Edith was learning about how observation, communication and, above all, logic, were vital in how ancient healers diagnosed the ailments of animals under their care.

But it was when she turned back to the book the Doctor had given her before they set out that her imagination truly took flight. As the Doctor snored upon her shoulder, she continued to read:

ABOMINABLES
by Ellen Bellamy

A LIFETIME'S STUDY IN THE NATURAL HABITAT OF THE HIMALAYAN YETI

It has been considered fashionable, among the zoologists of the last century, to dismiss the Himalayan yeti as a figment of the imagination. Perfectly sensible people will roll their eyes at photographic evidence of this ancient, proud and noble ape and insist that, far from looking at a picture of one of mankind's closest animal relatives, they are in fact looking at a goat on its hind legs, a prankster in a white furry suit, an unusual formation of cloud – or, most laughable of all, a simple snowman made to look ape-like and ferocious by Nepalese children. But to deny the existence of the Himalayan yeti is as absurd as to look upon a radish and declare, "I see a cucumber before me!" Dear Readers, the Himalayan yeti is as real as you or me. And I, Ellen Bellamy, have lived among them...

By the time the plane had touched down in Kathmandu, Edith knew all about Ellen Bellamy, the twentieth century's great explorer and conservationist, who had first written about the troops of yetis living in the Himalayas.

The Nepalese locals both revere and fear the great ape. Once there was an age when the yeti lived in the foothills, but for centuries now they have lived in the mountains' most inhospitable reaches, where none but the most fearless of hunters may tread. How many are left, we do not know. But this proud ape, which stands nine feet tall, covered in shaggy white fur to camouflage it against the mountain snow, is seen more and more rarely, and in the future will be seen more rarely still...

Edith knew that the Yeti was a gentle creature, living on grubs and vegetation high in the mountains. She knew that they lived in family groups called "troops". She knew that they lived in caves that they decorated with paintings on the walls, made by crushing the flowers of the blue Himalayan poppy and kneading it into the stone. And she knew that they had an instinctive fear of humans, made worse by all the centuries their ancestors had been hunted, that it had taken Ellen Bellamy half her lifetime to overcome.

But once this fear is overcome, the Himalayan yeti reveals itself to be a warm-hearted beast, capable of the most enormous intellect. Oh, dear reader, if only we spoke the same language – what wonders that might reveal!

Edith looked up from her reading and out of the window. It was a forlorn hope that she might spy any of the noble apes marching across one of the mountain ridges from this high up – but, in her imagination, they were down there, turning to watch the passing plane, and it was a magnificent sight.

As promised, Edith woke the Doctor once the plane had hit the tarmac in Kathmandu. From there they hurried to meet their connecting flight, an ancient eight-seater plane – complete with twirling propellers and rattling engines – that would take them up the mountainside to the small village of Jomsom, high in the Himalayan Annapurna mountain range.

This time, not even the Doctor could sleep. The plane, scarcely as big as a school minibus, seemed to labour as it took off. Edith worried they might drop out of the sky. But soon they were zipping past shining mountains, the bright sunlight reflecting off their snow-capped peaks. Edith could no longer concentrate on her book. Instead, she pressed her face to the window, drinking in the spectacular scenery – which only became more dramatic with each leg of the journey. Now, they were flying straight up into the mountain range itself.

Exhilarating didn't do this last leg justice. Eventually the noise of the plane's engine started to deepen, signalling they were slowing down and coming in to land. Rather than descend, though, the plane seemed to continue in a straight line – and, just as Edith started to wonder what was going on, they landed on a thin strip of runway, perched on the top of the mountain.

"It's a precarious place. When they take off to go back down, the planes just drop off the end of the runway." The Doctor's eyes twinkled as he watched Edith's incredulous expression. He flashed her a big grin. "We made it, Edie! Welcome to the Himalayas!"

It was a different world.

Any weariness Edith had felt from the journey seemed to evaporate the moment she walked down the steps of the aircraft. The bustle, noise and colours of the small mountain airstrip electrified her every sense. Following the Doctor across the runway, the plane's other few passengers fanning around her, she looked up and around.

It seemed like she was on the top of the world. The sky was the most brilliant cloudless blue. Mountaintops ringed the horizon and, as they walked towards the small airport building, Edith watched as a team of airport staff ran out to the aircraft and started hauling bags from the plane on to a metal trolley.

Even the air felt different up here. It was like every smell in the world had suddenly become richer and sharper.

Edith realized she had been marvelling at the halo of mountain peaks for too long. The Doctor was already at the door to the small airport building. From a distance, she could see him being greeted by a stocky Nepalese man with a square face and shaggy jet-black hair.

The trolley, having been piled high with bags, raced past her, driven by a team of porters, clearly in a hurry. Edith spotted her rucksack perched precariously at the very top of the pile, and as the trolley slowed to a stop outside the hut, the bags were rapidly swung down and placed behind a cordoned-off section of rope. Soon all the plane's luggage was arranged in a neat row by the doors.

Edith hurried to catch the Doctor up.

The rest of the passengers were already scrambling for the luggage, then heading off through the airport building to the mountainous village beyond, so for a moment Edith couldn't see the Doctor as people surged around her. When the crowd finally parted, she could see that he was embracing the man, as if he was a long-lost brother.

"Doctor!" the man exclaimed when they finally parted. "My dear old friend. It has been too long!"

"Khageshwaar," came the Doctor's reply, "I came as

soon as I got your message. Tell me, has the situation worsened?"

"I don't know, Doctor. I was in the mountains yesterday with Babu, but we saw few signs. We fear the worst. . ."

The Doctor stepped back, his cape fluttering wildly behind him in the stiff mountain wind, and for the first time, Edith could see this man, Khageshwaar, up close. He was younger than the Doctor, perhaps thirty-five years of age, with crinkles around his eyes and a smattering of dark stubble around the line of his jaw. His eyes were deep black but, even so, he had a boyish look about him. He shared this, at least, with the Doctor.

"Edie, might I introduce Mr Khageshwaar Khanal, a dear old friend and associate of mine. It was Khageshwaar who wrote to us to deliver us our mission in these mountains." Khageshwaar, this is Edith Wight – my niece."

Khageshwaar's face remained kindly, but a look of unease flickered across it. He was skilled at keeping it hidden, but something tensed in his features and he said to the Doctor, "Your niece, Doctor?"

"And apprentice," the Doctor confirmed, with a neat nod of the head.

This creased Khageshwaar's face further. Edith found herself flushing. What was so wrong with being the Doctor's apprentice?

"But, Doctor," Khageshwaar whispered, "to bring a young girl into these mountains. . . Does she know what's waiting for her?"

Edith tried not to feel affronted, but it was difficult. She still had the Doctor's books in her hands, and she held it up.

"I've been doing all my reading," she said, with a hint of defiance. "I know the yeti takes thirteen months to gestate its young. I know they live for one hundred and twenty years. I know their fur is three times as thick as a mountain yak, and that their hearts are shaped like three balloons tied together by string. I know. . ."

Khageshwaar flapped his hands. "Put it away, put it away!" he whispered. "And keep your voice down! You never know who's coming through this airport. Half the people here come dreaming of yetis. But you never know which of them come with hunting rifles in their luggage."

Edith found herself flushing, remembering how urgently the Doctor had spoken about the cloak of secrecy, all the way back in Forest Cottage.

The Doctor laid a hand on his arm. "Don't worry, Khageshwaar. Edie is proving to be a fine young veterinarian. She has already shown herself brave and cool in a crisis – with no less than a pegasus king." He lowered his voice. "She's talented, K. Talented in the same way as Wilma."

Khageshwaar's eyes widened.

The Doctor looked up at the ring of mountains all around. "I've been dreading this," he said softly, "but, now that I'm here, all that I'm seeing is how beautiful it is. How much Wilma loved it here." He shook his head, clapped his hands and said, "But we have a job to do, so lead on, my dear, dear friend!"

Khageshwaar grinned. "Wait here a moment," he said. He darted back into the airport building, returning a few moments later with a garland of bright orange flowers, which he looped over her neck.

"Thank you." Edith smiled back.

"It's a traditional Nepalese greeting for honoured guests. It is very nice to meet you, Edie."

It was but a short walk from the airstrip into the small mountain town. The dirt road had been freshly cleared of snow, but in places there was black ice underneath – and Edith soon found herself having to hold her arms out to keep herself from slipping. Villagers watched them from every one of the squat white buildings that bordered the track.

As for the Doctor, any of his remaining nerves seemed to have drained away at the sight of the mountains. It had been some years since he was last here, he said, but his feet seemed to remember the way. Soon, it was not Khageshwaar but the Doctor who was leading them into the middle of the village, with its stone and timber buildings and market square, above which sat a small clock tower and an old colonial-style hotel.

"How are you feeling, Edie?" asked Khageshwaar, as they fell into step behind the Doctor. "The air is very fresh here but wait until we go higher. It makes the heart sing!"

Edith wasn't sure about singing; she hadn't gone two steps out of the airport before she felt dreamy and light-headed.

"It's beautiful," she said. She put her hand to her chest. "I feel as though I can't take a proper breath."

"Don't worry," Khageshwaar said reassuringly. "You're panting because of the altitude. You're fit and strong – you'll get used to it quickly. There's less oxygen in the air the higher you go, so everybody needs a little time to adapt."

Edith was glad to hear it. She desperately didn't want to slow anyone down.

"Will I be able to breathe normally soon?"

"You'll be running up the mountains in no time! I can see it in you; you belong with us up here in the heavens!" Khageshwaar laughed. "I might have to watch out for my job if you stay too long!"

"What do you do?"

"I run tours and treks up the mountains for adventure tourists and explorers. I plan their routes, carry their bags and ensure that they stay safe."

"And that's how you know about the. . ." She dropped her voice to a whisper. "Yetis?"

"Not quite, Edie. That, young doctor, is an altogether older story."

Edith liked the way he called her "doctor". It made her feel important – as if all those years of skulking in the shadows at St Margot Montefiore's, all those years hiding from her mysterious headaches, had been practice for something so much more magnificent: this adventure she was on right now.

Up ahead, the Doctor had slowed down too. Evidently, he'd spied something in the scrub at the edge of the track, where a trail zigzagged up into the mountain crevices above, because he had dropped to his knees and was teasing his fingers together. Edith spied a small silver-and-black cat, with its face full of whiskers and a plump little body, crouching in the shelter of the thorns, considering her uncle suspiciously.

"When I got sent to Forest Cottage," she went on, watching her uncle and the cat, "he hardly wanted to know me. Then we found out about the voices..." She paused. "What *did* happen to Wilma?"

Khageshwaar said, "It is not my story to tell."

"She could speak to the animals too."

"She and the Doctor were a formidable team. The greatest of friends and the closest of partners. But then..." Khageshwaar trailed off and then looked at Edie.

Edith knew what Khageshwaar was going to say next. It was the word that had been stalking her, all the way from the headmistress's study to here, in the mountains at the very top of the world.

"The Syndicate," she whispered.

"Speak not of them," Khageshwaar said sharply, "for we face an altogether different danger today. Yetis are complicated beasts. My family have lived in these mountains since time untold, and we have watched and observed the yetis across the generations. In your book, they call them the *Abominables*. In these mountains, we call them the Guardians. They are, at heart, a gentle, loving ape. They have good souls. But *abominable* they truly can be. A yeti endangered is a wild animal, beyond our comprehension. They earned their reputation as 'abominable' by defending themselves from hunters in the only way they knew how – with the brute strength and raw power that nature gave them. Getting close enough to treat the sick yeti I saw will not be easy."

"Whats wrong with it?" Edith asked, pausing for a moment to catch her breath.

Khageshwaar twisted his head to look up at the high mountain peaks.

"I was up there," he said, "checking on a track in preparation for a guided trip to the summit – when I glimpsed one of the creatures, stumbling. Ordinarily, the great apes walk on their feet like men – but this one was frail, knuckling forward like a gorilla. A ten-foot tall, snow-white gorilla."

Edith gasped. "What happened?"

"Two of its family came down the mountain to rescue it. Their anguish was clear. And only your uncle – who is brave, selfless, and yes, slightly *strange* –" Khageshwaar's eyes crinkled warmly – "has the experience to save them."

"Because he's been here before, many years ago," Edith whispered. "When he came with . . . Wilma."

Khageshwaar's face clouded fractionally as a shadow passed over his face. "I wasn't sure he would be able to face coming back here. But he is the Healer of the Seven Kingdoms, and he would not let an animal like this down."

"The Healer of the Seven Kingdoms?"

"Your uncle earned this title many years ago. He has helped mythical animals on every continent of the world. The yetis will remember him. They will accept his help."

"Where do they live?"

With one hand, Khageshwaar reached out and pointed up towards the mountains. "You see that big mountain peak?"

Edith looked ahead. The horizon was ringed with mountaintops, all inspiring and impressive, but one peak in particular stood higher than the others, its sharp summit spearing into the sky with a rugged grace.

She nodded.

"The journey to that peak is hard and treacherous, but we will walk it together; you have nothing to fear. The place where we need to go is near the very top – a sacred haven where only a very few of us Nepalese have ever been permitted. It is where the yetis have their home in the mountain caves. And I will be taking you there."

Further down the track, the Doctor was waving them over.

"Come on," said Khageshwaar.

By the time they reached the Doctor, his excitement was bubbling over. The silver-and-black cat was still in the bushes, peering out.

"This, Edie, is one of the very few Pallas's cats that inhabit this part of the world. Nobody knew they were here at all, not until a few short years ago. But here he is. Isn't he a beautiful specimen?" The Doctor held his hand out at the suspicious little feline, who only cringed away from the touch. "Well, he's a friendly fellow, but he's still wild – and that's as it should be. Perhaps he's come foraging for scraps for his litter. What's he saying, Edie?"

She focused her mind. There had been an odd kind of silence on the journey to Nepal, with no animals chattering away at the back of her brain whilst she'd been on the aeroplanes, but now she could hear the voices of birds in the trees. And one particular, hissy, indignant voice coming out of the bushes.

"What, in the name of all the Nine Nepalese Feline Families, are you wearing, you strange man? A cape? In

the MOUNTAINS? *What are you, some kind of clown? My good man, take your hand away from me! You look absurd! I am a Proud Cat, and I can't be seen fraternizing with a man in a cape. What would the other cats think? They'd think I'd lost all my elegance! My grace!"*

The Doctor looked up with an infectious grin.

Edith felt herself flushing. The Doctor looked at her expectantly. "He's saying he loves your cape, Doctor. And your little cap."

Then she threw a wink at the wild cat and hurried on.

The Traveller's Rest was the only hotel in Jomsom and it comprised not just hotel, but meeting spot, restaurant and village store all in one. Khageshwaar led them through its doors, and to the check-in desk, where one of his old friends was happy to receive them.

Edith looked around. The reception hall was small and panelled in wood, with a seating area of plush velveteen sofas and a hearth-fire in front of which a domestic cat happily slept. On one side of the hall, wooden stairs twisted up to the bedrooms and suites above. On the other, through saloon doors, lay the hotel restaurant where a few local guides were drinking great pots of steaming tea and a lone guest was reading a magazine about the mountains.

"He'll take your packs to your rooms," Khageshwaar said, having spoken to the desk clerk.

"We're not going up ourselves?" asked Edith.

"One stop first," said the Doctor, "but we'll come back and get provisioned soon. By provisioned, of course, I mean a hearty meal and a warm, bubbly bath each. I'm sorry, Edie. We've come a long way. But first I owe Khageshwaar's mother a visit. She has been a dear friend to me, over the years."

Khageshwaar's family lived on the outskirts of the village, right where the mountain trails led to the crags hanging above. On the way there, the Doctor told Edith more about the yetis.

"The Himalayan yeti are an extraordinary species. And in spite of all the horrors mankind has visited on them – all the hunters who have come to these mountains, hoping to steal their cubs and put them in zoos, or to butcher them for their furs – they have always helped the people who live in these mountains. Go back far enough in the legends, and you'll see they leave signs in the mountains, to protect lonely travellers from avalanches or other mountain risks. They've rescued climbers trapped in storms. Indeed, once upon a time, that's how Khageshwaar's family came to know them."

"It was my grandfather," said Khageshwaar, "who also had my name. He got himself lost on the mountain. The clouds were low and the mountain treacherous, and he would surely have perished there when darkness fell – but one of the yetis led him to safety. Since that day, my family and I have pledged our lives to protecting them from discovery by the outside world. My brother Babu and I would rather lay down our own lives than reveal the secret of these mountains. We are the Keepers of the Yeti, Edie – and this is our home."

Home was a small stone and timber dwelling, and a patch of earth with a couple of lean-tos where three goats were tethered. As they approached, the steep escarpment of the mountain rising overhead, Edith could see the lodge interior. Somewhere inside, a fire was crackling. Its smoke curled up and over the mountaintop.

It took a moment for Edith's eyes to acclimatize to the dark interior of the house as she and the Doctor followed Khageshwaar in through the doorway. Two puppies were playing in the hall and Edith suppressed a giggle as they rolled around their feet.

"Quick!" she heard one of them chortle. *"New people. Once they take off their shoes, grab one! Grab two! Grab half a dozen! We can take it in the yard and hide it. They'll have to climb the mountains in their socks!"*

"Not if we grab the socks too!"

"Naked little toes, all dancing on the mountain snow! How funny!"

"Look, he's taking off his boot! We can tuck it behind the log pile..."

Edith's eyes widened as she watched her uncle kick off his boots – but, before she could warn him, one of the puppies had darted in, snatched a boot, and tumbled off with it, out into the yard.

"Stop!" Edith yelled. *"You cheeky little rats!"*

"Rats?" said one of the puppies, in horror. *"Who said that? Somebody's calling us rats! We're mountain dogs – brave and true! Rats indeed!"*

While Edith was staring after the scrapping dogs, a door opened at the end of the hall and out of it there stepped a man who looked almost identical to Khageshwaar, except that his head was shaved and he seemed a little younger around his eyes. In his hand he clutched a yellow neon woollen hat.

"Babu," the Doctor began. "It has been a long time, my friend!"

When the Doctor put his arms around him, Babu seemed less comfortable, somehow, than Khageshwaar had at the airport – but soon he gave in, and patted the Doctor on the shoulders in return.

"My brother, Babu," Khageshwaar whispered to Edith. "He keeps his head shaved to honour the passing of our father."

"I'm so sorry to hear that," Edith said. "I like your hat."

Babu grinned. "The tourists all know who to look for when they are seeking the best mountain guide."

Khageshwaar chortled. "They know that he lives with a younger brother who has a bright yellow hat!"

Edith smiled. "I am sorry about your father though."

"He had lived a long, happy life here in these mountains," Khageshwaar said. "He cared for the yetis before us. Devoted his life to them, just as we do. There can be few more special lives than this. It is sad that he is no longer with us – but his life was filled with joy. He was happy when he passed."

Edith wasn't sure she understood what Khageshwaar meant. How could somebody be *happy* to have died? Khageshwaar led them forwards and, quickly removing her own boots, and casting a glance back outside in case the naughty puppies were about to return, Edith followed them into the family living room.

It was a small room, with a few chairs and pillows around the fire, shelves filled with family heirlooms and old books on either side. In the corner was an old record player, and in another a blocky, old-fashioned TV. Small carved statues adorned a stone mantelpiece. And in the middle of the room, close enough to the fire to feel its prickling heat, there was a bed.

The Doctor knelt at the bedside. At first, Edith wasn't sure if there was anybody there at all. It was only when she looked closer that she saw the sleeping woman who was swaddled up there. Her eyes were closed and she looked as thin and wrinkled as the bedsheets themselves.

"My dear, dear Daxa," the Doctor said, taking her frail hand. "It has been too long." The woman did not stir, and he looked up at the brothers standing there. Edith noticed that, although Khageshwaar remained the same, Babu's face had scrunched up into a scowl. "How long has she been like this?"

"Since a few weeks after our father passed on," Khageshwaar began. "She sleeps most of the day. She takes a little water, a little soup. Binsa – that's my wife," he explained to Edith, "has been tending to her – but there's not much we can do."

"There's *everything* we can do."

It was Babu who had spoken. The ferocity in his voice startled Edith. She saw, now, how his hands were clenched into fists and his face turned to a mask of anger.

"Babu," Khageshwaar began. "This isn't the time. . ."

"Not the time?" Babu gasped. "Doctor, you must be

able to do something. It's you, Doctor, you who told me that human beings are just another kind of animal."

"Oh, Babu," said the Doctor, gently. "Your mother is..."

"Not past saving," Babu spat, "if only my *brother* would listen."

Khageshwaar remained calm. "A doctor came up from Kathmandu and made sure she was in no pain. It is simply her time. She will soon be with our father."

Babu pulled away and flashed an angry glance at Khageshwaar. For a moment, Edith thought Babu might hit his brother, and she flinched. But then, swallowing his anger at the very last moment, he turned and stormed wordlessly from the room.

Khageshwaar sighed. "Babu was always the wildest of us, even when we were small."

"Be kind to him, K," said the Doctor. "He is scared."

Khageshwaar nodded. "He still has not recovered from the passing of our father. He is angry with the world. He cannot accept that no medical care could help our mother, no matter if a hospital was built here tomorrow." He paused. "It is difficult for him. I have my dear Binsa – and our own child on the way. Babu has only my mother. When she goes..."

"Can't you fly her down the mountain?" Edith asked quietly. "Take her to a hospital in a city?"

Khageshwaar smiled sadly. "I fear she would not make the journey. Our mother is old. She wants to be at peace. She wants to be with our father – up on the mountain, where he is buried."

The Doctor stood. "There is no more difficult moment in life than this, my friend." He spoke softly, his eyes taking on a faraway expression. "Babu will no doubt come to terms with things in his own time. Grief is a difficult thing." Then he looked down at the sleeping lady. "I should like to see her, when she wakes," he said. "But now, Khageshwaar, we have come a long way. Food, and drink – and, yes, a nice bubbly bath. After that, we have much planning to do." He went to a window and, wiping away the condensation from the glass, looked up at the mountainside. "I only hope we are not already too late."

Back in the hallway, Edith was grateful to see that both her boots were waiting where she had left them. The Doctor, however, was not so lucky. He hopped around in a circle, one boot on and one boot off, his face screwed up in puzzlement.

"Better check behind the log pile," grinned Edith.

Khageshwaar and the Doctor both looked at her, the Doctor's eyes creasing with amusement.

"I'll go and look," Khageshwaar said, slightly uncertainly. Moments later, he was striding back through the front door with one chewed-up, and decidedly slobbery boot in his hand.

"It's here!" he called, laughing as the Doctor squelched his foot back inside. "And look, I found my old slipper hidden behind there as well!"

As they set out, back to the village, she could hear the whispery voices of the two puppies who watched them go.

"How did they find that so quick?"

"Old Khaggy must have smelt the boot – it really did have a whiff about it!"

"Best place for it out by the log pile."

"They nabbed the slipper as well. . . I loved that slipper!"

Edith looked around, thinking she might catch sight of the puppies scampering around in the yard, but they were nowhere to be found. All that she saw was the shadowy figure of Babu, who emerged from the lean-to where the milking goats had been tethered, his eyes narrowed with brooding anger, his face marked by the tracks of the tears he had been crying for his mother.

CHAPTER ELEVEN

*In which our intrepid adventurers
prepare themselves for a journey into
the wildest mountains on Earth – and
events take an unexpected turn...*

Edith had never enjoyed a bath as much in the whole of her life. In the hotel room at the Traveller's Rest, she dipped her head under the water, submerging beneath the bubbles.

It had been midday by the time they returned to the hotel. Khageshwaar would return the next morning when they would plan the expedition. The hotel was much grander than anything Edith had ever seen, and she and her uncle had a suite that was bigger and more comfortably provisioned than anywhere she had ever stayed before. Two identical rooms with a huge single bed and red shaggy rug on the floor were connected by a door into a kind of study, which held an ornately carved wooden desk and a large gold-framed mirror, along with two armchairs and a separate door leading off to the large en-suite bathroom in which she was currently very happily ensconced.

There were bubbles everywhere.

Once she had got out of the bath and dressed, she wandered back through to the lounge area.

"These rooms are amazing!"

"Nepal doesn't just cater for budget backpackers, my dear, although I'm not quite sure what we will do with all this space." The Doctor – who had cleaned himself already, but didn't seem to have noticed the bubbles still sprouting out of his left ear – was whirling around the room, pulling notebooks from his voluminous pockets, and placing phials and pens and medical equipment across every available surface.

"You must rest, Edie. Gather your strength, for there'll be little chance to laze around when we head into the mountains."

"Oh, Doctor!' she laughed. "Rest, when we've only just got here? I'm not tired one bit!"

"Lay your head on that mattress," the Doctor began. "Doctor's orders!"

And sure enough, as soon as her head touched the pillow, she realized that the Doctor was right.

It was nine p.m. when Edith awoke. Feeling parched and dazed – but very much rested – she sat up, blinking away the sleep. The room was dark, but a dim glow came through the open door from the other room. And there was her uncle, sitting at a desk in the window, his head in his books, one pencil tucked behind one ear and another gripped between his teeth. He appeared to be in the grip of some enormous medical problem – and, what was more, he didn't seem to have slept a wink at all.

"I told you so, Edie," he grinned, without looking up. "Now there'll be no excuses on the mountainside."

"But didn't you need to rest too?"

The Doctor, poring over some textbooks, gave a little chuckle. The feeble lamplight was doing its best to illuminate the pages but, at last, the Doctor flicked on the main light switch, blasting the room in brightness.

"No chance. Always so much to do. I don't need much sleep though; trick of the trade, you might say."

"What are you reading?" Edith rubbed her eyes, her

stomach rumbling as she realized she hadn't eaten since they'd arrived.

"Ah, a fantastic book! And very, very useful for what we've got ahead of us. It's a bit of a strange transcript, but I need to refresh myself. Yetis, you see, have a highly complicated digestive process. Antelopes have three stomachs – cows have four, of course – but yetis, being a bit more complicated, have five! They are wonderful animals, Edie. Do you know, they even have two rows of teeth! They grind their food over three cycles of rumination, in order to accumulate sufficient saliva to aid the digestive process. The saliva, being alkaline, counteracts the acid secretions from the first stomach and aids the digestive process further down the gut. Without it, the acid would build up and then who knows what would happen!"

Edith stood up and walked over to the desk, peering down at another textbook that lay open. She saw a picture on the page and the Doctor noticed her glance.

"Ah!" he said. "It's the Rod of Asclepius. An ancient Greek symbol that represents healing the sick through medicine. The serpent shedding its skin is a symbol of rebirth and fertility; the staff is a symbol of authority befitting the God of Medicine. Asclepius was the Greek god of healing."

"It's a bit of a strange symbol to represent healing."

"Well, truth be told, it's actually much older than that – it's believed to originate from the treatment for guinea worm disease."

"Guinea worm?"

"It's a parasite that infects people when they drink contaminated water. Initially there are no symptoms – but then a female worm forms a blister under someone's skin and the worm emerges over the course of a few weeks. Very painful. The females can be up to a metre long. Quite a size."

The Doctor raised his eyebrows as Edith listened attentively.

"Anyway, guinea worm infection used to be treated by cutting a slit on a patient's skin just in front of the path of the worm. As the worm crawled out of the cut, the physician carefully wound the pest around a stick until the entire animal had been removed. More than three thousand years ago, physicians would advertise that they could do this by putting a sign showing a worm on a stick in front of their house."

"How do they treat it now?"

"Well, they now use antibiotics to make the extraction easier and stop secondary infections – but in truth it's pretty much the same technique. Times haven't changed that much! The difference is that, nowadays, we try to prevent it rather than treat it." The Doctor chuckled. "Genetically, homo sapiens have virtually identical DNA to our ancestors even 50,000 years ago."

Edith's face wore a slightly confused expression.

"The point is, my dear, that whilst many treatments do evolve, the principles of medicine hardly ever change. Even if one patient dies, knowing what caused that patient's death can save the lives of others. The art of medicine needs a logical mind. And we'll need both of ours in tip-top shape if we are to help these poor yetis!"

Edith nodded thoughtfully, trying to take in what he was telling her. They were silent for a moment and then the Doctor smiled.

"You look famished! Betty would never forgive me if you starved before we've even left! Why don't you head down to the restaurant? I believe they are still serving food. Could you get me a plate of cheesy chips? Two things I find accessible almost anywhere in the world are cheese and chips. It's the food of kings and queens." He paused. "I'll take some marshmallows too, should they have any."

Edith wondered if many kings or queens actually did eat cheesy chips, but it sounded divine to her. Her tummy must have heard too, because all of a sudden it was rumbling uncontrollably – so, pulling on her shoes, she hurried downstairs.

As Edith pulled open the heavy glass door to the restaurant at the Traveller's Rest and walked cautiously in, it was much busier than she expected. The bar itself curved out from the back wall, facing towards rows of square wooden tables, each surrounded by red leather chairs. There was a faint smell of stale tobacco hanging in the air, but the light brown carpet – although worn and thin in places – looked clean and the atmosphere was buzzing with a crowd of patrons. At first, she wondered if an unaccompanied eleven-year-old really ought to be venturing into this noisy, smoky place alone – but, in fact, nobody batted an eyelid as she pushed through the press of people. In fact, most of the cosmopolitan characters lounging around the place stood out far more than she did.

There were some people dressed in brightly coloured Nepalese cotton garments. Others were clearly mountain climbers, busily swapping stories about their conquests up the perilous mountain routes. A few of the patrons looked like typical tourists, with rucksacks, handbags and maps.

However, the main reason people didn't notice Edith was because they were all too busy keeping an eye on one particular group who filled up a large space in the middle of the room.

Edith could hear them from halfway across the busy restaurant. As she weaved through the tables, heading for the bar where she hoped to collect two heaving portions of cheesy chips, she found herself edging closer towards the group with every step. And little wonder: although the rest of the restaurant was swarming, the area around the group was practically empty. Nobody, it seemed, felt comfortable about getting close.

It wasn't just the fact that so many of them seemed to have scowls fixed on their faces. Nor was it the fact that there were so many of them – there must have been fifteen or more, dominating the big table, all dressed in black combat fatigues. Nor was it, even, the troubling fact that there were many large knives, axes and even a rack of hunting rifles propped up against their table.

It was something else in the air. Something palpable and menacing. Edith had never felt a sensation like this before. It was like this group of people *smelt* of trouble.

Most of the group were big, burly men – but the figure holding court at the head of the table was a tall, striking lady with flame-red hair and piercing green eyes. Edith immediately sensed that she was probably the one in charge of all of them.

For the briefest of moments, the lady's eyes swept over Edith. She felt herself inadvertently flinch as if she'd suffered a small electric shock. Then, quickly bowing her head, she hurried past, ducking her head down until she'd reached the bar.

There, a kindly barman asked, "And what can I get the little miss?"

"Cheesy chips," Edith said, casting a quick glance over her shoulder. "Two portions please."

"Ah, the little miss is hungry tonight!"

"No, no," said Edith, distracted again by the red-haired woman. "One's for my uncle. And some marshmallows, if you have any?"

The barman grinned. "I'll see what I can do – and I won't tell if you won't. I'll let you into a little secret. I once ate *three* portions of our famous cheesy chips for dinner, and another one for dessert! Coming right up, miss!"

And he spun around on his heel to rustle them up.

Edith tried not to look back at the table where the big group sat, but it was difficult. There was almost something magnetic about the lady at the head of the table. A jagged scar ran the length of her cheekbone. It seemed to be a badge of honour.

Something told Edith she should stay away. Something else told her she should get nearer. That part won. She edged her way back across the restaurant floor until she could hear.

"And then I shot it in the chest. I thought it was dead. Assumed I'd hit its heart by the way it dropped. But when I walked up to it and crouched down –" She looked around at her audience – "its amber eyes locked on to mine. Dying it might have been, but this beast wasn't giving up. It reared up and pounced on me. A four-hundred-pound male lion had me pinned. . ."

The audience waited expectantly.

One of the men sported an eyepatch and wore a heavy gold ring on his little finger. Unbeknownst to Edith, the ring held the symbol of one of the deadliest biker gangs in the world, the Bandidos. His huge frame seemed to dwarf the other man standing next to him. He leaned forward expectantly, hanging on every word.

"I didn't scream. I didn't shout. I knew I had fractions of a second to live as it opened its jaws to bite off my face. Instead, I reached into my belt and pulled out my hunting knife."

The lady reached behind her belt and pulled a serrated blade from a sheath. It was a wicked-looking weapon, designed to deliver a killing stab with a single thrust. Its jet-black handle was embossed in gold with a flaming skull.

"This was the knife I used. The Syndicate awarded it to me after achieving my first hundred kills."

The Syndicate. Edith gave a little gasp.

A flicker of a smile played across the lady's lips as she paused for dramatic effect. "I thrust this knife, point first, deep into the lion's gaping maw, jamming my arm in-between its teeth. . ."

"It's a miracle you didn't lose your arm, Arabella," said the man with the eyepatch. The words were almost a snarl of delight.

Arabella sighed wistfully. Her lips curved into a cruel smile.

"Wasn't it a knife that took your eye, Salva?" she said to the big man with the eyepatch.

Salva shifted uncomfortably and reached up to run his fingers over the black eyepatch. Then he nodded silently, clearly hoping the conversation would move on.

"What happened?" rasped another of the men. This one, Edith noticed, only had one ear.

"I got stabbed, Basco," snapped Salva. "It happens when people like us upset each other."

Basco grinned. A knife had instantaneously appeared in his hand and Salva's remaining eye widened in surprise at the sudden glint of metal.

"But I'm not like you, Salva. I've still got both my eyes for a start."

"Oh, I forgot," Salva replied. "They cut your ear off with a pair of scissors. You don't actually know what a real knife fight is like, do you?"

"I'm a very fast learner, cyclops!"

Edith took a sharp intake of breath, convinced that

one of these villains was about to plunge a knife into the other. And perhaps it was only that gasp that stopped a bloody battle from beginning – for every eye at the table seemed to shift, to take in the little girl who was standing there, staring at them, with her mouth opened wide. The woman named Arabella had a particularly curious look on her face. She looked Edith up and down.

Edith felt sick. These people weren't just hunters of animals; they were killers.

For the first time there was silence around the table.

Then a call came out from the bar – "Cheesy Chips! Double Cheesy Chips for the little miss! And a bowl of marshmallows!" – and Edith, spinning around, dashed back to the counter to pick them up.

"One portion for you and one for your 'uncle', eh?" The barman grinned, and handed two enormous plates over, with a bowl of marshmallows balanced on top.

Back at the table where the brutish gang were sitting, the conversation had started again. With any luck, they'd forgotten completely about the girl who'd been staring at them, listening in. Now, they were talking about a whaling voyage, deep-sea fishing with big harpoons, and Edith slipped past unnoticed.

She hadn't forgotten them, though. They'd said that

single word which seemed to be stalking her from one side of the planet to another: *Syndicate*.

The Doctor, she thought. She had to tell the Doctor...

She was so focused on balancing the cheesy chips and marshmallows on top, repeating the names she'd heard – Arabella, Salva, Basco – under her breath so that she wouldn't forget, that she hardly noticed the little creature padding across the restaurant carpet as she hurried from the bar. In fact, it was only when the creature got entangled with her feet and she almost tripped that she slowed and looked down.

A cat with striking silver features was staring at her incredulously, as if affronted that it had almost been trampled underfoot. Then, quite haughtily, it sat down and began grooming itself.

"Stupid humans, messing up my fine coat!"

A thought occurred to Edith, and she focused her mind.

"Hello."

The cat stopped licking its leg and regarded Edith with what could only be described as aloof caution.

"Are you talking to me?" The cat's voice sounded slightly bemused and more than a little suspicious.

"Yes," Edith said. *"It's nice to meet you. I'm sorry for almost stepping on you."*

"Yes, well, were you to actually step on me, I can promise you'd regret it. I've got fleas."

"Fleas?"

"Indeed. Thousands of them. And they'd have jumped straight from me on to you – and what would your mama think of that?"

It was on the tip of Edith's tongue to tell this puffed-up feline that she wasn't here with her mother and, in fact, had no idea where her mother might be – but time was of the essence, and not only because the cheesy chips were getting cold.

"Do you live here at the hotel?" she asked.

The cat didn't reply, just casually resumed licking itself.

"Please?"

"Live here? This is my hotel. I own the place!"

"Own it?"

"Oh, those mice will tell you they own it, but don't you go listening to them. Scurrying about all day, leaving their scat. And no sooner have I hunted one, ten more pop up in its place! But they don't own the Traveller's Rest. I do, and that's the way it will remain!"

Edith decided that, if she tried to argue about any of this, she was bound to lose, so instead she cut straight to the point and asked, "Do you know the people in the bar?

The ones all dressed in black?"

This time, the cat narrowed its eyes.

*"I am not sure why I can hear you in my head – or
indeed how that is possible – but I am rather busy at the
moment."*

"You're just licking yourself."

As soon as Edith thought the words she regretted
them. The cat was clearly a prickly character.

The cat promptly stood up and started to walk off, its
tail high in the air, twitching irritably.

"I'm sorry!" Edith called after it. *"It's just they were
saying horrible things about killing animals and I wondered
if you might know who they are?"*

The cat stopped and turned its head round to regard
Edith with cool disdain.

*"They're hunters. Fine, fine hunters. A cat like me
respects a good hunter. Pounce, kill, pounce! Miss Arabella
and her team have a fine reputation for hunting."*

*"Hunters? Are they allowed to do that? Go into the
mountains and kill animals?"*

The cat almost seemed to smile. Its eyes glinted with
a hint of what Edith could only interpret as amusement.

*"Every species hunts in one way or another. You
humans are amongst the worst."*

"Can you go find out what they're doing here? What

they are planning to hunt?"

The cat turned the rest of its body round to face Edith, as if seeing her in a new light.

"Why? It's not a secret. Everyone benefits from them being here. Half the people in this hotel have come to hunt. They come, pay the price, fill the hotel rooms, eat in the restaurant, buy snacks from the shop. Money, little girl! It makes the world go round! Why, the Traveller's Rest itself would hardly be here at all without the hunters who make it their base. Jomsom – the whole village! – would just . . . disappear! The only ones who lose out are the snow leopards, barking deer or the bharals."

Edith had never heard of an animal called a bharal before.

"Bharals?"

The cat seemed to find this amusing as well.

"You seem a very innocent human. Bharals, tahrs, blue sheep – whatever you humans call them – are the wild, goat-like creatures up in the mountains. Plucky things, but they've got more courage than they have good sense. They make fine game hunting as well. Hunters come from all over the world to hunt them here." The cat began preening again. *"It's perfectly normal. After all, there's nothing wrong with a good hunt. Just ask my mice. . ."*

A chill ran up Edith's spine. She wasn't sure if she

liked this cat. Something of her distaste must have shown on her face because the cat was clearly enjoying itself. It continued after the briefest of pauses.

"That group, though, they haven't really come for the bharals. I know that, because it's my business to know everything that goes on in my hotel. Now, their hunting permit might say 'bharal' on it – but that, human girl, is NONSENSE. Oh no, these hunters have come for something much bigger."

Edith could hardly bring herself to think the word.

"Yetis?"

The cat stared intently back.

"So," it miaowed, "you're not quite as simple as you look, little girl. Yes, this lot have come with the biggest prize in mind. The pelt of the Himalayan yeti. The Abominable Snowman itself. The Guardian of these mountains. It's been a lifetime since one was actually hunted in these mountains, but hunters like these, they want the biggest prize possible. They want to go down in history. Many have tried before them. But this lot? This lot are serious. I know, for a fact, that they've hired the best guides money can buy. They claim to be the best hunters in the world, don't they? No expenses spared! And if there's one thing Arabella Spearstrike and her Syndicate want, it's the pelt of a yeti to call their own!"

CHAPTER TWELVE

*In which the best-laid plans are thwarted,
and the Doctor and Edith must set
off at once, into the storm...*

By the time Edith had hurtled back to the room, the cheesy chips were hardly hot at all – but the Doctor didn't mind. To him, they were still delicious. He set about mixing in the marshmallows with the cheesy chips and devouring them with gusto as, breathlessly, Edith explained everything that she'd heard.

"And you're certain?" the Doctor asked, wiping the last pieces of cheddar from his lips. A heavy shadow seemed to have passed over his craggy features, clouding his usually cheerful disposition.

"I heard them myself. They used the word Syndicate. What should we do, Doctor? Call the police?"

The Doctor thought for a moment, then shook his head.

"They haven't broken any laws yet. No, they'll have been careful. They will have permits to hunt in the mountains."

Edith marched, in frustration, to the window where the Doctor sat and looked out into the darkness, at the face of the frosted mountain, magnificent in the moonlight.

"Why would anyone want to come somewhere so beautiful to kill animals?" she exclaimed. "It's horrible!"

"Yes, Edie," the Doctor agreed. "For those of us who can't comprehend it, it is impossible to understand these people. Yet hunting is a right. A freedom of mankind to kill, take, or destroy whatever he or she wants. Life is about choice. These people choose to do this. In the eyes of the law, what they want is no more or no less important than what we want. Such are the laws and rules by which we live. Animals have no rights, no voice in this. If people pay a fee, the government let them take our creatures. We cannot change that."

"But the cat was saying that these hunters are here for the yetis! They can't have a permit for that!"

The Doctor shook his head. His lips were a thin tight line as he reached up and adjusted his cap.

"This Syndicate, Doctor. Are they the ones you talked about? The ones who hunt mythical creatures?"

The Doctor remained impassive. "This lady you saw, what exactly did she look like?"

"She was tall. With flaming red hair."

Edith saw the Doctor's face harden even further.

"Edie, this is important. Did she have a. . ."

"A scar, Doctor," Edith interrupted. "Her name was Arabella."

All at once, the Doctor stood up.

"Pack up your things. We must go to see K immediately." When he saw Edith open her mouth to ask some other question, he lifted up a hand. "There's no time for discussion," he said. "And bring your coat. We shan't be coming back to this hotel room tonight."

Outside, Edith's breath plumed in great white clouds before her as she hurried to keep up with the Doctor. With his cape flying behind him, he marched out across the freshly fallen snow of Jomsom, leaving the lights of the Traveller's Rest behind.

"Doctor!" she called out. "Doctor, please!"

"It's them, Edie." The Doctor panted as the cold air lanced into his lungs. "By the stars up above, I'd hoped never to see that woman again!" Suddenly, he stopped in the snow, skidded around so that he was facing Edith and braced her by the shoulders.

The Doctor started marching again, and Edith struggled to keep up.

"Doctor, I don't understand!"

"The lady you saw, her name is Arabella Spearstrike. Edie, I'm sorry I keep so much from you, but know this: the Spearstrikes have been at the heart of the Syndicate for generations. That family have been hunting animals for trophies for generations – no doubt their ancestors were the ones who wiped out the woolly mammoths and sabre-toothed tigers! Wanton killers! That's what they are! No more, no less!"

The Doctor's words had started to break up, the more furious he was becoming. He steadied himself with a few deep breaths. By now they had come to the outskirts of Jomsom village, where Khageshwaar's house sat, banked in deep snow.

"I have a lot of history with them, my dear. The Syndicate has been in these mountains before. They came hunting for yetis back then as well." He said it with such sadness that Edith knew there was an even deeper mystery here. "But I can't talk about that tonight. For now, just know that Arabella Spearstrike is ruthless. The Spearstrikes profit from the blood of the innocent creatures they kill. They have no code, no sense of honour, no compassion. Yet they are here and they are on the hunt again."

"Come on, Doctor," she said. "Let's hurry."

Edith tumbled down the hill to Khageshwaar's door, the Doctor running close behind. As they arrived at the doorway, the Doctor banged his fist on the door repeatedly until it opened a crack and a sliver of light spilled out into the darkness.

"Khageshwaar, my dear friend. May we come in? Most urgent, I'm afraid."

Momentarily startled at seeing the Doctor standing outside, Khageshwaar pulled the door open wider and beckoned them in. The puppies once again bounded around their feet playfully, excited by the return of the Doctor and Edith, before Khageshwaar shooed them away and gestured they come into the kitchen.

"Please, Doctor, Edith. Sit and tell me what's wrong."

The Doctor pulled back a simple wooden kitchen chair and hurriedly sat down. "Khageshwaar, my old friend, we have to leave. The Syndicate are in the hotel."

Khageshwaar's mouth dropped open slightly as he digested the information.

"I believe they must know, as we do, that there is an injured yeti. I intend to heal it. They have come to kill it."

"They won't be able to find the yetis," said Khageshwaar. "Only the most experienced tracker would stand a chance. They failed before, Doctor. They'll fail again."

The Doctor shook his head vehemently. "You know the cost last time they were here. They mean business. But how do they know? Somebody must have told them there was an injured yeti up there. Somebody must have summoned them in. Who else knows, K? You must think!"

Khageshwaar frowned and shook his head in bewilderment. "Only me, Doctor – and you can't possibly think that I. . ."

Edith cleared her throat. "I think they have hired a guide. That's what the cat said. . ."

Khageshwaar shook his head. "No matter who they pay to guide them up the mountain, they will not know where the yetis are. Even if they were able to get up into the remote peaks, there are many caves."

"Then how will we find them, Khageshwaar?" Edith asked.

"It is as it has always been. The mountain animals will lead us to them." Khageshwaar paused. "You know my belief, Doctor. The yetis must be protected at all costs. They are a part of the mountains, a part of us, as old as the rock beneath our feet. Without them, the magic will be gone." Khageshwaar ran his hand across his brow, as if he was trying to brush away a heavy shadow.

As Khageshwaar's voice tailed off, Edith watched her uncle. The Doctor had seemingly frozen on the spot, his head cocked on one side as he gazed out of the window into the blackness beyond.

"We have to go," he whispered. "Khageshwaar, we need a head start. We cannot let them win."

A sudden fury of snow plastered itself across the window, so that Edith could barely see the mountains on the other side.

"Doctor – it is too dangerous to go now," Khageshwaar said. "The mountains are unsettled. It's dark. It's cold. We would be in peril."

"The yetis are in peril! We have to go!"

The kitchen door creaked open. The Doctor, K and Edith all turned their heads.

A woman came into the room and calmly sat down, her hands gently resting over her pregnant belly.

"I have heard you talking. Khageshwaar, my dear, the Doctor is right. You must leave. Babu will be back soon.

He will take care of us until your return. I am not due for two weeks. You will easily be back in time. I will nurse your mother myself. But you have to go. This evil woman cannot win. Not ever."

Khageshwaar didn't say anything. He walked around to where his wife was sitting and knelt down on the floor, clasping her hand with both of his. Bowing his head, he touched his forehead gently to the back of her hand.

The Doctor gave a sigh of relief. "Binsa, thank you. We will have him home in a flash. But can you also do me a favour?"

Binsa lifted her head. "Of course, Doctor."

"Can you send an urgent message to Forest Cottage? I must inform Betty of developments."

Binsa nodded and the Doctor smiled his thanks. "We must leave within the hour."

Khageshwaar nodded and, laying a hand on his wife's shoulder for a moment, he left the room.

Binsa smiled across at Edith. "I will find you some mountain clothes. Before this," Binsa pointed at her pregnant belly, "I was almost the same size as you!"

Despite a sudden feeling of nervousness coursing through her, Edith laughed.

The Doctor cleared his throat and the two of them glanced across at him. He shrugged as if slightly apologetic. "Binsa, my dear, you don't happen to have a pen and paper, do you? I must write my message."

"What will you write, Doctor?" Edith asked.

"I will ask for Francis to join us immediately. It will put a strain on poor Betty, but needs must. When he arrives, Babu can lead him up the mountain to join us." The Doctor hung his head. "Oh, Edie, I am sorry. I didn't mean to bring you into such danger. I didn't think to. . ."

"Doctor!" Edith declared. "I won't hear a word of it! I *wanted* to come. I *want* to be here and do what I can and . . . and . . . well, if it wasn't for me, you wouldn't know the Syndicate was here at all. So it's a good job I came. Maybe now those yetis have a chance."

The Doctor thought for a moment, and nodded.

"And maybe I'll be able to help up there as well," Edith said, turning to face the mountains.

CHAPTER THIRTEEN

*In which Arabella Spearstrike
and the Syndicate embark on an
expedition of their own...*

In the restaurant at the Traveller's Rest hotel, Arabella Spearstrike pulled back her chair and cast her eyes around the menacing group of men seated around her. They were a fine bunch of killers – tough and ruthless – exactly what was required for the task at hand. As food was brought over to the tables and the bar had emptied of guests, Arabella considered that this could be the pinnacle of her hunting career.

Arabella Spearstrike still remembered the day she'd first dreamt of holding a yeti pelt in her hands. How old had she been? Five, six, seven years old? She'd been sitting there, in her father's hunting camp high in the Rocky Mountains, and, as the night drew in around them and the campfire crackled, her father had come to wrap the pelt of the grizzly bear he'd just killed around her.

Never before had she felt so proud. "Daddy," she'd said, "are you the best hunter in the world?"

Her father's eyes had gleamed. "Not yet, my treasure," he'd said. "I've hunted lion and elephant. I've hunted dragon and wyvern. But there's one pelt I've never felt, running through these hands. The pelt of a yeti."

And he'd told her all about those fabled beasts, high up in the Himalayan mountains, and how he longed to be the first huntsman in generations to drag one back to civilization. Alive or dead, he'd said, it didn't matter to him. It didn't matter to Arabella Spearstrike either. For thirty years, she'd been building up to this moment. Somewhere along the way, her father's dream had become her own. For years, the Syndicate had tried to kill a yeti; once, many years ago, they had even come close, but she had never had an opportunity like this – and now was her moment. She had the yetis right where she wanted them.

The door of the bar swung open and a short, stocky Nepalese man walked nervously over to the group.

"Our guide!" Arabella declared.

The guide bowed his head respectfully and Arabella looked him up and down. Casually, she reached into her pocket and withdrew a rolled bundle of notes.

Tossing it towards the guide, she flashed him a wolfish grin. "You know what we're hunting." She grinned. "And you know that one is sick. Show us where and I'll pay you ten times that bundle."

The guide fingered the roll of money and nodded his head quickly.

"Good," Arabella said, standing. "But you understand that we must reach it before it dies. The kill will be mine. Do you understand?"

Once more, the guide nodded his head.

"When can we depart?" she demanded.

The guide licked his lips, which suddenly felt very dry. "The paths are treacherous, Madam. The yetis are in the highest peaks. We should leave early and travel as lightly as we are able. It will be hard going but I can take you there in a day's trek. We must go quietly. Yetis are sensitive and they will hide if they have warning of our approach."

"We won't find them then, will we?" One of the men spoke up. "How can all of us creep up unnoticed?" He risked a glance across to Arabella, who fixed him with an icy glare. The man dropped his gaze back to his plate.

"It is true they will hear our party approach," the guide said. He swallowed. "But, you must understand, they are already expecting a party of humans. A healer has been summoned to tend to the sick yeti. As long as we get there before them, they will think we are the ones coming to help them."

Arabella Spearstrike digested this information.

So, she thought, *the Doctor has been called*. Their paths would cross again. Last time they had met, he had managed to foil the Syndicate – but it had cost him dearly. Arabella had enjoyed that.

Arabella Spearstrike could only smile to herself as imagined what would happen this time.

She fixed her eyes on the guide. "When was he summoned?"

"Immediately after the yeti was sighted," the guide replied. "The same day you were notified."

Arabella Spearstrike marched across the emptying room and stood at the window, gazing out through the strafing snow. Her eyes looked distant for a moment. Then she clicked a finger, instructing the guide to join her at the parted curtains.

"Yes, Miss Spearstrike?"

Quick as a poison dart, Arabella reached out and grabbed the guide by the chin, forcing his head around so that he, too, was staring, pinch-faced, out of the window. Then, raising one long finger on her other hand, she pointed through the snow-flecked glass, a furious expression coming over her face.

"Are those lights?"

The guide squinted. The mountain face was dark and swirling in snow. But it did look like torches playing on the crags out there: beams of light moving jaggedly up the mountainside.

He shook his head in confusion. "It must be tourists looking for their hotel. It is late. It would be madness for anyone to be out trekking at this time of night."

All at once, Salva, Basco and the other mercenaries from the Syndicate were up and out of their seats, crowding around Arabella.

"They're heading away from us," Basco spat. "Going up the mountain, by the looks of it."

"Could there be other hunters here as well?" Arabella demanded, her eyes flashing dangerously. "Hunters who know what we are after?"

"No," the guide said quickly. "I only called you."

Arabella stared at the lights, watching them closely. "Then it's the Doctor," she breathed.

The guide shook his head vigorously. "It would be madness for anyone to be heading out to the mountain at night. They'll slip and fall! They wouldn't risk it! If they perished on the mountainside, why, who would save the yetis then?"

Too late, the guide realized what he had said. Every eye in the Syndicate turned to stare at him.

"It *is* the Doctor," Arabella Spearstrike snapped, bringing back her hand and striking him once across the jaw, "and you *know* he is out there!"

Abruptly, she turned around. In front of her, all the mercenaries stared.

"Grab your bags and equipment. The hunt has already begun. GO!"

CHAPTER FOURTEEN

*In which our intrepid team battle against
the elements, braving snow and gales in the
mountain crags, quite unaware that the killers
are on their heels — or who is guiding them...*

Edith heaved in short, icy breaths of mountain air, forcing her legs to keep pace with the group. She could see Khageshwaar streaming ahead of her, cutting the path up the mountainside. Since they'd left his home in Jomsom village, barely a word had been spoken. The only sounds, apart from the low moan of the wind, came from the crunching of stone under their feet as they trekked up the narrow rocky mountain path. The snow was thick around them, but where they sheltered in a gully, the track was free from the powder and wound its way steeply up the mountainside, barely wide enough for them to walk in single file.

It was easier to see on the mountain than Edith had expected. The moon reflected on the snow, creating an eerie pale light. It wasn't as cold as she'd been anticipating either – even though she could already see crystals of frost forming in her eyelashes. As soon as Binsa had learned that Edith only had one jumper, she had quickly assembled a huge pile of mountain clothes for her to wear. After adding layer upon layer, Edith now felt four times her original size.

Khageshwaar led them at the front. He was carrying a box as well as a huge pack strapped to his back, but he was conditioned by and born of the mountains. Edith knew the strength of Sherpas was legendary and she marvelled that he didn't show a glimmer of fatigue as he powered upwards, effortlessly carrying his load.

Not once had she complained about the pace, but her legs burned and she steeled herself to keep them moving. She idly wondered what the other kids back at St Margot Montefiore's would say if they could see her now, hiking up a mountain in Nepal in a race to save a mythical creature. Despite the pain she was in, she smiled to herself. They would never believe it!

Behind Edith, the Doctor was lost in thought, his short legs moving quickly up the mountain. He hadn't spoken since they had left; her uncle seemed very preoccupied.

After several hours of hiking, as the moon arced across the night sky, and, after scaling a short but almost vertical section of the track, they reached a rocky ridge, where Khageshwaar stopped and passed around a water bottle.

The Doctor shook his head and moved away from them, quickly removing some items from his pockets as he did so. Sinking to his knees, he placed a small bowl on the ground and a small wooden mallet beside it.

"Uncle," Edith asked, "why have you got a bowl in your pockets?"

The Doctor, lit up in the snowy light, gave her a smile. "Always be prepared, my dear. You might be the best car driver in the world, but if you don't have a car, you'll end up walking, just like everyone else."

Khageshwaar laughed. "There are no cars allowed on the mountain, Doctor, you know that!"

"K, don't be frivolous; you know exactly what I'm doing and how important it is. We have to signal to the yetis and let them know we're coming."

Khageshwaar gave her a grin.

"We must tell the yetis we are coming in peace. If we don't, they may hide from us – or worse, cause an avalanche to deter us from approaching." Khageshwaar craned his head upwards, to study the night sky. He had told Edith this was how he judged the weather, the coming of the winds and snow.

Now the Doctor had set about placing a series of tea light candles around the bowl, and then he took a tiny vial of purple liquid and carefully poured a tiny drop on to each candle. Edith watched, her curiosity mounting as her uncle continued his strange ritual.

"Now, as I light these candles, please arrange yourselves behind me. Try to keep close together; this bit is always a touch fiddly. I don't want the candles to go out. We want them to pick up the scent."

A strong smell of perfumed incense drifted into the air as the Doctor lit the candles. Soon, the scent began to engulf them. The burning wick from each candle gave off a faint blue smoke which snaked into the night air and trailed off up the mountain, whipped away by the wind. As it travelled, it would grow fainter and fainter – human beings would not be able to sense it, but Edith knew from her reading that yetis had an incredibly strong sense of smell.

"Edie, please shuffle forwards a bit. K, get close. Try

not to inhale too much of the smoke – it will make you light-headed. Perilous business to be dizzy up here."

Edith shuffled forward and respectfully took her kneeling position directly behind the Doctor.

Her uncle closed his eyes and, for a moment, no one spoke or made a sound. Edith found herself almost hypnotized by the silence. Reaching out a hand, the Doctor picked up the wooden mallet and proceeded to drag it around the rim of the bowl, which he held balanced on his other palm. As the mallet rotated around the outside rim, a sustained musical note sounded out over the mountainside, echoing in the gully. The note soared in volume as the Doctor continued to slowly rotate it.

"He's sending the signal."

As soon as she heard the voice, Edith opened her eyes. Where it had come from, she was not sure. She looked around quickly, trying to seek out whichever animal's voice had made its way into her thoughts – but all that she could see were the rocks and the snow.

"Been a long time since anyone has observed the proper etiquette," came a second braying voice. *"Just like in times of old. Very respectful."*

"Strange-looking group though, aren't they? What's he got on?"

"It's a costume. Some sort of cloth hanging off his back."

"Can he fly?"

The two voices exploded in a riot of laughter in Edith's head.

"Why is there a little human with them?" another asked, with a note of outrage in its voice. "Little lambs should not be out on this side of the mountain at night."

"She hasn't even got a proper fitting fleece!"

"It looks warm though. Thick wool on her."

The voices cascaded into Edith's head but, no matter how hard she cast her eyes about the mountainside, she couldn't uncover their source.

"He's getting the volume up."

"Very impressive. Bound to get their attention with that."

"Yes. This will mark him out, all right. They'll be watching."

"That note was spot on."

There was a pause. Then:

"I'm a bit peckish. Do you think this will go on for a bit? Can anyone see any poppies about?"

A sudden skittering of small rocks on one of the crags overhead drew Edith's attention, and she craned around to peer into that particular pocket of darkness. Suddenly, she could make out silhouettes on the rocks above them.

Six shapes were looking down. To Edith, they looked like sheep – but not the usual type of sheep Edith had seen back at Forest Cottage. These were stockier. Each with a pair of curled horns. Some seemed to grow up and out from their heads like an upside-down moustache, while others were shorter and straighter.

She dared to speak. *"Hello?"*

On the crags above, the animals went rigid with the shock of hearing her voice.

"Are you hearing that?" one of them asked, in astonishment.

"Have you been grazing that lichen again?"

"Surely you heard her?"

Edith was going to have to try again. Edith tried to put her uncle's ritual out of her mind and focused her own thoughts on the silhouetted sheep above them. Such was the single-mindedness of her uncle's concentration that he scarcely seemed to notice as she slowly stood up to get a better view of the visitors.

"Hello, sheep."

The creatures skittered back, sending a small shower of stones bounding down the mountainside. Slowly, they edged forwards again.

"Oh, my goodness!" one of them indignantly called. *"It can talk!"*

"And," gasped a horrified other, *"she dared to call us sheep. Common sheep!"*

On the crags above, there was an outburst of such horrified baa-ing that even Khageshwaar looked upwards.

"It's all well and good speaking to us!" a domineering voice shouted out. *"But to call us sheep? My fleece might fall out with the shock of it."*

Edith held her arms out in apology. Being able to speak with animals was a gift more magical than any she'd ever hoped for – but somehow she always seemed to be saying the wrong thing. It wasn't good enough to be a telepathic polyglot, not if you always managed to unwittingly insult the animals you were trying to speak with.

"Sorry," she went on, *"I didn't mean to say you were a flock of common sheep. Not at all! Are you Himalayan blue sheep?"* She paused. *"Only you don't look very blue."*

One of the animals stamped its hoof in fury. *"We are not blue and we are not sheep. We are also not a flock!"*

"Sheep indeed! For a human lamb, you really have no manners."

Khageshwaar, who couldn't help but be alerted to the commotion above, suddenly widened his eyes in surprise. "Edith, look! There are bharals here. I wonder why. They live on the other side of the mountain."

"I'll ask them." Before she went on, she had a sudden thought. "Bharals? They aren't sheep, then?"

"No – they're their own species, more goat than sheep."

Edith nodded and looked back up the mountain.

"I'm so sorry. I'm learning all the time. You're bharals, aren't you? I'm with my uncle and his friend Khageshwaar."

"That's better," one of the bharals proudly announced, shaking his horns in pride.

"Maybe she couldn't see our herd properly."

One of the bharals, a younger one by the looks of him, stuck his head out of the crowd and said, *"Your little clown man down there. He's signalling the yetis, isn't he?"*

"He's a doctor. He's the Doctor. And yes, he's signalling them. We've come to help the sick yeti."

The bharals above broke out in another cacophony of baa-ing.

"Very respectful!" cried one

"We like the yetis!" cried another.

"But you won't be going far tonight, not with this storm coming."

"No, little lamb, you won't be climbing higher tonight."

"They'll have to find shelter."

"WE'LL have to find shelter!"

"This blizzard's going to be a bad one. I can feel it in my udder!"

Edith looked up and all around. The snow that had been falling since they set off was thin and raggedy, but something had changed in the half hour since they'd made base on this crag. The light of the moon and stars that had shone down, illuminating them as they travelled, was paler – and she saw now that this was because the clouds up above had hardened, growing deeper and thicker. The wind was picking up too, churning those same clouds into constantly shifting patterns. There was a different smell in the air.

She looked at Khageshwaar, who was watching her intently.

"They say there's a storm coming."

He nodded. "I am hoping we can stay ahead of it."

She looked back at the bharals. "My friend thinks we can stay ahead of the storm."

The bharals exploded into mocking laughter. "Your Sherpa friend is no bharal! Better than many men, perhaps, but what does he know about mountain storms? We say: BAAAAAAA!"

And, up above, the baa-ing echoed and echoed again. This time, even the Doctor was wrenched from his reverie. The tune he had been conjuring up was suddenly silenced.

Khageshwaar looked again at the sky intently for a moment and his expression changed. "Doctor," he said, "there's a storm coming. It is moving quicker than I'd first thought."

The Doctor peered up at the night sky. He could see it, too, the way the snow clouds were deepening. "If you think there is a chance we can stay ahead of it, K, then stay ahead of it we shall. The yetis may have heard my calling by now. We must make haste for them. . ."

Khageshwaar gestured at Edith. "The bharals are warning us – and nature always knows best. We should look for shelter until it blows over. We will be no good to the yetis if we get blown off the mountain."

A look of confusion flashed across the Doctor's face, before he spotted the inquisitive animals, who were watching them intently.

"What are they saying, Edie?"

"They think we're foolish, being out on the mountain at night," she said. "They say this storm – it's the worst in a generation."

The Doctor screwed his face up. "I should have come alone," he said. "I could risk it alone. But not with you, Edie." He stopped. The riot of baa-ing was fading away, and even the Doctor thought he could hear that the bharals were scoffing at them. "What are they saying now?"

Edith tuned her mind back to the conversation.

"They won't survive," one of the older bharals was saying. *"No chance to make it back down in time, no chance to make it to the top."*

"Humans are weak. When the blizzard begins, the little lamb won't last an hour."

The bharals bustled around each other, butting horns.

"We'd better go ourselves. We have to get to shelter before it hits."

There was a momentary silence on the crag above. Only then did the smallest bharal poke his horns up and boldly declare, *"But where's Ada?"*

By now, Edith was starting to make out the voices in the herd. This particular bharal may have been half the size of his herd, but there was as much boldness in him as in the rest combined.

"Ada will catch us up," said one of the older bharal, who Edith decided had the tone of somebody's stubborn grandmother. *"She just had to circle around. She'll be with us shortly."*

The little bharal clearly was not convinced.

"Snow leopards all over the place!" he declared. "We can't just leave her!"

"Rakshek!" the grandmother thundered. "You might think you're as brave as your father used to be – but you can't go up against snow leopards alone. We're bharals and we follow the herd."

"I don't see why I should!" the young ram hollered.

"Ada will find a cave and see us when this storm has passed. Rakshek, come!"

The rest of the herd, seemingly no longer interested in the human beings hunkered on the rocks beneath them, had started to turn around, their silhouettes vanishing into the night. Only Rakshek didn't move, lit up by the eerie light of the snow. Edith could see the fearless set to his snout, his two proud horns.

"What about the humans?" he called. They were truly magnificent, the way they could hop from rock to rock without slipping, even in these icy climes.

"The humans are not our concern, Rakshek," a voice sailed back out of the dark.

There was a silence, and then Edith said, "Why aren't you leaving?"

Rakshek stood defiantly against the night. "I won't! Listen to me, little lamb. My herd are right. You'll perish on this mountain if you're caught in this blizzard. Can't you feel it? It's coming, and it's coming quick. Come with us!" he declared. "Come with us! We know the caves and crags in these parts. You can shelter with us."

Suddenly, the Doctor was at her side. "Edie," he began, "we must make haste. If we're to reach the yetis before the blizzard comes. . ."

"Doctor, Rakshek here has a suggestion."

For the first time, the Doctor took in the lone bharal gazing down at them. "Oh my!" he explained, his breath pluming in front of them. "What a fine young creature you are!"

Rakshek himself did not seem quite sure.

"You won't make it," he said, "not if you head for the yetis. Their caves are too high. You'd have to walk into the path of the storm. You'll freeze yourself, even under all that fur."

Suddenly another bharal reappeared at Rakshek's side.

"*Grandmama,*" Rakshek declared. "*We're going to help the humans!*"

"*And why, you impudent young thing, would we do such a thing? Humans are hunters. Humans hunt us through these mountains. Humans. . .*"

"*Have come to the mountains to help the yetis! So they're coming with us, Grandmama, and that's the last I'll hear of it!*"

The older bharal was wearing such a curious expression that even the Doctor seemed to understand she was not used to being told what to do. At last, though, she tilted her head in agreement.

"Come on, K," the Doctor declared, "it seems our journey may take a little longer than we'd anticipated. Let us hope that this blizzard keeps the Syndicate at bay as well!"

Rakshek, proud as punch to be leading this strange group into the deepest crags, took a wild leap on to a precipice and began to pick a way further up, through jagged outcrops of rock and loose shale.

As the Doctor, Edith and Khageshwaar followed, the first wilder flurries of snow started to rapidly fall.

* * *

Dawn came with a blinding whiteness that Edith had never experienced before.

They'd followed the procession of bharals for half an hour, the storm advancing like a deep, impenetrable curtain of white, until at last they'd reached a cavern, set between two sheer pinnacles of rock. Edith had fallen asleep with her head resting uncomfortably on a rather oddly shaped rock.

Now she woke groggily and looked around, trying to take in the cavern itself. It wasn't vast, she realized, but it had saved them from the lacerating wind and the bitterness of the mountains at night. In fact, she realized, she was quite warm – but that might have been something to do with Rakshek, who seemed to have been using her as a pillow. As she awoke, Rakshek stood up. The rest of the herd were milling at the cavern entrance, eager to be gone.

From the other side of the cavern, she heard the low whispers of the Doctor and Khageshwaar. Evidently, just like the bharals, they were eager to be off as well.

Edith blinked herself awake, rubbing a sore neck.

"Rakshek," she whispered, *"are you OK?"*

"I'm furious, human friend. I have just been listening to the herd. They want to go back to our homelands on the other side of the mountain. Me, I want to go looking for Ada. They say she must fend for herself!"

"What will you do?"

The bharal thundered up and down, lowering his horns as if he was about to battle with a much bigger ram.

"They're calling me a black sheep – and all because I want to do the right thing!"

"Rakshek! Raa-aaa-akshek!" came his grandmother's call from the entrance to the cavern. *"It's time to leave!"*

But he paid it no mind, just kept charging furiously up and down.

"Edie! You're awake," the Doctor called out. Leaving Khageshwaar to ready their packs and dish out a breakfast of dried fruit and biscuits, he moved over to Edith's side. "I'm so dreadfully sorry. This really wasn't part of the plan. I should never have put you in this predicament. Betty will have words with me, I'm sure."

The Doctor crouched down and peered at Edith with a concerned look on his face.

"Uncle, I'm fine. It all seems a bit of a blur. All the snow and wind . . ."

"It would have been worse without your young friend there," Khageshwaar laughed, watching Rakshek still bouldering up and down. "What's got his goat?"

"He wants to go and find his sister. She got separated from the herd. There are snow leopards that hunt this side of the mountain. But the rest of the herd just want to go home."

"Sheep are the same the whole world over, I'm afraid. Anything for a quiet life." The Doctor paused. "Not, of course, that mountain bharals are just common sheep."

"That's what *they* said!" laughed Edith.

All at once, there arose a great chorus of desperate baas and shrieks from the cavern's entrance.

"Hunters! But we're not near any usual trekking paths!" Rakshek's grandmother was baa-ing. *"They're coming for us! They're coming for us!"*

Edith, the Doctor and Khageshwaar peered out. There, some distance below them, was a group, being led through the rocks by a figure in a bright yellow hat.

The Doctor looked at Khageshwaar, a dawning horror on his face.

"I am so sorry, K," he said.

Khageshwaar didn't say anything. His face seemed to sag.

"What?" Edith asked, confused.

"Edie," said the Doctor, "the party you see coming up the mountain behind us, are they the group you saw in the restaurant at the Traveller's Rest?"

To Edith, they were just tiny figures the size of dolls.

Even so, there was little doubt in her heart. From this distance, she could not make out their faces. But she could see their striking black uniforms. She could see the guns slung over their shoulders. She could see Arabella Spearstrike, with her red hair.

She could see the Sherpa, too, with his bright yellow hat.

"Babu," she said.

She turned to look at Khageshwaar, whose face was a rictus of disbelief and horror, whose hands were digging into his pockets as he focused on keeping his anger and betrayal inside.

"It changes nothing," the Doctor finally said. "We knew they were coming. We just have to . . ."

"It changes everything!" Khageshwaar exclaimed. "Babu is my brother! He knows, as well as I do, where the yetis dwell."

The Doctor nodded. "Yes, my friend. Yes, I know. Time is of the utmost. We must leave, now."

Rakshek sensed the urgency and the change of atmosphere. With another short bleat, he turned and skittered back to Edith's side.

"You need to get to the yetis before they do. Well, I'll take you!" he declared.

"What?"

"I don't care what the herd say. I'm not going home while Ada is missing. I can take you to the heartland of the yetis and I might find a sign of her on the way!"

The other bharal, who had heard Rakshek's declaration, set up another riot of baa-ing.

"Quiet!" Rakshek's grandmother finally baa-ed. "You'll bring those hunters right to us!"

"These hunters are not here for us," Rakshek declared. "It's yetis they seek!"

"Yetis!" the other bharals exclaimed, in a wild chorus of panic. "Yetis! Yetis!"

"Then we must go the other way – as far from the yetis as we can!"

"NO!"

Rakshek's defiant bleating was nearly enough to cause an avalanche.

The hunting party below stopped suddenly, scouring the mountainside for the source of the noise. The Doctor, Khageshwaar and Edith ducked back into the mouth of the cavern.

"No?" demanded Rakshek's grandmother.

"No! You take the herd as far from the yetis as you can – run away scared, like common bharals do! Ada is out there, all alone, and she's in the path of these hunters as well. I'm going to find her. And I'm going to take the Doctor and this *lovely human lamb – my new very best human friend in the whole wild world – with me!"*

Edith felt flattered to be declared Rakshek's best human friend in the whole of the world (even though, in all fairness, he probably didn't know too many humans).

"You're a black sheep, Rakshek! A black, black sheep!" the herd baa-ed as, without looking back, they began to cut a path up the mountainside, away from the hunters.

At last, Rakshek was the only one left.

"Well?" he said. *"What are you waiting for?"*

Edith took in the bewildered faces of the Doctor and Khageshwaar and said, "Uncle, Khageshwaar, the Syndicate might have a guide – but it looks like we've got one of our own!"

The path Rakshek chose was near-vertical, a trail not fit for human beings. More than once, Edith slipped, only to be caught by the Doctor or Khageshwaar as the bharal led them from outcrop to outcrop, leaping across narrow ravines, over jagged crests of rock and ice.

It was hard going. Even as they climbed higher, and the deep banks of snow that they had to clamber above began to fade away, the wind sliced deeper and deeper into them. Soon, Edith realized that she could hardly feel her fingers or her toes. Every time they reached what she thought was the top of the mountain, they clambered over a new jagged crest, only to discover yet another peak looming above them.

Eventually, Rakshek led them over a final lip of rock – and there, in a shallow basin below, they arrived in front of a cave that blended itself into the rock-face with amazing natural camouflage. This, thought Edith, was the sort of place you'd have to know existed in order to find. Only the narrowest of ledges preceded the dark arched entrance.

The Doctor was the next to clamber over the lip of rock. There, sheltered from the worst of the wind, he reached out for Edith and asked, "My girl, are you feeling OK?"

Edith nodded, catching her breath. She hadn't believed it possible, but the air was even thinner up here.

Edith nodded. "I'm fine. Uncle, we made it."

The Doctor seemed to sway, ever so slightly, for a moment.

"How about you, Uncle? Is everything all right?"

The Doctor managed a faint smile and gave a small nod. "Just shrugging off some memories of my last visit up these mountains. It doesn't do one any good to live in the past."

"Doctor!" Khageshwaar clambered up the rock face behind them. "I think Babu is closing in. I heard voices carry up the mountain. We should hurry."

"How far behind are they?" The Doctor took a few steps back to peer over the crest of rock and back down the mountainside.

Rakshek spoke up. *"They'll come from the other direction. A party like that wouldn't be able to follow the mountain road you three brave humans just followed! Honorary bharals, that's what you are! From now on, little lamb, you may count yourself a trueborn mountain goat!"* And Rakshek lifted his forelegs in a salute, shaking his curled horns merrily.

Edith repeated what she had been told and the Doctor nodded, his face filling with grim determination. "It may buy us some time. But we must hurry."

He turned to face the cavern entrance.

With a huge sense of trepidation, Edith began to follow, but Khageshwaar gave a polite cough.

"Doctor?" he said quietly.

The Doctor hardly paused. "K, not now, we must hurry."

"Doctor!" Khageshwaar said. "Listen. I have an idea that will buy you time. I will lead them away from this place. If I can speak to Babu, perhaps I can make him see sense."

The Doctor stopped in his tracks. His eyes searched those of his friend.

"Very well," he said at last. "We put all our trust in you."

Khageshwaar nodded. He looked at Edith and gave her a warm smile. "Be gentle with them," he said softly. Then he turned and was gone.

"Well, Edie," said the Doctor. "Just us, my dear."

"And Rakshek," Edith said quietly.

"I think your little friend might have other ideas," the Doctor chuckled, gesturing to where the bharal was wandering off. He gave a low bleat.

"I must look for Ada! I must, I must, I must!" He stopped. *"There's a clump of delicious blue poppies somewhere near here – the yetis love them, and Ada does too! She might be there! Good luck, little lamb!"*

Edith felt a tear in her eye as she watched him bound away. *"Thank you,"* she whispered – but, by then, the bharal had bounded over another outcrop of rock, and was gone.

Back in the cavern entrance, the Doctor held out his hand and Edith clasped it.

"Time to make some new friends, my dear. Are you ready?"

CHAPTER FIFTEEN

*In which Arabella Spearstrike and the
Syndicate close in on their prey...*

Babu felt the cool mountain air on his cheeks as he crested the pass. He had spent the long, frigid night silently wrapped up in his own thoughts, trying to block out the nagging doubts that raged inside him. Now, after hours battling the blizzard, he felt as cold inside as out. His heart was a piece of ice.

The hunting party Babu was leading had not been quick to follow him up the mountain trail, but they were the strongest he had ever seen. Not one of them had complained, despite the fact that he'd set them a steady and unrelenting pace. When the blizzard had been at its worst, he had led them to a large overhang where they waited until the snow clouds parted and he could blaze a trail further on. Not one of them had even muttered an oath at the icy terror of the mountains at night. People like this, Babu was beginning to realize, had been in worse situations and survived. Fear did not touch them in the way it did normal people. And this, perhaps even more than the flame-haired woman whose eyes struck such fear into him, was what unnerved him so as he led them up the mountain pass.

He hadn't chosen the most direct route. With all the guns and equipment the hunters were carrying, he had followed a slightly gentler and more circuitous path to reach the mini plateau halfway up the mountain. The blizzard, too, had slowed them down. But, even so, Babu was certain that the Doctor and little girl would not be able to keep ahead of the likes of Arabella Spearstrike and her killers for long. They would have taken shelter from the blizzard as well. . .

A shudder ran through him when he thought about how they would have coped with the storm. His brother Khageshwaar was one of the best Sherpas in Jomsom, but not even he would have predicted how quickly the storm had come on. If they had been caught out in it, they could already be buried somewhere on the mountain behind him. Frozen to death.

Babu felt a deep sadness catch in his throat. Khageshwaar was his brother. The Doctor had been a great friend to his family, over the years. No matter the deal he had struck with the Syndicate, he hoped desperately that they had survived the night.

Babu stopped, surveying his surroundings as dawn broke. The mountains were always stunning first thing in the morning, when the sun kissed their snowy slopes. Everything seemed peaceful, cloaked in a natural beauty that still gave him a thrill, no matter how many times he gazed upon it.

He rubbed his temples. His head hurt. He had done a terrible thing. This much was true. He had betrayed his brother, betrayed his father's memory, betrayed – perhaps worst of all – the yetis, up here in the mountains. The roll of money Arabella Spearstrike had given him felt heavy in his pocket. It felt like guilt.

He had to keep reminding himself that he simply had no choice. His mother was dying. Khageshwaar wouldn't listen. They needed money, he told himself – money to get their mother out of Jomsom, money to take her to the best hospital in the land, money for the very best doctors. Where was the treachery in that?

They were only yetis. They did not matter as much as his mother.

Yet, even as he voiced the thought, he found that he did not believe it. His family had been guardians to the yetis since a time untold. He would be the first to break the promise his great-great-great-grandfathers had made.

Suddenly, he was itching to move on again, keen to get the whole thing over and done with. Yet something held him back. No matter what he was doing here in the mountains, a bringer of death and destruction, the rites still had to be respected. No doubt his brother would have performed them with the Doctor, so the yetis would be expecting a group of humans, but tradition was ingrained in him, so Babu slid his rucksack to the ground, readying himself to perform the ritual.

He looked back down the mountainside. The main group of the hunters were still some distance behind, but Arabella Spearstrike was almost on top of him. She had been close on his heels the whole time; the hike seemed no more than an effortless stroll to her. Flashing Babu a smile, she watched as he began to unpack the items from his rucksack.

"Which way now?" she demanded.

"We must pause for a time," Babu replied cautiously,

raising his hand to shield his eyes from the glare of the sun.

"Pause?"

Babu dared not reply, but he dared not remain silent either. "It won't take long."

"How long until we get there?" demanded Arabella.

"The sick one will be with his family in a cave on this side of the mountain. It will take maybe another hour of climbing." Babu looked up, though he dared not look Arabella Spearstrike directly in the eyes. "I don't know which cavern they've taken shelter in – but, if I go ahead, I'll identify it and find the best trail."

Arabella Spearstrike pushed her face close to his. "Why are you waiting here then?"

Babu trembled. "You'll keep your promise? You'll only kill the sick one? There are four others in his family. You'll let the healthy ones escape?"

Arabella fixed Babu with a piercing gaze, pausing for a moment before she spoke. "Of course.

That was what we discussed. We don't want them to die out, do we?" A smile flickered at the sides of Arabella's mouth. Sensing his angst, she placed her hands on his shoulders, her grip hard. "All species need managing. If the old or the sick need culling, it can be a kindness. Think of the agonizing death we will spare the poor beast, not to mention the money I will pay you that will allow you to get the treatment for your sick mother. Everyone gains."

Babu nodded. It was exactly what he had needed to hear to steady his nerves.

"Madam, I need to perform the rites before we go higher up the mountain. To pay my respects to the yetis. It is a sacred tradition."

Arabella laughed. The tone of her voice hardened in an instant.

"No, you don't, Babu. You need to take us where we're paying you to take us. There is no time for sanctimonious rituals. Besides, we're all long past any hope of receiving some sort of blessing for what we're about to do. We must get there before anyone else."

"But, Madam!" Babu protested. "We must perform this ritual at the pass. If we don't show respect, we will be cursed. The yetis may even run!"

Arabella's eyes flashed. "On your feet, Babu! Find the

cave before your brother does. The only curse you need to worry about is mine."

Babu flinched.

"Go!" she ordered. "You have your radio. Leave markers and signal to us when you've staked out the best route for us to follow."

Babu nodded. Feeling wretched, he scooped up his bag and disappeared up the mountain.

As she watched him go, Arabella sighed a deep sigh. Babu was vital to their mission – but she could have lived without the self-pity. It made a person weak.

Soon, she was aware of a large shadow looming over her.

"What is it, Salva?" she said, half turning to look at him.

The big, burly mercenary arched his eyebrow, and held up his hand showing five outstretched fingers.

"Not a word," Arabella said. "Babu must only believe we're hunting one or his resolve will crumble. He must not know we intend to kill every yeti on this mountain until it is already too late." She paused. "Is the helicopter on standby for collection of the bodies? Loading five will be a job. We'll need to move fast to get them off the mountain."

Salva nodded slowly. "We just need to radio for it. If

we have all of them . . . their skins will become priceless. Irreplaceable."

Arabella licked her lips. "We'll sell them as the last five yeti skins in the world. We cannot let this chance slip through our fingers. This is the closest we've ever been." She opened her arms, as if she was speaking not only to the group who now gathered around her, but to the mountains themselves. "I already feel the thrill of this hunt. Everything is at stake. We must do whatever it takes to get those skins. We cannot fail. Do not let any of the beasts escape alive." The next words she spoke were for Salva alone. "I will ready the rest of the team for what will need to be done. You need to follow Babu. He may not like our plan as it unfolds. I can already see he is beginning to have second thoughts."

Arabella looked hard at Salva as he registered the implication.

"Do you want me to kill him before we get to the yetis?"

"As soon as we know where the cave is and how to get there, do what you like with him. We cannot risk him interfering with the hunt." She smiled her wicked smile. "Throw him off the mountain."

Adjusting the gun strapped to his broad back, Salva gave a final glance towards his boss before heading off, moving surprisingly lightly for such a big man.

Arabella smiled. It was all coming together. Within a couple of hours, she would be in possession of some of the most sought-after treasures in the world. She turned her attention towards the top of the mountain, scanning the cliff face, watching for movement. A surge of satisfaction coursed through her. After all the years the Syndicate had been hunting down the yetis, *she* was going to be the one to triumph.

Babu had set off fast. Not having performed the rites made the deep feeling of betrayal that weighed on him with every step feel so much worse. His family had been performing that ritual for generations. Hundreds of years had gone by – and now he, Babu, was the person to break the chain. It made him feel sick to his very soul. But, as he kept climbing, he reasoned that Arabella Spearstrike was right; his soul was already cursed. Leading her to the yetis would damn him for eternity. The mountain spirits would hate him soon, whether he performed the ritual or not.

He shook his head, trying to clear an ever-increasing feeling of worry. What if Arabella and her Syndicate killed *all* the yetis and not just the sick one? What would he do? He could see the greed in her eyes. Would she even pay him as she'd promised? Would he be able to buy the medicine to save his sick mother? Would he ever be able to look any of his friends or family in the eye again after they discovered what he had done?

Had he made a dreadful mistake?

Babu realized he was muttering under his breath. He was begging the mountains for forgiveness.

An icy gust of wind caught him full in the face. There was no going back now. If he ran off or didn't signal to the hunters when he found the cave, Arabella and her men would track him down.

Yes, he thought – and found himself momentarily paralysed with fear – *I have really made a dreadful mistake.*

As he scrambled over a rocky outcrop, he didn't see the boots resting on the trail until he had almost tripped over them.

"Babu."

The word cut across him like the flick of a weathered whip.

"Babu."

The word sliced across him again.

Babu looked up. His brother was standing above him, the wind raking through his black hair. He gazed into Khageshwaar's expressionless face.

"Brother," Khageshwaar gasped. "You can't do this."

For a moment, Babu didn't say a word. He simply climbed on to the narrow ledge and faced his kin. The silence between the two brothers stretched on and on as they faced each other.

"I must," Babu eventually replied, his voice sad and heavy.

When Khageshwaar replied, his tone was soft, almost pleading. "There will be another way."

"But there isn't," said Babu, and Khageshwaar heard the genuine anguish in his voice. "Oh, Khageshwaar, you don't know what I've done."

"I know you're leading them up the mountain. I know you agreed to be their guide. I know you betrayed everything our fathers stood for."

"I did it for Mother!" Babu's sudden cry echoed across the mountaintops, stretching far and wide. Khageshwaar thought he heard it a hundred times: *Mother, Mother, Mother*, all over the mountains.

"Our mother will die without treatment," Babu tried to explain, more softly now. "Treatment we can never afford. The Syndicate are only going to take the sick one. He's beyond all help anyway – just like you think our mother is! But what they give in return could save her. I can get her out of Jomsom. To the private doctors in Kathmandu."

"And you believe them?"

Babu didn't say anything. His eyes brimmed with tears.

"Our mother would never trade her life for one of our sacred yetis, Babu. You know this! She will not accept help like this – not from anyone! She's dying of old age. It's her time. But the Doctor has come. He can save the yeti. Please," Khageshwaar begged, "think of what you're doing."

"Brother – this tears me apart. I know the price of this is my soul. To break every promise our family made. But with the fee they have pledged, I can save Mother. Maybe even build a hospital in the village! It's not just our mother I can help – everyone could benefit!"

Desperation was flashing in Babu's eyes and Khageshwaar realized he was trying to convince himself as much as he was trying to convince his brother. It gave him some hope. Perhaps, it seemed, his brother was not beyond being saved.

"The Syndicate do not care for us," he whispered, reaching out as if he might take his brother's hand. "They don't care for Jomsom, or any of the mountain people. They just take what they want. They will not stop at just killing one of the yeti family, Babu. But I think you realize this already, where it matters – right here, in your heart."

Khageshwaar reached out to place his hand on his brother's breast. Their eyes locked for a moment. Khageshwaar thought he saw, then, that Babu finally understood. His desperation had led him to the edge of something truly evil. But there was still time to save his soul.

Babu made as if he was going to say something, but a sudden noise startled both men and they turned their heads as a large shadow fell across them both.

"Well, well, well. What have we here?"

While they had been arguing back and forth, Salva had appeared on the ledge behind Babu. His gun was aimed at Khageshwaar but he swung it briefly towards Babu, giving him a wicked grin.

"Funny place for us all to bump into each other. I'm guessing the family resemblance must make you two brothers?"

Babu nodded mutely. He knew all too well that Salva was one of Arabella's most merciless killers,

"I thought this cave we're going to was supposed to be a secret location. What was the plan – a family picnic?"

"Khageshwaar is just giving me some supplies," Babu said, speaking fast and flashing his brother a quick look.

"Really?" Salva replied, his voice tinged with amusement. He fixed a steely gaze with his one good eye on Khageshwaar. "Aside from a supply drop, I assume you're the one taking the Doctor to the yetis?"

Khageshwaar said nothing, but Salva edged closer, bringing Babu with him. Khageshwaar tried to shuffle around, until at last they were standing on opposite sides of the ledge again, each where the other had once been.

"Is the cave close?" Salva hissed.

Khageshwaar's eyes darted to Babu.

"Salva, forget my brother" Babu exclaimed. "We don't need him. I can take you to the cave. Let's just move on. Khageshwaar is no threat to us."

"I'll be the judge of what is and isn't a threat," Salva replied sharply. "Where is the cave and where is this Doctor?"

As Salva spoke, a deep noise seemed to reverberate through the mountain.

No sooner had the men shared bewildered glances than another rumble, this one coming from much higher up the mountain, seemed to shake the very cliff on which they were perched. They looked up as a sudden shower of pebbles slid down on to the ledge between them. Khageshwaar stretched a hand towards Babu as the pebbles became a surge of rocks, but he couldn't reach his brother. Khageshwaar jumped back just in time. Rocks were cascading between them now and pounding into their shoulders and backs. Even Salva, by far the biggest and burliest of the three, recoiled in alarm. Cursing, he raised his arms to protect his head – but the rocks just came faster and faster, driving down into him as, from somewhere up above, an avalanche took hold.

Salva's shouts became cries of pain as a huge boulder piled into his shoulder. Khageshwaar watched as, face twisted in fear, his knees buckled. Then a huge cascade of stones poured down the mountain, sweeping the ledge clear.

Salva was gone.

And so was Babu.

"Babu!" Khageshwaar called. "Brother!"

Khageshwaar stood in total shock and disbelief. The noise was deafening. The rocks too many. He staggered back and watched as the rocks built a vast wall between him and the place where Salva and his brother had once stood.

After what seemed like an eternity, the cascading stone eased back into a trickle, then stopped, as if a tap had been turned off.

Khageshwaar caught his breath.

"Babu?" he ventured.

In reply, there was only silence.

Khageshwaar waited and waited, listening carefully for any sound of movement. And then, finally, he heard a voice. "Khageshwaar, are you alive?"

"I'm here! Babu, I'm here! I'll try and find a way through." But, no sooner had Khageshwaar started digging at the rocks, than something shifted. Fearful of triggering another landslide, he stepped back. "I can't get past. Are you hurt?"

"Battered," came Babu's voice. "Bruised. Nothing more."

"And that man?" Khageshwaar called. "Is he with you?"

"I can't see him!" Babu replied.

"He would have killed us both," Khageshwaar shouted. He paused. "You must see now they are going to kill all the yetis. Even the mountains themselves know it! These people are evil!"

On the other side of the landslide, Babu's voice was barely audible when he spoke again. "Brother," he breathed, "I'm sorry. But ... we can put this right, can't we?"

Khageshwaar looked around and remembered how, in the confusion of Salva's gun being pointed directly at him, they had circled each other on the ledge. Now, it seemed, he was stranded on the very same trail Babu had been following as he climbed up the mountain.

Only now the way was blocked. His eyes darted back down the slopes. "The Syndicate are coming," he gasped. "I can hear them somewhere below. Listen, brother. You should go. Warn the yetis."

"Can't you climb over?" Babu yelled.

Khageshwaar's eyes took in the wall of rocks before him. If he dared to try, he was certain to fall – to join Salva in his tumble down the mountainside.

"It has to be you," he said. "Get to the Doctor and warn them."

There was a moment of silence.

"I'm sorry, Khageshwaar. This is all my fault."

"We don't have time for laying blame, Babu. We just have to put this right!"

Babu spoke in a soft voice, "Will you tell Mother?"

Khageshwaar's voice sailed up and over the landslide. "I will tell her how we saved the yetis together – and you will be with me when I do so."

"I'll do it, Khageshwaar. I'll find the Doctor. But what will you do, brother?"

Khageshwaar looked down at the ground. A vibrant patch of colour had caught his eye. Bright yellow. He picked it up, out of the rocks. It was his brother's hat.

"I'll do what I can to mislead the hunters. To buy you some time."

"They'll kill you if they realize you're not me!" Babu exclaimed.

He was right, thought Khageshwaar. "They won't want to kill me till they know where the yetis are. This avalanche will give us time. I'll lead them astray. I'll do what I can."

The sound of shouting echoed up the mountain and, on opposite sides of the landslide, both men froze.

"Quick, go!" Khageshwaar cried out.

He raised his hands to his head in silent prayer, then jammed the hat on his head and began to climb.

Everything was in the balance. He just hoped his plan would work.

CHAPTER SIXTEEN

*In which, in the secret caverns at the very
top of the Himalayas, Edith meets some of
the last surviving wonders of the natural
world – and, together with her newest friend,
sets out on a quest to save them, even while
the dreaded Syndicate are closing in...*

Edith blinked as she tried to accustom her eyes to the
dark. After the startling brightness of the mountain, the
blackness of the cave was a stark contrast. With every
step that she took, she felt as if she was being swallowed
by the rocks themselves.

Pulling a small head-torch from a pocket beneath his
cape, the Doctor fitted it over his cap. The light seemed

feeble as the cave walls folded in around them, but at least it helped them see a few metres ahead. Soon, the Doctor had started to quietly sing to himself as he led them on.

Edith tucked herself close behind him, trying not to think about what might happen if the Syndicate were closing in on them with guns and evil on their minds. She thought of Khageshwaar and gave an involuntary shudder when she imagined what they might do to him if he was caught.

The roof of the cave was high, at least twice the height of the Doctor, but as they progressed, it became increasingly narrow. The path weaved between huge rocks that jutted out at every angle from the walls on either side.

"Uncle?"

The Doctor stopped humming and turned his head towards her, the torchlight shining straight into her eyes.

"What if they aren't here?" Edith asked. "What if we're in the wrong cave? We could be trapped."

The Doctor blinked as if the thought hadn't occurred to him.

"Edie, stay close behind me. Put your hand on the wall – can you feel it?"

Edith put her hand on the side of the cave wall and

gave a small gasp. There was buzzing in the stone. It was vibrating.

"They're humming," he said. "Yetis love to hum. You know how cats purr? That deep, rich purring from deep in their belly? Well, it's how the yetis communicate too. Their humming comes together. It comes from the heart. It calms them, makes their families feel as one." He paused, pressing his own ear to the rocks. "The wall is carrying their sound. I believe they are just up ahead. Not far to go now. Are you ready?"

Edith could just make out the white of the Doctor's teeth as he flashed her a smile. Then he turned back and continued on, almost daintily stepping forward as the tunnel rounded a slight bend.

A faint light seemed to emanate from somewhere up ahead. Edith felt her heart beating faster. All of a sudden, the Doctor stopped, reached behind him and took hold of Edith's hand.

"We're here."

After a few more steps, they made a sharp turn. Edith felt the space immediately. The ceiling seemed to soar upwards, jagged rocks protruding from far above, like ragged mountain teeth. They had stepped into a vast subterranean chamber. Sunlight, which came from holes in the far wall of the chamber, streaked into the cave, bathing it in an eerie glow that added to the spectacle.

The floor seemed to have been polished smooth, but, as she blinked into the space, Edith could make out the extent of the chamber walls. Sitting at the far end were five huge, shaggy shapes. At first glance they looked like human beings, but no human being was ever this size. No human being was covered in thick, pale fur.

The Doctor reached up to his head to turn off his head-torch. Each figure sat absolutely motionless. The silence was unnerving.

The yetis looked like nothing Edith had ever imagined. She'd seen the pictures in Ellen Bellamy's book, and read the descriptions in Hugo Ethelred's, but not even the detailed writings of those naturalists could have prepared her for what she saw now.

They were monstrous – and yet somehow perfectly simple and gentle, exuding a calm at odds with their size. To Edith, they seemed somewhere between a gorilla and a human being, and near twice the size of either. They sat like humans, but had hunched muscled shoulders like the great apes, with long arms that seemed to stretch down their bodies, and big, flat, leathery feet covered in yet more fur.

One of the yetis lifted its head to consider the two

tiny, pink apes who had wandered into its cave. Its features were soft and covered in hair, just like its entire body – varying shades of white and silver and grey that seemed to ripple in the low cavern light – but it was the eyes that really struck Edith.

Each yeti had eyes of the most startling green – their gaze was both sharp and piercing. They also, Edith realized, didn't seem to blink. Whilst the hair that covered their faces was quite thick, she could clearly make out their noses and mouths as being much like her own. All of that she could relate to, even the very small ears she could just about see underneath the hair; but it was the unblinking eyes, radiating a power and aura, that unnerved her most. Their gazes had such intensity she felt they could see right through her.

The smallest yeti was about the same height as Francis, but twice as wide again. It was lying on the floor with another sitting close by, tenderly stroking its head, grooming the thick hair with a paw that showed partially webbed fingers tipped with sharp nails. The nails looked like claws and seemed to stretch a good two inches beyond the end of the fingertips. Edith knew instinctively that they were mother and her son. The son, it was clear, was the sick yeti that Khageshwaar had seen.

It was the mother, the one doing the stroking, who

first acknowledged the presence of the Doctor. She seemed to nod slightly in welcome as he and Edith edged cautiously into the chamber.

"Doctor?" Edith whispered.

But the Doctor only lifted a finger to his lips. "Give them time, Edie. All of this is very new to them. It has been some time since I was last among my yeti friends."

Glancing at each of the other yetis in turn, Edith thought she could also tell which ones were male and female. The females had slightly softer faces, while the males were heavily muscled and seemed to take on another dimension in stature.

The largest yeti, who sat furthest away from the entrance to the chamber, was one of the biggest creatures Edith had ever seen. He was about twice as wide again as any of the others. Had he been standing, he would have been nearly as tall as the cave. Indeed, he seemed to fill the back of the chamber. His shoulders bulged with enormous power and a large hairless scar ran diagonally down his chest.

The other two yetis, both female, were a similar size to the mother tending to her sickly child. They sat calmly on the floor, unmoving, just watching Edith and the Doctor with their glittering, unblinking eyes. Their hair, resembling a horse's mane, thickly cascaded over them from the head down, making their bodies almost flow as Edith watched it glimmer in the faint light.

After a moment, the Doctor stepped forward. He gave a small bow, spreading his hands out wide, his palms facing upwards.

"He has come."

The voice boomed in Edith's head.

"We are here to help your young one," Edith said to the yetis.

As one, the family of yetis suddenly sat straighter, each of them shifting to face Edith. Even the Doctor could see the way their expressions changed, first to surprise, then apprehension, then wonder.

All at once, a cavalcade of voices tumbled through Edith's mind.

"The human child speaks!"

"You are just like her – only younger. You can understand us like she did!"

"We thought there was no one else, that she was unique!"

Edith forced herself to think words of reply.

"I can speak to other animals. I am here with my uncle, the Doctor."

The Doctor showed no reaction as the yetis all murmured around the chamber, other than to tilt his head to one side, as if straining to hear Edith speak.

"Then there is something we would like you to tell him for us – on behalf of our family, and all yeti-kind." It was the big male speaking. *"Tell him our pain is shared. I should have gone down the mountain and checked for traps. She should not have died."*

Edith repeated the words slowly, wondering what the exchange meant.

The Doctor nodded, his eyes looking distant for a moment.

"Is he talking about Wilma, Uncle?"

Edith couldn't help herself. The question had escaped her lips before she could stop it. The Doctor turned his head to look at her and Edith's heart lurched. His eyes seemed to well with emotion. He gave a small nod, then turned back to face the yetis.

Edith could see the pain in the Doctor's eyes, just as she could see the pain in the yetis'.

The voice of the big male boomed out again: *"Thank the mountains that you came with the Doctor, child. You must tell the Doctor: the transformation period is almost upon me. Tell him now – we did not know how we would convey the danger."*

The Doctor had seen the way Edith's face creased in confusion. "What is he saying, Edie?"

Edith shook her head. "I don't know what it means."

The Doctor took a step forward. He looked so tiny, standing in the shadow of the great hairy beast – but the look on his face was turning from wonder to fear. "The words, Edie. What were his precise words?"

Edith said, "He said, *the transformation period is almost upon me.*"

"What are the odds of that!" the Doctor replied quietly, shaking his head.

"What does he mean? What transformation?"

"It means," said the Doctor, "that we must be quick and careful." He pressed his hands together, as if making a wordless plea to the yetis. "It's hard to believe, Edie, but yetis and elephants have a common ancestor. Male elephants go into musth each year – a periodic condition caused by a surge in hormones. It makes them somewhat unpredictable, dangerous even. Male yetis undergo the transformation too. It's very similar – except that they become even more unpredictable and dangerous than crazed bull elephants. The saving grace is that their transformation lasts for a much shorter period of time. I understand it can come on quite quickly, and only lasts a few short hours."

Edith looked up at the enormous yeti. In his eyes there was apprehension, but also a kind of shame. It seemed to Edith that he did not want to enter his period of transformation at all.

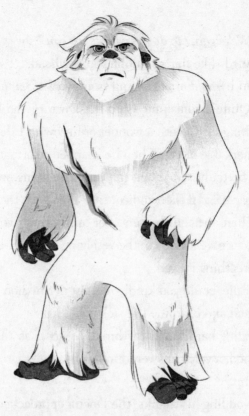

"How long do we have?" Edith asked.

"You are wise to ask, little human. It could come at any hour. When it happens, I will not know myself. Please don't judge me unkindly. I wish that it was different."

Edith took a stride forward, entering the space where the yetis gathered, and lifted up her hand. Down came the enormous male yeti's finger, to touch the point of her own.

"We're going to do everything we can," she whispered, the words like fizzing bubbles in her head.

"Any friend of the Doctor is a friend of yeti kind."

"Quite astonishing," said the Doctor, who had been watching Edith with a wonder of his own. "Edie, you are a remarkable child." Then he snapped to attention. "But we'd better hurry. When the yeti transforms, we mustn't be near – and if the Syndicate are already on their way. . ."

There was little time for any other words. The Doctor's gaze shifted to the yeti lying on the cavern floor, his breathing ragged.

"Edie, could you kindly request permission for me to proceed and examine the sick one?"

Edith hardly had to think. As soon as the Doctor finished, a voice answered in her head.

"Yes."

Nodding his thanks, the Doctor approached the sick yeti, kneeling down near its large head and beginning to closely examine it. His fingers reached out to feel around its neck and throat.

"His lymph nodes feel a normal size. I don't think this is a typical infection. They would be much bigger. Could you delve into the pack and pass me my stethoscope, please?"

Steeling herself to keep calm, Edith quickly grabbed

the stethoscope from the Doctor's pack and placed it at his side. In silence, she looked down at the sick beast. The small fine hairs on her arm were standing on end. It was such a beautiful sight. It was not right that something as wondrous as this animal should be on the edge of death.

The mother yeti who had been tenderly stroking the sick one, slowly reached out and placed her hand on Edith's head.

The moment her fingers touched, Edith felt as if a bolt of energy was passing through her. It must have only lasted seconds, but it felt longer. As the hand gently rested on the top of her head, a feeling quite unlike anything she had ever experienced before washed through her. All her aches and pains seemed gone, the tiredness vanished and she blinked in surprise.

"Does that feel better?"

Edith nodded, dumbfounded, as she watched the yeti reach over and do the same to the Doctor, who blinked a few times and then continued with his examination.

"Edie, dear, could you ask when this one became sick, if they have any idea what caused it?"

Edith focused on the words, making sure the yetis understood. Then she let the mother yeti's own words wash over her. She had a soft, purring voice and Edith realized, without needing to be told, how much fear and devastation the poor animal was keeping inside.

"Doctor," Edith finally said, "they think he was poisoned."

The Doctor raised his eyebrow and paused his examination. Then he nodded to himself and looked at Edith. "That would make sense. There are some neurological symptoms. See the eyes tracking slightly, almost as if they're watching a tennis ball being hit backwards and forwards? It's called nystagmus. Has he had a fit?"

Edith relayed the question yet again, as the mother yeti purred and purred, making soft noises of explanation.

"It happened a week ago," she finally translated. "They were up even higher in the mountains when he collapsed. One minute he was OK, the next he suddenly fell to the ground twitching. He was sick. . ." Edith could almost see it: the way the yetis had gathered around their convulsing brother, as his eyes rolled back and he doubled over in pain. "He seemed brighter afterwards, but then he had another fit – and they just didn't stop. About every half an hour for two days. He couldn't eat, couldn't drink. His fever was raging. They all tried to heal him but nothing would work."

"I see." The Doctor pondered the information and

then went on. "I assume that, when the treatments weren't working, they made the decision to come down from the higher altitudes and find sanctuary in this chamber?"

The mother yeti purred, and her words drifted into Edith's mind.

"That was when we saw our good friend Khageshwaar walking on the mountain. We knew he would send for the Doctor again. It has been so long."

Edith nodded. "That's it, Doctor. They knew that, if Khageshwaar saw them, he'd know something was wrong – and send for you!"

The Doctor cleared his throat. He closed his eyes for a moment, forcing his own memories down before speaking again.

"Edie, I need to be clear about the danger we are in. Take a look at our friend at the back, over there." Edith's eyes revolved to the towering male, whose eyes shone with fear of his transformation to come. "See the scar that marks his breast? I watched it happen. The very last time I came to these mountains, the Syndicate did this to him. Their bullets raked the mountainside. He was fortunate to come out of it with his life. The wound got infected. He had sepsis, a horrible infection – he almost died at the Syndicate's hands. Fortunately, I was here for him with antibiotics, a simple tonic and some acupuncture – we pulled him through. But then. . ." The Doctor's voice tailed off.

The Doctor shook his head, as if trying to clear water from a blocked ear. "The important thing is: back then, even with the Syndicate circling, I knew what I had to do. I've treated sepsis before. I had the antibiotics. But this?" He looked down, sadly, at the ailing yeti. "This is quite different. Far more complicated. Oh, if only I had my laboratory, I could run tests! This poor creature is on the very brink of death. Clinging to the edge of survival!" The Doctor began tapping the yeti's stomach and watching the skin closely; his belly seemed hard as stone underneath his fur. "What do they think caused the poisoning?" His tone was urgent.

Edith looked at the mother and asked her.

"He hadn't eaten anything out of the ordinary," she said. *"The only thing he did any differently at all was to go out that morning looking for a harvest."*

"Ah yes," said the Doctor, when Edith had translated, "a harvest of blue poppies. Yetis love them. Did he bring any back? Did any of the others eat them?"

Edith asked the question.

"No. He came back to lead us there. He said they were very fresh and tasty."

"Perhaps they were poisoned," the Doctor said. "I wouldn't put anything past Arabella Spearstrike and her blasted Syndicate."

"But – the bharal!" Edith exclaimed, in horror. "Rakshek! He said there was a new patch of poppies nearby – it was where he was going after he led us to the cave! What if he. . ."

The Doctor's eyes opened wide. "It can't be a poison," he muttered. "I can't believe it. Those poppies are a rare treat on the mountainsides. Animals flock to them from all over – we'd find the results of that poison up and down the trails. Dead or poisoned animals everywhere. There must be something else. Some kind of contamination, perhaps. . ."

The Doctor reached over to his case. Rummaging around, he removed several small vials which he began to shake vigorously. That done, he placed them to one side and pulled out a needle and syringe. Attaching them together, he then used the needle to pierce the top of each vial in turn, sucking its contents into the plastic chamber.

"Shake this for me, please."

Edith took the syringe and did as she was told.

"What is it, Doctor?"

"It's a combination of drugs to work as a powerful muscle relaxant. The metabolism of the yetis is five times that of a man. We need a huge dose. Mix them well, Edie; we have to give these quickly – it might buy us a little time to figure out what's going on here."

The Doctor rummaged again in the suitcase and brought out another syringe.

"We'll also give him some anti-inflammatory – it'll bring down his temperature and make him feel slightly better whilst we collect a sample of the poppies. We need to move fast – time is paramount! Arabella and her blasted Syndicate outside, a dying yeti inside, a yeti about to undergo the transformation. It's almost too much to bear! We must hurry!"

With that, the Doctor drew up another injection and, retrieving the other syringe from Edith, he swiftly stuck them into the front of one of the yeti's hairy legs.

The prone creature didn't flinch in the slightest as the Doctor gave the jabs.

"Rectus Femoris – it's a good muscle to inject into. It helps avoid accidentally hitting any nerves – but it can smart a little. Runs straight down the front of the thigh. Anyway, if our friend did feel that in any capacity, it won't matter now because I think it's working." The Doctor watched as the yeti almost immediately relaxed even further into the floor of the chamber. "Rest easy," the Doctor whispered, "we're doing everything we can."

Edith had crouched to take the sleeping yeti's hand, when a sudden deep rumble erupted from the back of the chamber.

She could feel the tension in the room. It was like one of the headaches of old, a blossoming of pain behind her eyes. She darted a look at the Doctor. He darted a look at her. Then, as one, they both turned around.

At the back of the cavern, the big male yeti was edging away from the group.

Edith tried to send her thoughts out, but when the yeti replied, all that she heard was a low moaning and jumbled words.

"Doctor," she whispered, "I can't hear his voice."

"It's the transformation," the mother yeti said, still not leaving her son's side. *"It's starting."*

No sooner had the mother yeti spoken these words, than two of the others lumbered to their feet and moved gracefully to flank the big male. When they stood, they towered over Edith – great shambling giants of flesh and fur. She tried not to cower from them, but her instincts took over and she drew closer to the Doctor.

Watching closely, she saw that the male yeti was moving into a recess in the rock face itself. The two others who had approached him were now rolling rocks across the front of it. Between them, they managed to heave slabs of stone across the recess, sealing in the huge male.

"They're barricading him in, Edie. It is for our own safety – and theirs." The Doctor hung his head sadly. "The timing couldn't be worse."

Just then, footsteps echoed in the cave behind them. Edith turned on the spot, peering into the gathering darkness.

In the cavern, everyone – even the two yetis barricading in the big male – suddenly froze.

"Doctor, somebody's coming."

The Doctor picked himself up from the side of the sick yeti. In the same second he turned around, a figure materialized out of the darkness down which Edith and the Doctor had first entered the tunnel. They could hear the sound of running and breathing, desperate, fitful bursts – as of a man who had run all the way up the mountainside. The figure rounded the corner and burst into the chamber.

"Babu!" the Doctor cried, immediately recognizing the man. He rushed forward. "Have you led them to us?" The Doctor's face was thunderous. Edith had never seen him like this. Every feature was contorted into pure rage.

Babu saw it too. Instinctively, he stepped back.

"Doctor, no!" he gasped, still taking great gulps of air. "I've come to warn you!"

"Warn us?" The Doctor laughed. "You have betrayed your people. You have betrayed these animals which desperately need our help. And you have betrayed me, and the memory of my dear Wilma, who died on the mountainside at the hands of the very same people you now serve! Arabella Spearstrike and the Syndicate!"

Edith took a short, sharp breath. So that was the truth of it, the truth the Doctor hadn't been able to speak out loud: Wilma, dead at the hands of the Syndicate, dead on these very same mountains. It was, she realized, the very reason he hadn't wanted her to come to the mountains. He wasn't being cruel. He had been seeking to protect her.

"Doctor," Babu gasped, "you have it wrong. I met Khageshwaar on the mountainside. They tried to kill him. But he got away and..."

"Is he OK?" Edith blurted out.

"There was an avalanche. We were separated in the landslide. I came to warn you and he..."

"He what?" the Doctor snapped.

"He's leading the Syndicate away from here. He has my hat. They'll think he's me."

Everyone paused to draw breath. The Doctor gave Babu a hard look.

"I'm sorry, Doctor." Then Babu turned to the yetis and threw himself on the ground. "I'm sorry," he pleaded with them. "I was taken in. They promised me riches, so that I could save our mother. But they mean to kill us all. They'll stop at nothing to get these animals' pelts. They'll kill every beast on the mountainside, human as well, to take the yetis' hides. It's my fault, Doctor. But we have to put it right. I have to have that chance!" He paused. "There's still time, isn't there? There's still hope. The Syndicate aren't here yet."

The Doctor muttered something to himself and then, dismissing Babu with another angry glare, he put an arm around Edith. "Edie, ask the mother if there is another way out of the chamber."

The yetis sensed the tense atmosphere of the meeting and exchanged looks with each other. Edith was aware of some muted communication going on between them, but couldn't hear anything in her mind. She fixed the mother yeti with her eyes and concentrated on forming the words.

"There's a passage to the other side of the mountain. We can take you there – to where the poppies grow wild."

"Then it's decided," said the Doctor, readying his bag. "Everyone must leave here, to escape the Syndicate and find the flowers. Edie, I'm going to have to ask you to be brave. Braver than I've any right to ask of you – you who have been so courageous already."

"I can do it, Doctor."

He looked at her and smiled. "You can, my dear."

As if on cue, the two yetis who had been barricading in the giant male finished loading rocks in front of the recess and then moved back into the centre of the chamber, where they bent down to pick up their sick brother. The mother yeti stood and walked over to the opposite wall. There, gripping a massive rock with both hands, the powerful creature heaved aside a huge section of stone.

Bright light streamed into the cave, accompanied by a blast of fresh mountain air. A path, clearly visible thanks to the daylight streaming through it, led out of the chamber, into the snowbound wonderland on the opposite side of the mountain.

Edith was fastening her coat again when she saw that the Doctor was rooted fast, staring at Babu – who still remained, kneeling on the ground.

"Where is K?" he demanded. "The truth, Babu. If you ever truly loved your family, you must tell me the truth now. What have you done with him?"

"I told the truth, Doctor," Babu said, more calmly now. "I have seen my mistake. I must make amends. My brother's trying to lead the Syndicate away – it was the only option we had. I would have done it myself, but the landslide came, and. . ."

Babu's voice tailed off. He looked desperately at the Doctor and then at Edith.

"You were leading them here," the Doctor said bitterly. "We can't trust you."

There was a tiny silence, and then Edith said, "He's telling the truth, Doctor."

The Doctor flinched. "How can you tell?"

"You're the one who told me that human beings are animals too. I can't read his mind, but . . . I can feel it. I *know* he's not lying."

She felt it with a strange certainty, like it was something she'd known all along, a memory from long ago that was only just resurfacing in her mind.

The Doctor whirled around. "Edie," he declared, "you have to go and find the poppies. We need to discover what could possibly have contaminated them. Whatever it was, it got into this poor yeti and has taken him to the very brink of death. If we're to have a hope of setting things straight again, we must know what it is, test them for a poison, a toxin, anything that could have turned those poppies bad. Follow the yetis to the flowers." The Doctor delved his hand into one of his wondrous pockets and pulled out a clear plastic bag, which he handed to Edith. "Pick some samples and place them in one of these."

Edith had already taken the bag when a sudden thought occurred to her.

"What do you mean ... *I* have to go?" she asked, confused, as a kernel of fear took root inside her. "Doctor, aren't you coming too?"

"Edie, dear Edie. You must understand this already. What I am asking of you, I have no right to ask – and yet ask it I must. I need you to be braver still – you who have already been so courageous. I cannot come with you. Arabella and her hunters may yet find this place, no matter what our friend Khageshwaar is trying to do out there on the mountain – and, if they do, someone has to stop them. Or else they will hurt that yeti in there." The Doctor glanced over towards where the huge male was barricaded in the corner of the cave.

He paused and took a deep breath. "I have to stay near the cave. I have to distract them if they get close and prevent them from finding this place. There is no other way. I have sworn to protect all the yetis, and there are now two in desperate peril."

"No!" Edith's voice sounded panicked. "We'll take him with us! We can hide on the other side of the mountain! The yetis can block up the chamber once we are through!"

The Doctor shook his head. "That yeti is about to undergo the transformation. You must trust me on this – I have seen a yeti in the throes of transformation before. A madness will grip him. He is trapped here for both his safety and ours. He will be a raging, unstoppable beast – and not even you, with your special talent and kind, kind words, will get through to him. So I will stay and make sure the Syndicate don't unearth him as he hides."

"They'll shoot you!"

The Doctor shrugged. "I cannot promise you that they won't. But there is yet hope. I will lead them on a merry chase." He stopped. "You must be gone, Edie. Every second counts – for all of us, now. Get me the poppy. When the transformation is complete, I'll find you on the ridge at the very top of the mountain. We will then cure the young one."

The Doctor put a hand on Edith's shoulder and flashed her a smile. Somehow, that smile seemed to steady everything inside her. She felt her heart start to beat less wildly. All her panic was slowly turning into courage again. "I promise you that."

Babu's voice sailed up out of the darkness, thick with emotion. "What about me, Doctor?"

The Doctor spun around, his cloak fanning out.

"Edie believes you are telling the truth, Babu, and I will choose to believe her. So look inside your heart and tell me – what do you choose?" He paused. "Rest assured that whatever you decide in this moment will live with you the rest of your life. Rest assured, too, that should we fail in our endeavours on this day, the Syndicate will be merciless with you – there will be no kindness to a man who took their money and then betrayed them."

"Better betray them," breathed Babu, "than keep on betraying my friends." He got to his feet. The emotion had leached out of him. Edith sensed some new courage, some new resolve. The light from the new tunnel, where the yetis were already heading, shone with the brilliant blue of the mountain sky and drew Babu's gaze. He shook his head as if trying to rid himself of a fog of confusion.

"I will go with them, Doctor. I'll be their guide on the mountainside. I'll look after your niece, and I'll die before the Syndicate lays a finger on any one of these noble animals."

The Doctor hesitated, casting a glance at Edith, before giving a curt nod.

Soon, Edith and Babu had crossed the cavern floor, heading towards the shambling yetis who were already halfway down the tunnel, heading towards the light. The bright blue sky beckoned them forward.

"Doctor, I'm not sure I can do this alone."

Edith's voice sounded small in the space – but no sooner had she spoken, than there came a clattering of hooves, and a voice popped into Edith's head. To everyone else, the noise came across as a plaintive bleat.

"You're not alone, little lamb! I'll come with you!"

Edith turned on the spot. There, in the jaws of the same tunnel along which they had first come, stood Rakshek.

The small plucky creature walked up to Edith, his little hooves clipping softly on the stone floor. She reached out her hand and the bharal touched it with his nose.

"I've been looking for you human monkeys all over the mountain. I found Ada, she is safe and well, so I went off looking for the poppies, but those hunters we saw are climbing this way too. Can't leave the little lamb to fend for herself against those hunters."

"What is he saying?" The Doctor's voice was louder than he intended and he couldn't mask a hint of urgency as his eyes darted between Edith and the bharal.

"The Syndicate are coming up the mountain. They're nearly here. But Rakshek said he can come with me."

The Doctor opened his arms and took Edith into a warm embrace.

"You've made yourself a fine friend here, Edie. Stay true, and stay courageous, my girl. You yourself are one of nature's wonders. We cannot lose another like you. I'll be with you once the transformation is over – the yeti through there can guide me to the ridge where you'll be safe – but, should I not be with you in three hours' time, you're to get off the mountainside and get out of Jomsom. The hotelier at the Traveller's Rest will make arrangements for Francis to find you. Do you understand?"

"Uncle," she whispered, "I'm not leaving you behind."

"I hope it doesn't come to it. But, Edie, do you remember what I told you before we set out on this expedition? That you must do exactly what I ask of you, when I ask it of you?"

Edith nodded.

"Well, now is the time, my special girl. Off with you, now. Be brave, be kind, be loyal! Now, go!"

CHAPTER SEVENTEEN

*In which Edith and her intrepid band discover
that the animal kingdom is much richer and
more magical than any of them had known . . .*

The mother yeti was the last to leave the chamber, turning to pull the rock back into place with surprising gentleness. Her unblinking gaze lingered for a moment at the far recess of the cave where the male yeti was temporarily entombed; then she leaned sideways and the rock rolled across. Edith stood behind her giant form, Rakshek at her side, as the hidden exit was once again sealed from within.

"He's your mate, isn't he?" Edith asked.

"What is . . . a mate?"

"The one you're with for the rest of your life."

The mother yeti turned and looked down at Edith.

"Then, yes. He is my . . . mate."

The two other yetis were carrying their sick brother between them, and as their mother paused in her reply to Edith, she watched them adjust his weight and take their first steps along the mountainside.

"He is brave and strong. But now the transformation comes, as it must. We must be patient and keep our distance. I only pray that, when it is over, his son is alive to welcome him."

The way to the poppies was up and further up, the trail little more than series of ledges cutting a zigzag up the slope. Rakshek was already bounding ahead, crying back for Edith to follow, but the yetis were slower. Babu had plucked a pair of binoculars from a pocket and, with them, he searched the mountainside.

"No sign of the Syndicate. Luck may be on our side."

The brilliant blue of the sky made Edith squint as they set off. She felt as if she had been transported to another world, Soon, the gloom of the chamber became a distant memory in the bright light.

"What is your guide searching for, human?"

"He's afraid of hunters. That the Syndicate are out here. They should be on the other side of the mountain, but he fears. . ."

Too late, Edith realized what she'd said.

"Syndicate?" the mother yeti breathed. *"The Syndicate are here?"*

Edith cast her mind back, and realized with mounting horror that it wasn't until this precise moment that the yetis had been made aware that the Syndicate were here in the mountains as well. She could almost see the understanding flicker across each of the yetis' faces. The mother looked at her and, though it was difficult to read her lined, furred face, she saw anger and fear and rage, all mixed together in its glittering, unblinking green eyes.

"We thought we were taking you to the poppies, to treat our son."

"You are!" Edith cried out, desperate to be understood. *"That's why the Doctor stayed. To lead them away from your mate. The hunters are on the other side of the mountains."*

"But how did they find us?"

Edith cast a look at Babu. She saw his tear-stained face. She saw his determination. She remembered that feeling she had got when he was trying to convince the Doctor that he was telling the truth. She decided, there and then, that she would not tell the yetis what he had done.

"I don't know," she said. The lie stuck in her throat, but she could feel the yetis' fear and did not want them to hold Babu responsible. *"If we can get to the poppies, we can try and figure out what's wrong with your son – and we'll be hidden from the Syndicate if we stay this side, won't we?"*

The mother yeti looked back down the mountain, at the tunnel from which they'd emerged. *"The Doctor cannot possibly hope to stand against them alone."*

"It's what he told us to do!" Edith insisted, remembering her promise. *"Please!"*

For a time, the mother yeti was silent. Then, she said, *"I will not be stranded in the open, not if the Syndicate are here. We have to move quickly."*

"That's the spirit!" brayed Rakshek, stamping his hooves. *"We can be there in a matter of hours if..."*

"Hours is too long!" roared the mother yeti.

And, in one fell swoop, she reached down and snatched Edith up from the ground.

"Calm," the mother yeti whispered. *"You'll be safe in my arms. As will you, little sheep."*

Rakshek was about to yell out in indignation, *"I, madam, am not a common sheep!"* – when the mother yeti swooped him, too, into her arms.

"I'm a bharal, I don't need to be carried!"

"You do where we're going," the mother yeti said. Then, with a curt nod to her daughters, she said, *"The other human too."*

Babu had watched Edith be swept into the yeti's arms with mounting horror – but it was nothing to the stomach-churning lurch he felt when the two yetis came apart, one bearing her brother's weight effortlessly alone while the other reached down and plucked Babu off the mountainside. Edith could hardly keep herself from grinning as she saw Babu's shocked face when the yeti tossed him up, sat him on her shoulders like a toddler, and scrambled up the rocks.

"This is going to be bumpy," the mother yeti said, inside Edith's mind. *"Hold on!"*

Then they were off.

Edith didn't have time to be afraid. She told herself not to look down, and wrapped her hands in the yeti's fur, Rakshek pressed up tight beside her, his horns interlocked with her arms.

"Don't look down!" he bleated – and Edith didn't need telling twice.

The yetis were unstoppable. Using just one arm to pull themselves up the mountain, somehow they leapt from ridge to ridge, clutching on to jutting outcrops, hauling themselves up. Their strength and speed were breathtaking and, within moments, they were hundreds of metres above the cavern, disappearing into the mountain range beyond.

Edith looked over her shoulder. Babu had his eyes clamped closed. For a fearless expert mountain guide, she thought, he was certainly out of his comfort zone, and he wasn't the only one.

"I'm not sure we're going to enjoy this... Baaaaa-aaaaa-aaaaargh!" Edith clung on to Rakshek's horn as his voice projected into her mind. *"I'm right here, little one!"* he called out, as if he had any choice in the matter.

And the mountains kept flashing by.

The air was getting thinner up here. Edith was certain of it. She had to bury her face in Rakshek's fur just so that the wind wouldn't steal away her breath, and even then, the air was so light she found herself taking great gulps of it, sucking in all the oxygen she could. It wasn't until the mother yeti paused to get her bearings, perched on a peak still ringed by taller crags, that Edith was able to properly catch her breath.

She gazed out across the mountain range, seeing further than she'd ever seen before. The peaks of smaller mountains stretched to the horizon, their snow-capped tops glistening in the sunlight.

"It's beautiful," she whispered.

"Put me dooooooooooooooowwwwwwwwwwwwwn!" yelled Rakshek.

Soon the other yetis joined them on the peak. The mother yeti looked at her sleeping son with lines of worry etched into her furred face. The daughter who carried him had finally started to lag behind, slowed by the weight of her brother despite her colossal strength, but on catching up, she gazed at Edith implacably. For the first time, Babu – up on the other daughter's shoulders – opened his eyes.

"I've never been so high," he said in wonder – and would have said more, only, at that precise moment, a deep, bass rumble shook the mountainside.

They all looked back down the sheer slopes.

"What was that?" Edith asked.

"Not a landslide," Babu replied. "Not a gunshot either."

It dawned on Edith that there was only one other thing that could have made such a noise. She clung on to the mother yeti and asked, *"What was that roar?"*

The mother lifted her nose to the pure mountain air and drew in a deep breath.

"The transformation," she whispered – and, around her, the other yetis grew agitated, jostling Babu and the sleeping brother. *"The madness has come upon him. It will be over in a few hours. But until then. . ."*

Edith had just one thought in her mind. If the roar had reached this far around the mountain, then there was little chance Arabella and her hunters wouldn't have heard it.

It was the very same thought spooking the other yetis. *"Mother,"* one of them said, *"it will draw the Syndicate."*

"We must trust the Doctor," the mother yeti replied. *"And his friends. This one's family have been looking after us for generations."* And she looked directly at Babu, who flushed.

"My uncle will find a way to protect your father," Edith said, desperate for it to be true. *"If the Syndicate find the cave, he'll think of something."*

None of the yetis replied. Instead, some imperceptible signal passed amongst them and moments later, they were loping up the mountain again, bound for the highest crags. As they went, the mother yeti spoke a few last words, which echoed in Edith's mind.

"You mistake me, little human. I worry the Syndicate is no longer the thing the Doctor must fear the most."

"What do you mean?" asked Edith.

"That roar was heard for miles around. It must have come from outside the chamber. It is possible my husband has escaped."

They were moving faster now, the yetis taking huge

bounds. Edith tried to think positive thoughts about her uncle's predicament. Perhaps he was no longer in the cave at all. Perhaps he was out on the mountainside, trying to find Khageshwaar and help him lead the Syndicate astray. But every time she tried to picture him, something terrible was befalling him – and, in the end, she had to cast those thoughts aside. "I have a job to do," she told herself. "The Doctor is counting on me and so is that yeti, still on the edge of death."

The power of the mother's legs propelled them up seemingly impossible distances with each and every stride. Moments later, they were cresting a ridge high up on the plateau, before dropping down again into a rocky crevasse.

The mother slowed and came to a sudden stop, lowering Rakshek and Edith back to the ground. Soon, the other yetis and Babu dropped into the crevasse as well.

Rakshek shook himself like a dog. *"Well, I never! The herd had better never hear about that. A creature like me, born of the mountains, being carried like a sack of stones? I could have got here just as fast!"*

He shot the mother yeti an aggrieved look and Edith wondered if she could make out the small semblance of a smile on the huge creature's lips.

"Is this it?" asked Edith. *"Is this where the poppies are?"*

Only yards from where they were standing, beyond jagged outcrops of stone, the mountains fell away. Taking her by the hand, the mother yeti led her to the very edge. Out there, the mountains plunged into a deep, unending ravine which echoed, already, with their voices. But, when she looked down, she saw that the walls of the ravine were coated with small blue flowers, each one glistening as they danced in the sunlit breeze. There were ledges down there where a yeti might cautiously clamber down. A bharal, too – and, indeed, Rakshek was already guiding himself over the lip, drawn by the blossom's scent.

Rakshek looked back. *"Come on, little lamb! Slowly is the only way. If you slip you will fall. Grab my fleece. These poppies are a tasty delight!"*

"You mustn't eat them," she told him. *"The yeti, we think they made him sick."*

Stretching out a hand, she gripped a handful of Rakshek's wool, and together they lowered themselves on to the first ridge, where the poppies made a perfect blue blanket all around.

"Do they ever run out?" Edith asked, basking in the sea of flowers.

"Poppies have grown here for a thousand years. We only

pick what we need and always plant the seeds from the last poppy we take." It was the mother who had spoken. When Edith looked up, she could see her above, peering down from the top of the ravine.

As Rakshek set up a baa-ing complaint about not being allowed to gorge himself on the poppies, Edith studied the plants carefully. They seemed perfect, each one an exact replica of the one next to it. She wasn't a botanist but it was plain, even to an eleven-year-old girl, that the poppies were healthy.

Gently, she reached out her hand and picked one, holding it up to the sunlight to examine. Then, still clutching it in her fingers, she gazed up at the mother, whose unblinking eyes watched the little girl carefully.

"What do you think? You are the Doctor's apprentice, are you not?"

Edith suddenly felt the weight of the world on her shoulders. Up until that moment, she had believed that, when she got here, she would find some sort of a clue. Now, there was nothing. She wasn't really a Doctor's apprentice at all. She was a child, stuck on the side of a mountain with a bharal and a yeti.

A tear welled up in her eye. Quickly, Edith tugged her sleeve at it, forcing herself to get a grip. She had to focus. She had to think.

"You still think they could have been poisoned?" Rakshek asked. *"I'm telling you, they're delicious! I could eat the whole lot! In fact, I just might!"*

Before she could stop him, Rakshek had dropped his snout to the flowers, ripped up a huge clump, and begun to turn them between his teeth.

"NO!" Edith yelled.

But it was too late. Rakshek was already spitting the poppies out.

"Yuck!" he cried out. *"I've never tasted CRUNCHY POPPIES before!"*

Edith froze. She looked hard at the bharal. *Crunchy poppies?* she thought. *But how could flowers CRUNCH?*

Rakshek spat the last flakes out and, in the very same moment, realized that Edith was staring at him.

"What?" he asked, puzzled.

It wasn't, she realized, the only voice.

She'd been too focused on the hopelessness of being here on the mountain, without a clue in the world what to do next, to notice it at first. She looked up, saw the yetis peering over the ledge above her, saw Babu standing between them, saw Rakshek with his eyes creased up in concern. But, she realized they were not the only ones here.

It had been a tiny buzzing sound, growing more

frenzied when Rakshek crunched his way through the poppies. She tried to follow it with her eyes. It seemed to be most fierce on one of the ledges underneath her – so, steadying herself on Rakshek's horns, she picked her way down the face of the ravine, dropping on to one of the lower ledges. The poppies were growing in even more abundance here.

"What is wrong?" came the mother yeti's sonorous voice.

Edith looked up to see the mother yeti lowering herself, hand over hand, on to the ledge where she stood. The great creature made sure she was within reach of Edith, clearly concerned she might fall.

"I can hear another sound. It's in my head. It's constant, all around us... And Rakshek, when he ate the flowers, he was CRUNCHING through something as well. There's only one thing I can think of..."

Reaching out, Edith plucked a handful of poppies closest to her. The buzzing was persistent now, even louder. She shook her head. This was very strange. Was she about to have one of her attacks? It had been so long. She was doing so well. She didn't want to faint – not here, not on the top of the mountain, not when there was so much else at stake.

It was in that moment that Edith noticed something

on the stem of one of the poppies. It was tiny, but it was also definitely moving. Peering closely and carefully, she found that she could make out a very small snail working its way towards the leaves.

Edith's eyes were transfixed on the snail. As she watched it, the whining noise intensified.

Carefully, she examined each of the poppies, one after the other. Sure enough, she found more snails. They were each about the size of half a pea with very pale green shells – and, as she spotted each one, the whining noise became stronger.

"Speak to me," she said, looking hard at one of the snails.

She hadn't dared to dream it would work, not really – and yet, as soon as she spoke, the buzzing came to an abrupt halt.

Edith focused harder, opening her mind. Was this real? Could she communicate with a snail? There was, she thought, no reason why not. She'd chatted to spiders and earthworms back at Forest Cottage. All animals had languages, even down to the tiniest ones.

"I can hear you," she said. *"Can you hear me?"*

In return, Edith got a small pulse of response. Not a word or a language. Just a tiny buzz that flashed across her mind.

She turned and looked at both the mother yeti and Rakshek.

"Do you know about these snails? Have you seen them before?" she asked.

Rakshek seemed too busy spitting out bits of snail shell – for it was these that he had been crunching – to answer, but the mother yeti hunched down closer to stare at the molluscs.

"I have not seen these before. They must be new to the mountain."

Edith felt a tremor of excitement. Perhaps this was a clue.

"Maybe it isn't the poppies," Edith said. *"Maybe it's the snails. Perhaps a bird brought them up here or they were carried up on the boot of a hiker. They found the poppies and the snails bred. And then maybe your son ate them."*

The mother yeti regarded Edith calmly and turned her head to look at Rakshek.

Edith knew what she was thinking before she spoke.

"Maybe they don't affect bharals? You have different digestion systems. You have an extra stomach. Perhaps bharals can eat them and not be harmed."

Edith lifted a snail on the tip of her finger and brought it level with her eye. It seemed so tiny. How could anything so small hurt a creature as big as a yeti?

"Are your kind in the yeti?" she thought, focusing as much as she could on the snail. *"Do you make yetis sick?"*

Again, there came a pulse of response. It made Edith's heart leap – for now she was certain that they could hear her. She just had to try harder to be understood, try harder to hear what they were saying in return. But even as she began to collect her thoughts together, a nagging doubt crept into her head. Could snails *really* be the cause of this? She thought back to the book the Doctor had given her to read on the plane journey. There had been a whole chapter on poisons – but nothing on snails. Something still didn't make sense.

With the greatest of care, she gently put the poppy and the snail into the bag the Doctor had given her, and stood up. The Doctor would know what to do. He would lead the Syndicate away from the cave, he would escape their guns and he would save both of the yetis. He had to. He was their only hope now.

At the top of the ravine, the other yetis were waiting with Babu. While Edith had been on the ledge, they had lain the sick yeti down. His condition had definitely settled since the injections the Doctor had administered back in the cave, but how long would they keep his sickness at bay? Now he rested with his head cradled in his sister's lap, while Babu kept watch with his small pair of old battered binoculars. As he leaned over a smooth, jet black boulder, scanning the surrounding peaks, he caught Edith's eye and shook his head. No sighting of the Syndicate – and no sighting of the rampaging male yeti either.

The sick yeti was all that mattered now. Somehow, by keeping this simple thought in her head, Edith found she could forget about everything else. Carefully, she walked over and knelt beside him. The other yetis parted to give her space and she felt shielded by a huge wall of hair as she reached out her hands tentatively.

She saw, now, that, while they had been down on the ridge among the blue poppies, the sick yeti had opened his eyes. Her heart gave a beat. Surely this had to be a good thing? But when she looked into their unblinking depths, she saw that his eyes were pinched from the pain and exhaustion that wracked his body.

She concentrated hard. *"I need to ask you about the poppies."*

If the yeti was surprised that she could speak to him, he didn't show it. Perhaps he was too sickly to even realize it was strange.

"I am fading. . ." His voice was like a distant whisper in her head, but she was certain there was something else

here, too – some other, even more distant voices swirling inside him. She looked at the little plastic bag in which she'd slipped the blue poppy and its tiny green snail. Yes, she thought – she was on to something. . .

"Did you eat many of the poppies that morning when you became unwell?"

"I can't remember. A few, I think."

"I need you to relax. I might have an idea as to what has made you so ill."

Edith screwed her eyes up tight, placed her hands on the yeti's stomach, and felt the warmth from his thick hair as her fingertips worked their way down to the skin underneath.

Focusing her thoughts on the contents of his stomach and visualizing a snail, Edith opened her mind. Her power felt stronger as she directed it around the yeti's abdomen, channelling her thoughts through her fingers, reaching out to the internal organs of the huge beast she was so desperate to help. She had never done this before, but she could think of no other way.

"Hear me," she said.

All at once, an image came into her mind. But not of a snail. She focused further, tried to shut out the wind that howled around the mountainside, the shuffling of the other yetis behind her, the crunch of Babu's footsteps as he prowled the boulders, scanning the slopes for signs of the Syndicate. She tried to separate herself from the world and focus on nothing else but this tiny image – and there it was, crystal clear in her mind.

It was not a snail, she realized. It was a worm.

A white worm, wriggling and writhing in the belly of the yeti – and, all around it, thousands more . . . and fragments of snail shell.

Edith looked up. The faces of all the other yetis were peering into hers.

"You know something!" the mother yeti exclaimed. *"Tell us!"*

"It isn't the snails," she said, and delved into the plastic bag to pull out the little green creature. *"They're harmless. But inside them, there are parasites. Worms!"* She focused her mind further, tried to sink into the buzzing. *"Can you hear me?"* she said to the snail. *"Can you. . ."*

A little voice popped into her head. *"What, in the name of the Holy Blue Poppy, is going on?"*

"Don't be afraid," Edith began. *"I need to ask you something. There are worms inside you – parasites, living in you. . ."*

"Oh, THEM!" the little snail squeaked. *"Horrible little things, sneaking into our bellies and setting up homes there. Wriggle, wriggle, wriggle, all day long!"*

"But they don't do you any harm?" Edith asked.

"Wriggle, wriggle, wriggle, I said! All that squiggling!"

At least they aren't killing them, thought Edith, as she looked back at the yeti. These microscopic worms, so harmless inside the snails – and apparently the bharal, Rakshek – were deadly to the yeti. And they didn't even know it.

She pressed her hands back to the yeti's hard stomach, focused her mind until the pulsing buzz got stronger and the image of hundreds, perhaps even thousands, of tiny worms, multiplying inside the yeti's body, popped into her mind.

It was time to send a message.

"Please!" she called out. "You're killing him!"

In that instant, the buzzing stopped and the worms in her mind became still.

"Can you hear me?"

The buzzing began again.

"You must leave him," she said. "He's dying. He is not your natural host. He accidentally ate the snails in which you live when he was grazing the poppies."

"But it's lovely down here!" came a vast chorus of voices. The worms were speaking as one and their voice became a harmony in Edith's head. "Our people have lived in the snails for generations – but here we are, in wild, uncharted lands! It's fabulous! So much space to live! So much room to explore!"

"But he'll die," Edith said.

There was much buzzing and whispering among the worms.

"Die?" they asked, as one.

Edith remembered something she'd read in the Doctor's book. "And if he dies, your world in there – that will be over as well. Don't you see? You can't stay. You have to leave."

"But . . . it's . . . so . . . lovely!"

All at once, more than a thousand worms started weeping and wailing in Edith's mind.

"I'll take you back to the poppies," Edith promised. "You'll find more snails. You don't hurt them. Live your lives! But let this poor yeti live his. Please."

"How do we know we can trust you?" the collective voice replied.

As Edith considered their question, her eyes landed on Babu. "Sometimes," she said, "you just have to believe."

There was a pause. The buzzing had stopped. The voice didn't reply. Then suddenly, like the sound of rushing wind, there was a noise that made Edith's eyes fly open in alarm.

The yeti seemed to spasm beneath her.

"*What's happening?*" he gasped.

Edith staggered back. A horrible, peaty smell was rising up from where the yeti lay. She thought she knew exactly what that was.

"*Quickly now,*" she said. "*You need to get back down to the poppies. Don't eat any – just wait. When you last ate the poppies, you crunched up the tiny green snails that have been living there. I thought, perhaps, it was the snails that had made you sick, but it isn't – it's worms that live inside them. Little parasites that make the snails their hosts. Those worms got inside you. They started breeding, spreading out all through your digestive system. Your body – it's a paradise for them! But they are making you sick and now they're going to leave.*"

"*Am I going to be OK?*"

"*You're going to be fine.*"

Edith looked up and around. She took the mother yeti's hand as the others picked up their sick brother and helped him over the ledge, to where the blue poppies grew.

There came a deep rumbling – not from the mountains this time, but from the yeti's stomach. One of his hands clutched at his tummy.

"*I need to hurry!*" he said.

Edith watched as the yetis guided their sick brother over the cliff edge, taking him back down to settle in the poppies below. As they went, Edith wrapped her arms around Rakshek.

"He's going to be OK," she said.

"But where is he? What are they doing?" Rakshek looked confused. He cantered to the edge of the cliff, stuck his head over and peered down on to the ledges below. *"I think I can see him, he seems to be almost sitting amongst the poppies. Just sitting there."*

Edith started to laugh.

"He's just having a moment."

"A moment?"

"Some private time – like we all need sometimes."

A sound like wet thunder echoed over the mountain.

Edith watched Rakshek's face change with dawning understanding. Then Edith saw something else she had never expected to see before: a bharal in hysterics.

Rakshek's laughter was infectious. Soon, Edith was laughing again too. She whirled around, called out to Babu, "Babu! He's going to be OK!"

Babu, who was still up on the boulder, his binoculars in hand, turned around and cried out, "Edie, this is the greatest news! The Doctor is going to be so..."

He never got the chance to finish that sentence. For

at that moment, a succession of short, sharp explosions rocked the mountainside.

All the colour drained out of Edith's face. She scrambled up on to the boulder and hunched down at Babu's side, gazing out across the snow-encrusted slopes underneath.

The explosions sounded again, and Babu gripped her by the arm.

"It's the Syndicate," he whispered. "They must have found the Doctor!"

CHAPTER EIGHTEEN

In which the Doctor comes face to face with his oldest foes, and a yeti in the midst of transformation proves to the Syndicate that theirs is not a species to be hunted so easily...

"Hurry, K!" the Doctor said. "Pace is everything. We need to draw them away from the chamber. What's the quickest way up the ridge?"

The Doctor's voice was matter-of-fact as the two men frantically traversed the cliff, desperate to distract the hunters from the yeti's cave.

"There's no shortcut on this open stretch," Khageshwaar replied, still astounded that the Doctor seemed to have appeared out of nowhere. "There's nowhere to hide. They'll see us too clearly." The wind momentarily stole Khageshwaar's breath. "When they see you with me, Doctor, they'll know something's wrong."

The Doctor nodded. "Arabella Spearstrike will recognize me in an instant. They'll either assume Babu has double-crossed them, or realize you're not Babu. Either way, with the two of us together they'll think we're heading to the cave and take chase."

The Doctor winced as his foot slipped on some loose rock, threatening to turn his ankle.

"Doctor, be careful."

"I'm half mountain goat – have no fear!" As the Doctor was righting himself, he caught sight of something far below. "I can see them – down to our right. Keep that hat on, K. It's the perfect beacon."

Khageshwaar strained his eyes and saw the cluster of hunters huddled below.

"They look like they've found something."

"Yes," the Doctor cut in, "perhaps they have – but rest assured it is not your brother. He came to us in the chamber. He is alive and well."

"What happened?"

The Doctor grimaced. "Edie, Rakshek, Babu and the yetis have left in search of whatever poison has affected the youngest one. The slight complication is that the male is about to undergo the transformation. He's currently residing within the chamber. Khageshwaar, my friend, we are the decoy to pull them away."

Khageshwaar's eyes widened in horror.

"You think he will come out?"

"Dearest K, I am quite sure he will emerge at some point. The boulders securing him would be no more than cherry stones to a creature that size. It would seem prudent that we were not here when he breaks out though, wouldn't you say?"

Khageshwaar risked another glance towards the Syndicate. Now there was no doubt they'd been seen. Thuggish fingers were pointing directly up at them.

The Doctor turned to look as well. As he did, a glint of light flashed in his peripheral vision.

"K!" he cried out. "I think they're going to shoot at us. MOVE!!!!!!!!!!!!"

As he spoke, the Doctor reached forward and pushed Khageshwaar hard in the small of the back. In an instant, both of them lost their footing, then slid a few metres down the rocks before recovering their balance. At almost the exact moment they stopped sliding, the unmistakable crack of two rifle shots whipped through the air.

The bullets went high above them. Had the two men

stayed where they were, they would have been hit.

"If you can climb to the crest, there's a path that will take you up and out of sight!" Khageshwaar shouted. "Doctor, I'll draw their fire. You must escape and climb higher!"

Before the Doctor could stop him, Khageshwaar leapt down the mountain towards the hunters.

The Doctor watched in shock as his friend began a further uncontrollable slide downwards. More bullets whipped up the mountain and spurts of dust erupted as they ricocheted off the cliff near his feet.

"Climb!" came the shout from below.

Ignoring Khageshwaar's command, the Doctor immediately jumped off the cliff edge to follow, his cape billowing in the air behind him.

Both men careered another few metres down before landing awkwardly behind a huge rock, momentarily shielding them from the guns below. Khageshwaar looked round in surprise as the Doctor landed lightly beside him.

"What are you doing?" he said breathlessly.

"Currently wondering why we're going towards them?" the Doctor replied with a smile, straightening his cap with a flourish.

"I'm drawing their fire so you can get away!"

Khageshwaar said, desperation creeping into his voice.

"I prefer the option where we both survive this together. On the positive side, I think we now have their undivided attention. If they're looking for us, they're not looking for the yetis."

The Doctor paused to peer around the edge of the rock. Another bullet chipped into the stone, missing him by a fraction.

"They are quite determined. However, they have rifles, and rifles only take one bullet at a time. Is there a route out of here, K?"

Khageshwaar looked around, searching for landmarks and possible avenues of escape.

"I think so. If we can drop down another few metres, they'll need to reposition to see us. It will buy us time to cut behind those boulders over there." Khageshwaar pointed diagonally down the mountain to three huge boulders. "If we can get to them, there's a track that will take us further down the mountain and hide us whilst we figure out a way around."

"Give me Babu's hat," the Doctor said.

Khageshwaar looked baffled, but handed over his fluorescent hat to the Doctor – who flashed him a large grin and picked up an elongated rock, about a foot in length.

"Get ready to slide. We'll have a few seconds whilst they reload those blasted rifles." The Doctor chuckled to himself, almost as if he was enjoying the drama. Then he put the hat on to the very tip of a rock. With some caution, he then slowly poked it out, just a few centimetres from the edge of their hiding place.

Within seconds, two bullets shot into the hat, sending it jumping into the air.

"Now!" the Doctor shouted, hurling himself and Khageshwaar down the mountain.

The two men once again careered downwards, scraping their bodies on the stones as they crashed into a heap against another huge boulder.

Khageshwaar quickly peered down the mountain.

"We're hidden for the moment. We can edge round these boulders and drop down on to the track."

The Doctor nodded, momentarily unable to speak as he recovered his breath from the slide. Within moments, the two men steadily lowered themselves down on to the narrow track.

It was a small scrape of rock that alerted them first, but as they twisted around in the direction of the noise, the sound of a gun being cocked made them both freeze and look up.

There stood Arabella Spearstrike.

Arabella's eyes flashed with vicious triumph as she watched the Doctor slowly straighten and meet her gaze. Her group of hunters stood in a semicircle, casually surrounding the two men, hidden on the opposite side of the huge boulder which they had assumed would provide them sanctuary. Basco waved his pistol upwards, indicating the Doctor and Khageshwaar should raise their hands in the air, which they slowly did.

"Now, why would you run away from the cave when you were so close?" Arabella said, her voice like cracking ice.

Neither the Doctor nor Khageshwaar spoke.

"You could have warned the yetis we were coming but instead you decided to run back down the mountain."

The Doctor cleared his throat. "Arabella Spearstrike. It's been a while. I see your appetite for blood is as ravenous as ever." The Doctor couldn't keep the venom out of his voice, his eyes boring into hers, unyielding and unforgiving.

"This is no time for a happy reunion, Doctor. The only pleasure I have in seeing you again is knowing that I'm going to kill you shortly. In fact, the only reason you are still standing upright is because something doesn't add up. Why risk so much, only to turn tail at the last minute? What trick are you playing?"

The Doctor shook his head. "No trick, Arabella, simply a desire to avoid being shot by your mercenaries. The obvious escape was to drop back down the mountain."

"No, it wasn't. The obvious escape was to run to the cave. When those idiots missed, you had a clear opportunity to cut across the top. We all saw it. Your decision to slide back down the mountain doesn't make sense."

She took a couple of steps forward and then jumped down next to Khageshwaar, her eyes boring into him.

"You must be Babu's brother. Your brother will find his final resting place on this mountain. He will never return home. And neither will you. No doubt your dying mother will see you both soon. Quite a family legacy."

Khageshwaar looked at Arabella with a blank expression. It seemed to enrage her that her taunting provoked no reaction at all.

"Where are they?" she hissed.

Khageshwaar didn't speak, just dropped his gaze and stared at the ground.

"I have spent years tracking, hunting..." Arabella continued.

"Killing," the Doctor interjected, his voice hard.

"Killing." Arabella repeated the world slowly. "Yes, I do a lot of that, Doctor – as my father did and his father before him. You know all about our ability to kill, don't you?"

The Doctor once again met Arabella's gaze steadily.

Arabella's smile widened as she continued. "To enable me to kill so effectively, I have to read prey, and I can read you. If you were so determined to warn the yetis, to help them escape, you wouldn't have abandoned your quest so easily. Where are they?"

"For some people, family means their world," the Doctor said simply. An image of Edith flashed across his mind and, despite the situation, he felt a warm glow of pride that she was his niece.

Arabella tipped her head back and roared with laughter. "Family can mean love, but family can also mean opportunity. Irrespective, my family – and our Syndicate – is determined to get those skins. Basco, my patience is worn through. I think the Doctor's guide should look a little bit more like you. Please cut the ear off Babu's equally stupid brother." She pointed at Khageshwaar as she spoke.

Basco was beside Khageshwaar within seconds and his knife flashed. Before he could move, Basco had him in a vice-like grip. He fell to his knees, yelling in pain and clutching the side of his head, a pool of blood appearing on the rock floor.

"You should be thanking me – it's a neater job than I had!" he hissed.

The Doctor ran to Khageshwaar's side, struggling to support his weight.

"You witch!" The Doctor's eyes flashed with such fury that even Basco hesitated.

"Keep your wits about you, Doctor," said Arabella. "I need you focused. The deal I offer you is simple. Take us to the yetis or we will leave pieces of your friend all the way up the mountain. It will be a much slower death for him than the alternative."

Arabella's voice was ice. There was no emotion now. She was all business.

The Doctor was about to reply when there an almighty explosion of rock sounded from somewhere above. The roar that followed split the air with its deafening ferocity.

"What was that?" Basco said.

Arabella said nothing. Instead she craned her eyes upwards; then a sharp intake of breath betrayed her excitement. Forgetting her captives for the moment, she jumped up to the huge boulder that had previously shielded the Doctor and Khageshwaar from the sharpshooters. Standing tall, she gazed across the sweep of the mountain.

"One of the yetis is on the cliff!" She gazed, absolutely

transfixed. "Just one. A huge male. The others will surely be near – they always move in packs. Be quiet and still – we mustn't warn him of our presence."

The rest of the hunters shuffled together in trepidation.

It was at that very moment that the Doctor and Khageshwaar made a break for it. With neither Basco nor Arabella watching them, and the rest of the group distracted by the prospect of finding their prize, the Doctor seized Khageshwaar's arm and gave it a firm squeeze.

With a flash of his cape, the Doctor sprang forward, pulling Khageshwaar with him – and surged down the mountain, away from Arabella and her men.

"Stop them!" Basco shouted. His knife flew through the air, missing the Doctor by a whisker.

"QUIET!" Arabella commanded. "No firing or shouting. You will give our position away. We have bigger prey to deal with now – our prize is in sight. Let them go – we'll hunt them down later. It won't be hard to follow the trail of a bleeding man."

Basco cursed and scooped up his knife, before climbing back up to join Arabella.

"I'll track them down soon enough," he snarled.

"I know you will, but regardless, they have failed. The yeti has come to us!"

Arabella drew in a slow breath of cold mountain air. Her revenge on the Doctor would come soon enough, but now it was all eyes on the prize.

"Is that the sick one, do you think? They're bigger than I imagined." Basco spoke somewhat nervously, craning his head as he caught his first sighting of the huge creature.

"He looks perfect." Arabella's eyes glistened.

As Arabella began to calculate her options, two shots abruptly rang out. Two marksmen she had left behind to shoot the Doctor and Khageshwaar had spotted the yeti descending the mountain towards them. Now they crouched low, their weapons raised, peering through their telescopic sites towards the creature they had just shot.

"Fools!" Arabella snarled.

Another roar echoed over the rocks as the yeti dabbed at the pinpricks of blood that had appeared on his arm. The bullets had grazed him, but they didn't seem to slow him for a second. Without a moment's hesitation, he began to charge towards the two men.

The two mercenaries stood and turned to run. Arabella waved frantically, indicating for them to climb up towards the group. Then she signalled for the rest of her hunting party to fan out along the path.

In a flurry of activity, the men dispersed, checking their weapons. Only Arabella and Basco could see events unfolding on the mountain, but all of them could hear the shouts of alarm from their colleagues. The yeti was gaining ground quicker than they had imagined possible.

"Shall we attack?" Basco asked, licking his lips. "If we use the guns, we might slow him and give our men a chance? We can close in as he tires and finish him off. It will ruin his skin but. . ."

Arabella shook her head. "No," she ordered. "Stay still. Look at the mountaintop."

Following Arabella's gaze, Basco looked up. There, he saw the silhouettes of more yetis standing motionless in a line.

"The rest of the family," he said quietly.

As both he and Arabella watched, two much smaller figures became silhouetted on the mountaintop.

"Humans," Arabella hissed. "They must have split off and sent the Doctor to distract us. It all starts to make sense."

As they continued to stare upwards, a smaller yeti suddenly crested the ridge and moved towards the others. The group visibly reacted, clustering around the newcomer, embracing it one after the other.

"Very sweet," Arabella commented acidly. "A family

reunion. Those ones must be the females and the children. They're all much smaller than the monster heading down the mountain. Let's use him as a distraction, keep their attention focused. If we attack right now, the others might run off."

"What are your instructions?" Basco asked calmly.

Arabella's teeth flashed in a smile as she spoke. "Tell the men to stay behind the line of boulders and keep hidden. Move them into a higher position so we can get clean lines of sight across this whole side of the mountain. Take out the family group first. Knives would have been nice, but they'll be useless out in the open. Too much space for them to evade us. Stick to rifles for this. We'll patch up their skins after we finish them at close quarters – it'll be easy when they're down on the rocks. You and I will stay here and take out the brute once the others start shooting."

"What about our two men in the open?" Basco added quietly, watching the two exposed hunters running away from the crazed yeti.

"Those idiots will have to take their own chances. Use them as a decoy whilst the rest move into position. At least their lives won't be in vain. They'll serve some actual purpose for a change."

Basco allowed himself another smile. Fewer hunters

meant more money for him. Fewer people to split the rewards with when the skins were sold.

Shuffling back from around the boulder, Basco quickly arranged the remaining hunters into pairs.

He rasped out instructions. "Take only your rifles. Find vantage points as you climb. You need to have clean shots that cover the sweep of the mountain in case they run. Go for head or heart. Clean kills. There are four on the ridge. Take the smallest first, fire in rotation between you and your partner. Arabella and I will finish the big one whilst you pick off the others. The humans. . ."

He hesitated, knowing what the answer would be. Nevertheless, he called out the question.

"Arabella – what about the Doctor's companions who are with the yetis?"

"What of them, Basco?" Arabella replied. "They have made their decision. If they die today, the fault is theirs."

The men wasted no time. Their blood was up, the anticipation of a kill powering them onwards. Besides money, this was what they lived for. They scrambled up the track, each pair breaking off along the way to find a vantage point from where they could best shoot across the mountain.

It only took a minute before the huge male yeti, seemingly unhindered by the bullets that had hit his arm, reached the two men who had been unable to keep up their run through the challenging terrain and lay cowering behind rocks.

The yeti's mind was in the full grip of the abominable madness that had made yetis legend. He let out another deafening roar that seemed to reverberate around the entire mountain. The first of the men stood up and tried to make another bolt for it, but he wasn't quick enough. In the blink of an eye, the yeti surged forward and grabbed him by the neck, flinging him into the air in one swift movement. His body arced through the space, his screams fading abruptly as he landed against the cliff face.

It was just as the yeti was about to grab the second hunter that a stone hit him square on the head. He swivelled his gaze, immediately forgetting the hunter at his feet. Another stone arced through the air to strike him, this time on the shoulder. The yeti felt nothing, only the awareness of a new source of attack. It triggered his instincts.

Abruptly he turned and leapt further down the mountain with another roar.

The fight was on.

* * *

Edith bit her lip in frustration, peering anxiously down the mountain.

"We can't just stay here," she said impatiently to Babu, whose binoculars were fixed on Arabella Spearstrike. "How can we do nothing? The Syndicate are there – they're going to attack!"

"Edie, the Doctor told us to wait. He'll come to us – I know he will. We're safer up here."

"Little lamb." Rakshek's words popped into her mind. He was pawing the ground with his hoof. *"I'm with you, you know that. We can charge down the mountain! We bharals are fearsome when we want to be!"*

Edith felt a surge of love for the plucky little bharal.

The mother yeti reached out her arm and gently brushed Edith on the shoulder with her fingertip. *"Your spirit is strong. You have healed my son. Knowing you are safe will give the Doctor the strength to do what he needs to do – but, please listen, we cannot fight the Syndicate."*

"They might kill your husband!" Edith's voice sounded harsh in her mind as she stared, bewildered and uncertain, watching the small figures scurrying amongst the boulders.

"He's in the grip of the transformation. None of us could aid him."

As the mother yeti spoke, Edith saw the huge male

reach the two hunters who had been further down the mountain. Her mouth dropped open in horror as she watched the confrontation.

"He is amongst them. They will unleash all their weapons on him now." The mother's voice spoke the words simply, heavy with sadness.

"Edie!" Babu's voice sounded panicked.

Edith turned her head sharply. The expression in Babu's eyes filled her with a sense of foreboding.

"I think they've seen us. I saw a flash of movement behind those rocks. They could be coming. We should hide."

Panic and indecision flooded Edith's mind.

"What is it, little lamb? You look pale. Are we readying for a fight?" Rakshek edged closer to her, his expression almost eager.

Edith didn't answer. Instead, she turned to look at the mother yeti, whose eyes were fixed on pinprick figures down the mountain.

"Can you hear the noise?"

"What noise?" Edith looked around, confused.

"We have company."

All the yetis seemed to have heard the same sound. Edith watched as they moved uneasily together.

Then Edith heard it too.

It was soft and distant at first. Then it slowly got louder. It sounded rhythmical, like the knocking of waves against a ship, or the heavy beat of . . . wings.

Shadows flickered over them. All the yetis craned their heads upwards, gazing towards a flock of dark shapes that passed overhead.

Edith and Rakshek scurried to the opposite side of the ridge, away from the cliff face where the Syndicate were climbing. She gasped as she looked down the slope.

Below them was a mini plateau, a flat expanse with a sparse covering of boulders and loose rocks. Standing in a close-knit group among those boulders were twelve gleaming white creatures that made Edith's heart sing with joy.

"Pegasi!"

Figures seemed to be perched on some of their backs. It was hard to see, because the elegant creatures' muscular wings blazed in brilliant white against the bright blue of the mountain sky, the sweat on their coats glittering like diamonds.

As Edith put her hand to her mouth, the King, standing a hand taller than all the others in the middle of the herd, raised his noble head and nodded at her.

"Humans think we can't understand their

language – simply because we choose not to speak it." The rich sound of his voice filled Edith's head like a wave unfolding itself on to a shingle beach.

"Quite a journey!" Betty laughed, as she dismounted. She was clutching a large bag in her hands.

"We went very high, Edie!" Francis chipped in, as he too slid from one of the stallion's backs. He was carrying something in his arms – a large, brown, hairy something.

"Arnold!" Edith shrieked.

The dog wobbled on his feet for a moment, then gave a huge wag of his tail, shaking his body as he charged over to Edith.

"I've missed you! Oh, Edie, you're OK! I was worried about you, you know. I wondered when I was ever going to get a secret sausage again."

Arnold rolled over, inviting Edith down on to the rocks to scratch at his belly.

Edith laughed with joy, her spirits soaring as she met her friends – no, not just her friends, her *family*. Tears of happiness welled up in her eyes.

"The King had just arrived for a check-up when we received the Doctor's letter," Francis explained. "One minute Betty was reading it to me in the barn; the next, there was a sound like thunder and the rest of the herd of pegasi arrived on the lawn outside. Even the little one!" Francis's face cracked into a warm smile.

Edith quickly scanned the herd again. Sure enough, a foal was present, nuzzling up to one of the creatures Edith assumed must be its mother. As she watched, it danced quickly in a circle, clearly delighted to be on such an adventure.

"Is he cold?" Edith asked.

"We should have got a jumper for him." Francis glanced at Betty.

"Well, if Gerry can be persuaded to give it up, there's a jumper under him in this bag," Betty said, giving Edith a wink as she slid her hand into the backpack tied to the stallion's side and began to ferret around inside.

Gerry poked his head out of the bag and saw Edith. He gave a squawk.

"Are we here? Oh! It's so cold! I needed that jumper but ... well ... just this once!"

Edith turned to Betty. "But I don't understand..."

"It's quite simple, dear. The Doctor sent us a letter, asking Francis to come. The rest of us decided to tag along."

"Yes, Binsa posted the letter – but how did you get here so fast?"

"The pegasi fly at incredible speeds," Betty replied.

"It has been something of an adventure. We can't tally long, mind; the animals at home will need their evening meals."

"Oh," Edith said, as if it was the normal explanation in the world. "Thank you all so much for coming."

She paused a moment, then looked at the King and repeated the words in her mind. *"Thank you!"*

"I understood you the first time, little one."

"Edie dearest, where is the Doctor?" Betty's voice sounded calm, yet Edith could see her eyes moving around the group of yetis and frowning not to find the Doctor standing among them.

"I'm not sure. We think he's somewhere down the mountain. But—"

Before Edith could explain, a sharp crack sounded across the mountainside. Almost simultaneously, the surface of one of the rocks exploded in a shower of dust and fragments of stone.

The King whose focus had been on Francis as he tried to wrestle the jumper on to the foal, beat his wings. *"Gunfire!"* he whickered. *"Tell everyone to mount."* The King fixed her with large, soulful eyes. *"We must hurry. Edith – you will ride with me."*

The King tossed his head in her direction, flexing his mighty wings.

"What is he saying, Edie?" Francis asked.

"Back to the skies," breathed Edith, as the King's words continued to pour through her mind. "Back to the skies and then..."

"Then what, my dear?" Betty asked quickly.

"Then they take us to battle," Edith said simply.

"About time!" a voice bleated out, as Rakshek pushed himself forward. *"Which one shall I ride?"*

CHAPTER NINETEEN

*In which old friends and new come
together on the frozen mountainside,
and the Final Battle begins...*

The Doctor tugged on Khageshwaar's sleeve as they scrambled around a tight corner, a few loose rocks scattering in their wake. His cape flapped around them both as they heaved in gulps of air.

"Stop, K! Those fiends have given up the chase. Let me look at that wound." The Doctor pulled Khageshwaar to a halt. The track down which they had plunged had twisted and turned on its way down the steep mountainside and now they were well hidden from the Syndicate above.

"Why aren't they following us?" Khageshwaar asked, his face a mask of pain as tried to cup his hands over the side of his head.

"They have bigger prey to contend with. Prey we need to help in more ways than one."

"What do you mean?" Khageshwaar panted through gritted teeth.

"We have to try to protect the yeti. But there's something else. We have to save the Syndicate as well."

Khageshwaar gasped. "But, Doctor. . ."

"We can't let the yeti kill the Syndicate's hunters. If dead bodies are found strewn over this mountainside, it will raise questions the Nepalese authorities will be forced to address. In short, the yetis will be exposed."

Khageshwaar nodded. "I see. It would be difficult to blame their deaths on an avalanche over such a large area. The Government would be forced to take action to make the mountain safe."

"The Government would declare the yetis too dangerous to be allowed to roam free. There would be an official hunt. The Syndicate would get what they wanted after all."

"What shall we do?" Khageshwaar asked.

"Firstly, we shall bind your ear. Do you have a knife handy, my dear friend?"

The Doctor reached for the end of his cape as Khageshwaar silently passed him a pocketknife. Using it to make a cut in the material, the Doctor tore a strip off the cape and, reaching forward, tightly bound it around his old friend's injured head.

"That should stop the bleeding. Here, take these."

Deftly pulling a bottle of tablets from a pocket, the Doctor shook out two small white tablets into the palm of Khageshwaar's shaking hand.

"Are these a special medicine, Doctor?" Khageshwaar asked.

"No, just paracetamol, I'm afraid," the Doctor replied "You need to rest. The wound needs time to clot and you have to stop moving. I'll have to leave you, old friend. I must draw the yeti away from the hunters."

"Doctor, no. Let us both go, we can distract the yeti together."

"The huge male is in the grip of the madness. He has broken free of his chains and he was charging down the mountain as we escaped. We need to keep him away from the Syndicate and the Syndicate away from him. I will be best at this alone – one target for him to chase."

Khageshwaar shook his head. "But if you draw him off, he'll come after you. How will you survive? You'll have both the hunters and the yeti after you."

"I will move like the wind! We can't give up, K. Not after all we've been through." The Doctor flashed a grin. "Besides, if we don't try, how will I ever look Edie in the eye again? She'd be up there in a heartbeat, we both know it!"

Khageshwaar gave a weak laugh. "Yes, she would. I hope we see her again soon. She will not forgive me if you do not return from this adventure." He looked upwards. "Do you think they've made it to the ridge?"

"If they're on the ridge, they'll have been able to see the danger below."

"Will they hide?"

The Doctor shook his head slowly. "I doubt it. They will be watching. They'll want to help somehow given half a chance."

"Doctor, please. If you won't let me come with you, let me go further down the track. I will find a safe place for us. When you run, draw the yeti down the mountain and I'll have found us somewhere safe where we can hide. Hopefully the other yetis on the ridge will follow."

The Doctor nodded. "Let's do it, K. Good luck, and find us somewhere small!'

Khageshwaar nodded and set off down the winding mountain path.

The Doctor waited for a minute to give Khageshwaar

a head start; then, adjusting his cape, he too began to move. Climbing up the mountain, away from the path and scaling the broken rocks, his head crested the cover and he scanned the mountainside. Not far away, the towering figure of the yeti loomed in front of him, poised above the second hunter.

Without a moment's thought, the Doctor picked up a stone, drew back his arm and launched it as high and as hard as he could.

It struck the yeti directly on the back of the head. Quickly, the Doctor bent down, chose another stone and threw that as well. The creature paused, searching for the source of the attack. Then, as he swivelled his head, his eyes fixed on the Doctor's position.

It was at this moment that a flurry of shots rang out from higher up the mountain. The Doctor, distracted, looked up, and gave a gasp of horror. He could see the rest of the family of yetis clustered together on the top of the mountain – and also, to their right, pairs of hunters lined up on the cliff edge, unleashing volleys of fire at them.

"No," he said under his breath. Then, a deafening roar blasted towards him and the huge male yeti, forgetting about the prone hunter at his feet, took a stride in the Doctor's direction.

The Doctor hesitated. His plan was falling apart. He had assumed the Syndicate were closing in on the male yeti; he hadn't realized the rest of the family were now in peril. The Doctor cursed. Arabella Spearstrike was never to be underestimated. She had been using her hunters as a distraction and then the male yeti, all to get her mercenaries into position to attack the entre yeti family.

They needed his help. The yetis – and presumably Edith – had made it to the ridge as he knew they would, but now they were under attack. The hunters had it all. Arabella had planned everything perfectly. By sacrificing the two hunters on the mountainside, she would be able to kill all of the yetis with multiple assaults. But multiple assaults would mean. . .

He looked up again at the top of the mountain, his mind whirring in the microsecond he had to decide.

Suddenly another shot echoed out, this one much closer. The Doctor watched in horror as the colossal figure of the male yeti staggered.

A patch of red exploded on its chest.

The yeti dropped to his knees.

"NO!" the Doctor roared, scrambling forward.

A familiar figure stepped from behind the male yeti and his heart sank. Everything was unravelling. Arabella Spearstrike wasn't with the rest of her men. She had waited to kill the male when the time was right. She had split her force so they could all attack at the same time.

Of course, the Doctor realized, her personal desire would have been to kill the biggest and strongest.

"You can't do this, Arabella!" he cried. "You have to stop! This slaughter will not go unpunished!"

Arabella seemed to notice him for the first time. She began to laugh. She raised her hand to signal, and Basco appeared from behind a boulder, his high-powered rifle balanced easily in his left hand.

She pointed at the Doctor. "Kill him if he moves!" she shouted. "I will finish the yeti."

With a flourish, Arabella pulled her knife from her belt, angling the blade towards the prone creature.

"Why not kill me now?"

"I want you to watch this, Doctor. All of this time, since your dear little Wilma died on this very same mountain, and you still haven't learned your lesson, have you? The Syndicate takes what the Syndicate wants. A silly little veterinarian with a fancy cap and cape isn't going to stop that. Wilma understood that in the end, didn't she? When she was lying there, twisting and turning in one of our traps. But you – you're so much more stubborn." Arabella's eyes glittered with evil delight.

The Doctor's teeth clenched together. He took a deep

breath. A sharp stab of pain coursed through him as the memory returned.

Arabella laughed. "You're pathetic, Doctor! It should really have been you in that trap, instead of Wilma. It would have saved us a lot of trouble over the years, repeatedly getting in the way of the Syndicate's plans." Arabella paused. "But at least this time it's different. This time we have the family pinned down so they can be slaughtered. It's almost perfect."

Arabella gave a cackle of laughter as she approached the prone male yeti.

"He's still breathing, Doctor. Any last words you want him to hear before I drive my blade into him, and then Basco puts a bullet through your heart?"

The sudden gust of wind came from nowhere. It was so powerful, it almost knocked both the Doctor and Arabella off their feet. They staggered in an effort to keep their balance, arms flailing.

The gust came again, even stronger. Arabella's face went white with shock as a huge shadow passed overhead.

The Doctor looked up into the sky and his heart skipped a beat.

"It would seem your hunters have just become the hunted!" he thundered, unable to keep the rising hope from his voice.

Arabella Spearstrike's mouth dropped open in surprise.

Darts of gleaming white surged through the air above them. The pegasi glided into position – and, as if in well-practised formation, they lined themselves up to approach each pair of hunters from above. As both Arabella and the Doctor watched, they arced through the sky and, with a thunder of hooves, dived down upon the attackers with pinpoint precision, giving the hunters no time to react or aim their guns.

The pegasi attacked without hesitation. One beat of their huge wings was enough to knock the grown men off their feet. Lashing out with their teeth and hooves, they scattered the Syndicate over the rocks. Soon, the hunters were huddling together on the open mountainside, slack-jawed in amazement and fear.

The power and speed of each pegasus was terrifying to behold. The hunters didn't stand a chance. Within moments, the group was disarmed and huddling in fear surrounded by a ring of the imposing winged horses.

A few pegasi still circled overhead. As the Doctor watched, he could see figures clinging on to their backs.

"Betty! Francis!" he shouted, waving his arms in delight. "And Edie, my dear girl!"

Hearing his cries, they slowly descended. Their

hooves touched down on the mountainside with surprising lightness – and, within moments, the figures who had been clinging on so desperately slid gratefully to the ground. The pegasus foal, not part of the attacking force, landed as well, his hooves skidding on the rocks alongside them.

"Doctor!" Francis boomed.

Wagging his tail madly, Arnold bounded over to his master.

"By all the pointed peaks of a dragon's brow, how on earth did you. . ." The Doctor didn't get to finish his sentence because, at that moment, Arnold crashed into him, sending him staggering back a few steps.

"Your letter, Doctor," Francis explained. "The King was with us when we received it!'

The Doctor grinned, stepping forwards and embracing them all.

Sliding off the King's back, Edith ran over the rocks to wrap her arms tightly around her uncle's waist.

"Edie, my dear. You're safe!" The Doctor breathed out as he spoke, an invisible weight lifting off his shoulders.

"I'm fine, Uncle. It was snails that did it – well, worms in the snails!"

The Doctor looked confused as he studied his niece.

"I mean, worms in the snails on the poppies which had infected the yeti. They didn't affect Rakshek, though; he's fine. It's just yetis who are susceptible to them. A new species on the mountain. And then the Pegasus saved us all. All the yetis are fine. A couple have minor wounds but they're all right, all of them except for. . ."

Edith looked down over at the fallen male yeti lying

at their feet. Her happiness evaporated like morning mist as she took in the extent of his injuries.

"We're too late," she breathed. "I was too slow."

"He's been badly hurt," the Doctor said.

"Did they shoot him?" Francis asked.

"It was Arabella Spearstrike."

Betty's knuckles tightened, gripping the bag containing Gerry. Sensing her anger, Gerry gave a sharp squawk. "Where is she?"

The Doctor spun round, scanning the mountainside. There was no sign of Arabella or Basco.

"She's run," he cursed. "But she can't have gone far. We must find her – but first, the yeti."

The Doctor began to move carefully towards the fallen yeti, whose chest heaved with each laboured breath.

"He's in a bad way," Francis said, moving alongside the Doctor. "Shot near the heart. His lungs are filling with blood."

Betty shook her head in despair as the Doctor crouched and tentatively touched the yeti's bloodstained fur. As his fingers made contact, the huge creature twitched and gave a low groan.

"We have to stop the bleeding," he said calmly. "The bullet has torn through the muscles and tissues after passing between his ribs."

"But what can we do?" Betty replied, her voice quiet. "It's internal."

A voice that only Edith could hear sounded out.

"Edith, tell them to move back. I can help him."

Edith looked back at the King.

"What is it, Edie?" the Doctor enquired.

"The King wants us to move back. He wants to help the yeti."

As they shuffled back, away from the dying creature, the King slowly stepped forward. As he moved, the play of his muscles rippled under a gleaming white coat. Lifting his left foreleg, he gently pawed at the ground by the side of the yeti, before steadily lowering his head, and touching his nose to the bullet wound.

Time seemed to stand still. The pegasus held that position with his eyes closed, his head bowed and his powerful neck arched with swanlike grace.

The magic was subtle, almost invisible, yet Edith could see a slight shimmering of his wings as power radiated out from the King, pouring over the body of the prone yeti.

It took a few seconds for things to take effect, but then the yeti's breathing began to slow into a much steadier rhythm. Soon, the heaving of his chest seemed to settle; then, the yeti's hands started to twitch as if being pricked by a thousand needles. Finally, his arms jerked as they were drawn back under his body.

The King, raising his majestic head, gave a snort and stepped two paces back. As he moved, so did the yeti, who heaved his shoulders off the ground and drew himself up into a kneeling position.

The Doctor, Betty and Francis tensed and took a step back. Edith did the exact opposite. Instinctively, as if drawn by some irrepressible urge, she stepped forward.

"Edie!"

There was a note of panic in the Doctor's voice, but Edith ignored it. Without any hesitation she placed her hand on the shoulder of the great creature who remained motionless, dazed and unblinking, drawing deep breaths of mountain air as if waking from a deep sleep.

As his green eyes locked on to those of Edith, a calmness seemed to flow from him. The crazed glint had gone. The magic had healed him physically and mentally.

"The transformation has passed," the Doctor said, once again in awe of his fearless niece.

The King snorted and pawed the ground.

"He will be dazed, Edith, with poor recollection of what has happened. I will tell his family it is safe to come down the mountain. Stay with him. Talk to him."

The King's voice reverberated in Edith's head as his hooves suddenly clattered on the rocks and his legs powerfully launched him into the air. His wings beat a breeze over them as he soared up the mountainside.

Edith smiled at the yeti as she concentrated her thoughts.

"How do you feel?"

"Tired. I must have escaped the chamber – did I hurt anyone?"

"I'm not sure," Edith replied carefully, casting a glance at a figure slightly further down the mountainside – the hunter that the yeti had attacked. As she watched, the hunter seemed to move slightly. He wasn't dead.

"My son?"

"He is well." Edith laughed out loud, unable to contain a burst of happiness that bubbled up from within. Less than half an hour ago, everything had seemed so desperate and now, here they were, all together. She turned to look at her uncle, who beamed broadly back and tipped his cap in gentle salute.

The yeti's gaze swept around the group before coming to rest back on Edith.

"Thank you."

His eyes drifted over to the Doctor, and they exchanged a solemn nod.

The Doctor caught sight of Babu, who lingered back a few paces. "You proved true, Babu. Your brother is alive but he needs help – he's been injured by one of Arabella's henchmen. If you go down the mountain a few hundred yards, you'll find him. Bring him up to us."

Babu nodded and set off down the mountain, calling Khageshwaar's name.

Edith stepped back, feeling a sudden and almost overwhelming sense of fatigue. She wanted to sit down, close her eyes for a moment, but a movement caught her attention.

Looking up the mountain, she saw the pegasus foal was wandering off by himself. Smiling to herself and wondering what mischief the foal had in mind, she walked slowly after him to make sure he didn't stray too far away.

The Doctor, having watched his niece silently communicate with the yeti, glanced across at Arnold. The lumbering dog was snuffling around the rocks behind the group, but stopped suddenly to scent the air.

"Arnold?" the Doctor said.

Arnold looked over at the sound of his name, but quickly turned back to the rocks. Distracted by Arnold's antics, the Doctor watched him for a few moments as the big dog continued to snuffle about, scenting something amongst the stones and boulders dotted over the mountainside. Suddenly, Arnold lifted his snout to sniff at the air and began to whimper and whine with increasing fervour.

The Doctor looked around, searching out Edith so that she might translate – but the young girl was nowhere to be found.

"Francis," the Doctor called out – and the big man turned around, instantly alert. "Quickly now! I've seen that look on Arnold's face before, whenever an intruder wanders into the grounds of Forest Cottage. Something's got his attention – and I don't like the sound of it at all."

CHAPTER TWENTY

*In which at the very moment when all
seems saved, Arabella Spearstrike makes
one last desperate attempt at glory...*

"All is not lost, Basco. You still have a chance to earn your money."

Arabella Spearstrike and Basco lay flat on their stomachs, peering through a crack in the rocks as the Doctor and his companions gathered round.

Pegasi, Arabella thought. Of all the things that could have spoiled the hunt today, she hadn't thought it would be them.

"I've heard of pegasi and their power, but to actually see it in action. . ."

They watched the injured yeti recover and get to his knees.

"Such power," Arabella whispered, in absolute awe.

Despite what had happened, Arabella was not feeling despondent. Her plan had been thrown into disarray and her men scattered – but they were only mercenaries, after all, and replaceable. Now, her cruel eyes sparkled with an unforeseen opportunity.

Using the sudden arrival of pegasi to make her escape, she had run back up the mountain, the last direction anyone would expect. Basco, having observed Arabella making her getaway, had climbed quickly from his vantage point to join her. The two of them now hid out of sight, having slid into a large gap between two massive boulders that completely sheltered them from both above and below.

At first, it had felt like certain victory had been flipped into a crushing defeat, but now – as Arabella hid here in the rocks and *watched* – it felt as if events were moving once again in her favour.

Despite their current predicament, she grinned with anticipation. She had devised a plan that would restore all of her fortunes.

"Pegasus wings would be worth more than all the yeti skins put together," she rasped. "This would salvage everything. But we will have to be quick. Look!"

Another stroke of luck: one of the pegasi had strayed from the herd. A little one. *A foal*, thought Arabella. Like all curious youngsters, it had wandered away from the cluster of people around the yeti. It was exploring the mountainside, nibbling any small plants it came across – but now it was within ten metres of where Arabella and Basco were hiding.

"Maybe we can shoot it without them hearing?" Basco replied. "We can quickly cut a wing off and escape."

Arabella didn't say anything. She was far too busy thinking.

"I have a clean line of sight."

"Don't be stupid!" Arabella's eyes flashed in the gloom. "We can't shoot it. The moment the gun goes off, they'll be on to us. If it keeps moving in this direction, it will pass between the rocks. We can jump down and finish it quietly. The others mustn't notice. It will take us a few moments to cut off those wings."

"You think we'll have time to take both wings?" Basco asked curiously.

"You saw what the big one did. It healed the mortally wounded yeti. The power is in their wings. We'll take all the feathers we can, sell them to the highest bidders. Imagine what each one would be worth – it would be criminal to leave one behind."

Basco smiled grimly in the darkness. His bounty would go up. Pegasus wings did indeed sound like a priceless treasure.

"We'll have to move fast," said Basco, a nagging doubt in his mind. "Once we get the wings, we have to get into a populated area. The other pegasi won't want to be seen so we'll be safe where there are houses. We'll need to get down the mountain – and fast."

Arabella took a sharp intake of breath as she noticed something else.

"There's a girl out there. She's broken off from the group. She's following the foal." She narrowed her eyes. "I saw that child at the Traveller's Rest. Staring at us before we set out. I didn't realize she was with the Doctor. This day is full of surprises."

Basco peered through the crack, angling his head for a better view. "Do you want me to kill her as well? Some sort of payback for what he's done?"

Arabella shook her head regretfully. "Killing a child on the mountain will attract attention and the authorities will investigate. With so many witnesses, we can also no longer frame things on the yetis. You go, dispatch the foal. If the girl gets too close, I'll try to distract her."

"And if it doesn't work and she sees me?" Basco enquired, his voice emotionless.

"Those wings are our objective – if the girl interferes, we'll have no choice. The yeti skins can wait for another day." Arabella Spearstrike leaned forward. "Whatever it takes, Basco."

Basco gave a soft grunt of acknowledgement, then quickly slid back between the boulders. He was both agile and fast. With great care, he levered himself out between the boulders and held himself ready, poised to leap down on to the unsuspecting foal's back as soon as it walked below him.

Edith glanced up. She was getting closer to the foal but it was still twenty metres ahead of her and heading out of sight.

Suddenly, a stone skittered on the rocks to her right and she paused, wondering where it had come from. Another one followed it and she hesitated. She had a creeping feeling that something wasn't right.

Picturing the foal in her mind, Edith momentarily closed her eyes.

"Don't wander too far. Wait for me."

The foal, just edging his way under the boulder where Basco was poised above, stopped in his tracks as Edith spoke to him. Startled, he gave a little wicker.

It was at that exact moment, the killer made his move.

With all the skills of an assassin, Basco jumped off the top of the boulder and landed heavily on the foal's back, which skittered sideways under his weight and went down on to its hind legs.

The foal panicked, flapping its wings in an effort to pull away, but Basco's bodyweight tugged him sideways and it scrambled on the loose stones. One of his wings flapped helplessly as the assassin adjusted his position and tried to drive his knife in.

Edith sprinted forward. Without a moment's thought, she hurled herself at the man.

Basco was about to strike again when Edith grasped his arm. Swinging his fist backwards, he sent the little girl flying – but the distraction was enough to enable the foal to push itself forward slightly, throwing off the man's next slice with the knife. Basco's blade managed to make contact with one of the foal's wings, causing it to whinny in pain.

Looking briefly behind to make sure the crumpled form of Edith wouldn't interfere with his plan, Basco readied himself to approach the foal again. By now, the animal was covered in its own blood and unable to use one wing. It was time to finish the job.

"We're making a mess of this," he hissed through gritted teeth, "but it'll be over soon."

It was at this moment that a sudden bray sounded from behind him

Basco turned his head just in time to see a blur of wool and horns come out of nowhere and launch itself at his chest. Before he could react, he had the breath knocked out of him as he crashed hard into the mountainside.

Rakshek hadn't been able to ride with the pegasi down the mountain. Francis was the only one strong enough to carry a passenger and he had taken Arnold, so the plucky bharal had remained with the yetis, who had watched impassively as the winged horses once more took to the skies. Determined not to miss out on the action, however, the bharal had given a determined bleat – and launched himself off down the mountain in hot pursuit.

"Rearguard action!" he'd told himself. A strong rearguard can make all the difference in a battle. He was determined not to miss out on the fight.

He'd seen Edith dash between the boulders as he had hopped down the crags of rock and headed after her. As he rounded the rocks, he'd taken in the scene: Edith lying on the ground, the foal badly injured, and a brute with a knife – and, in that instant, an anger had flared inside him that would have given him the strength to face a mountain leopard.

Without hesitation, the bharal had lowered his head and charged full tilt at the man. His horns were strong and broad, and the power from his legs meant that the blow carried the strength of a sledgehammer as he slammed into Basco.

Basco felt all the air leave his chest and his feet leave the ground as he was lifted upwards and fell back with an almighty jolt. Yet Basco was an experienced mercenary, who had been in more fights than most hardened soldiers, let alone a mountain bharal. His instincts were those of a trained killer – and, even as he landed, gasping for breath, his knife flashed upwards.

As Rakshek charged again, once more lowering his head, he was oblivious to the danger.

"YOU WILL NOT HURT MY FRIEND!"

His bleat ended abruptly as the blade entered his neck.

Rakshek felt the strength suddenly go out of his legs. Momentum carried him forwards – but, as he once again crashed into Basco, part of him knew he wouldn't be getting up again.

With a final last effort, he pulled back his head, the pain from the blade searing like the burn from a fire, then drove it down with one last blow, knocking the man backwards as he crumpled to the floor.

Arabella watched with growing disbelief from her vantage point. The spectacle of Basco tussling with a little girl and a mountain goat was quite unexpected. She held her own knife in her hand and weighed up the options as to what she might do next.

She made her decision.

Arabella readied herself to jump down and go after the foal. She could already hear Basco calling out for help, but he was of no use to her now. All she cared about was the pegasus wings. She would finish the job Basco had started.

Then she saw the enormous shadows starting to fall.

Yetis, she thought. *Yetis everywhere.*

Basco had started screaming even more fearfully now, but they could have him.

No, thought Arabella Spearstrike. *The Syndicate must live to fight another day.*

* * *

Edith shook her head, trying to clear the heavy fog that seemed to be weighing her down. Her nose hurt terribly and she knew she was badly bruised, but nothing felt broken. Her eyes flickered open as she remembered what had just happened. A shout of alarm was on her lips. She staggered to her feet, preparing to launch herself back at Basco, but then she took in the scene in front of her.

The yetis towered around her, the mother staring deep into her eyes with its unblinking gaze showing a look of deep concern. The eldest daughter was cradling the injured pegasus foal in its arm, which was clearly distressed and in pain from the savage attack, but not in any mortal danger. The second daughter stood close by, her head tilting this way and that as if looking for more assailants. The father dangled Basco upside down by his leg. His huge muscles and size made the assassin seem as if he was merely a feather. Arnold stood inches from the man's fear-stricken face, fully in the grip of his wolfish ancestry. Yet it was the fifth yeti that drew Edith's attention. The yeti she had saved, among the field of blue poppies. Now he was bent double, his great body shielding something small and limp from Edith's view.

"Rakshek?" Edith whispered. "Rakshek?" She limped over to where the yeti stood.

The yeti turned and looked deep into Edith's eyes.

"He is dying." The voice reverberated inside Edith's skull, heavy with sadness.

Edith dropped to the ground, her knees falling heavily on to the rocks.

"Let me hold him," she said, tears welling in her eyes.

Gently the yeti lowered the broken body of the bharal across her lap. Edith cradled his head as Rakshek's big eyes met hers and his body twitched as if trying to will himself better.

Within moments, the solid shape of Francis was kneeling beside her and the Doctor was in front, his hands assessing Rakshek's injuries.

"He has a very deep stab wound to his neck. He has lost a lot of blood."

"Can the King help?" Edith asked desperately. *"Can you?"* Edith screwed up her eyes as she thought the words, tears spilling down her cheeks.

The King was hovering up above with the rest of the herd, beating his magnificent wings.

"My power needs time to replenish. I am sorry, Edith. It takes many days. I have used all I have for the yeti."

"But he's dying," Edith sobbed, looking around at everyone, as though hoping for some miracle. "Rakshek can't die. Uncle, can't you do anything? Please?"

The Doctor reached forward and placed his hand on

her shoulder, his own eyes welling with emotion. "Only certain stallions in each herd have the power. Those who reign and those who will. None of the others have the magic, Edie. Rakshek can't. . ." The Doctor's voice broke slightly as he looked at the bharal. He took a deep breath. "He can't be saved."

It was a high-pitched snort that made Edith twist her head. The foal, wrapped up in the yeti's arms, had started to wriggle and the yeti gently lowered it to the ground.

The foal looked dreadful. Its shoulder was slashed, one wing drooped uselessly by its side, but it tossed its head and started to totter over to where Edith knelt with Rakshek in her lap.

There was a collective air of unsettlement amongst the herd as all eyes were drawn to the slow movements of the foal. Some of the magnificent creatures landed on the rocks around them, stamping their feet and tossing their heads. The yetis exchanged looks and the doctor gave a meaningful glance at Francis, who edged back to make space for the injured animal.

Seemingly unaware of the attention it was drawing, the foal continued to inch its way over to Edith before finally stopping and raising its head towards the King, as if seeking permission.

There was a pause. All of the pegasi herd were still.

Edith swivelled her gaze and looked up at the wise eyes of the powerful stallion, who now held the attention of everyone assembled. With a great nod of his head, the King gave a snort and gently beat his wings once, a breeze of air pushing up all around them.

Edith had no idea what had just transpired, but it was clearly symbolic, as the herd once again became agitated and the foal, teetering on the rocks, pushed his muzzle into Rakshek's tummy.

Edith froze, watching as the bharal lay limp, small shallow breaths the only sign that he was clinging on to life. The foal trembled all over, trying his hardest to see if he had the power of a potential King.

Nothing happened.

The foal stepped back. For a moment, he seemed on the brink of collapse. Francis placed a huge arm around its back to steady it. The King tossed his head anxiously.

"Please." Edith looked up the foal, who was clearly exhausted from his effort. *"Please try one more time."*

The foal moved forward once more, thrusting his muzzle harder this time against Rakshek's limp belly. Again, he started to tremble – but, after a moment, his good wing also began to beat. As it did so, the damaged wing gradually started to twitch in rhythm. Then a light began to grow out from the foal, radiating from its body, bathing them all in a glow that became so bright that Edith had to shield her eyes.

As the group watched, Rakshek was still taking shallow breaths, but the foal seemed to change. His damaged wing was now beating in time with the good one, completely healed. Somehow, as it stepped back, it looked bigger, stronger and completely transformed from the broken creature it had been just moments before. It tossed its head in the air, before bowing it towards the King, as the rest of the herd snorted and stamped in amazement and celebration of the spectacle.

The King's reaction was immediate. He reared up on his hind legs, his almighty wings beating twice, propelling him up in the air. His whinny echoed across the mountainside.

"A new king has been born, Edith. This is a coming of age for our herd. Two kings. Our future has been reborn!" The voice in Edith's head was rich and happy, and Edith felt a great surge of hope.

The foal pranced around in a tight circle, testing his muscles and limbs, before moving forward once again to thrust his muzzle a final time towards Rakshek.

The plucky bharal came around with the same gradual awareness that the yeti had. At first, he lifted his head and gave Edith a curious look of surprise. Then he twisted his body as he surveyed everyone looking at him.

"Why am I lying in your lap? This is most unbecoming for a warrior of the mountain!"

"Rakshek!" Edith wrapped her arms back around the little bharal – and, as the Doctor and Francis both hugged and shouted in joy, even the yetis seemed to savour the moment, smiling with their unblinking eyes and grunting with happiness.

Arnold, forgetting Basco for a moment, bounded forward and gave Rakshek a huge slobbering lick with his tongue.

"Oh, the indignity!"

Edith laughed. Her eyes met the Doctor's. Right there and then, in this remote part of the world, far away from everything she had ever known, she thought she had never been happier in all of her life.

CHAPTER TWENTY-ONE

In which Edith realizes that her world will
never be the same again – and that there
are many more adventures still to come. . .

Betty held Edith's hand as the two of them stood together, surveying the sweep of the Himalayas.

The yetis had gone, having first woven a string of snail-free blue poppies into Edith's hair, their eyes speaking more gratitude than words could ever say. The family had been solemn and dignified as they said their goodbyes and climbed back up the rocks, melting into the landscape as if they were part of the mountain itself. Edith wondered if she would ever see them again.

Some of the pegasi also stood ready to depart. Francis

was mounted with Arnold, who gave Edith a plaintive look.

"Hurry back!" he insisted. *"I need someone to sneak me a few of Cumberland's finest."*

He had spent the previous half an hour playing with both Rakshek and the pegasus foal. They had all skittered and chased each other amongst the rocks, the foal flying up into the air any time Arnold got close, and Rakshek leaping over the rocks as only a nimble bharal can.

"What will happen to the Syndicate's hunters?" Edith asked, looking at the sorry group of men who were all bound together in a line by a thick climbing rope. They had made a few stretchers out of coats and jumpers so they could carry the injured ones down the mountain.

Babu, who had emerged from the mountain trail with his brother propped up on his shoulder, was already starting to march them down the mountain. Khageshwaar and the Doctor were ready to move as well. The King and two other pegasi glided high overhead, ready to form part of the escort down the mountain where they would be met by the authorities. They wouldn't be visible from the ground, but the mercenaries knew what would happen if they tried to cause trouble.

Khageshwaar had used a radio found in one of the men's backpacks to send a message down to the village and his own Sherpa team were already en route to provide additional support in the event anyone tried to make a break for it when they got close to civilization and pegasi couldn't fly down.

"Most of those men will be taken and questioned by the police," Betty said evenly. "They are soldiers hired by the Syndicate – I suspect some of them will have international arrest warrants served against them already."

"Already?" Edith asked.

"These are bad men, Edie. The Syndicate attracts people with no good conscience who will do anything for the money." Betty took a deep breath. "Most will be released – they will say they were hunting bharal and there is no evidence they weren't. They have hunting licences, after all. But no matter what happens to them, I doubt any would dare come here again. Not after this."

"What about *him*?"

Edith pointed to the figure of Basco. He was separate from the rest, hunched and dejected, his teeth still chattering fiercely as he remembered how close he had come to the yeti's jaws.

"He should answer for cutting off Khageshwaar's ear," said Betty. "But I don't know if that will happen."

"How do you mean?" Edith asked.

"He was Arabella's second-in-command – he could

give some useful information as to where she has gone. It all depends on whether they can keep him in prison. The problem is, we have no proof of what he did." Betty's voice had hardened and a touch of frustration had crept in. "It is all so unfair, but if we were to tell the authorities what this man did, it would bring attention to the existence of the yetis. And that is the last thing we want to do. Sometimes I wonder if we shouldn't wreak some justice on these terrible people ourselves. But we can't, Edie – we can't ever become like them."

The old lady sighed.

"What is it, Betty?"

"She got away again. Arabella Spearstrike. Oh, I shouldn't think it, my dear – but I do detest that evil woman."

"Where did she go?"

"We looked everywhere. Even the male yeti tried to track her. We found no sign. For all her faults, she is an accomplished hunter; she can hide her tracks up there with the best of them." Betty glanced across at the little girl walking alongside her. "She escaped," she said simply.

"Perhaps learned her lesson?" Edith felt a glimmer of hope in her heart, but it didn't have a chance to grow.

Betty let out a sudden bark of laughter. "No! Someone like Arabella Spearstrike doesn't ever learn a lesson. I'm sure we'll have the unfortunate displeasure of meeting her again. But for now, Edie, she is gone – and you, my dear, have been magnificent."

Betty looked around. Francis and Arnold were already saddled up and ready to fly. Another pegasus waited, its head bowed down and its wings folded back, as if to invite Betty aboard.

Betty wrapped her thin arm around Edith's shoulder and gave her a squeeze. "It hasn't been easy for either you or your uncle on this trip. You have helped him more than you know."

"Betty, you don't have to tell me. I know about Wilma. That was why my uncle was so distant, back at the beginning. Why he didn't want me at Forest Cottage."

Betty drew a long breath and slowly nodded her head. "When your uncle last came here, he brought Wilma. They were very much in love. Devoted to each other as much as the mythical creatures they sought to help. It was on their way back down the mountain that the tragedy occurred. Wilma got caught in one of the Syndicate traps. They were designed for the yetis, so she didn't really stand a chance. Your uncle never forgave himself for what happened. It broke all our hearts."

"And I look like her?"

"More than that, Edie. You not only share the same

gift, but the same fiercely independent spirit." Betty cleared her throat. "You came along at the right time, my dear. The Doctor needed to be reminded that, sometimes – just sometimes – human beings are worth every bit as much as the animals he builds his life around. We've always wondered what would happen when we got too old to do it, how we could continue, and then. . ."

"And then?" Edith asked.

"And then, we found you."

But it wasn't Betty who had spoken. It was the Doctor, striding away from Khageshwaar and the roped-up hunters, his cape flying behind him.

"You're the future of our family, Edie," said the Doctor, "just like that foal is the future of theirs." He pointed at the pegasus foal, still playing with Rakshek. "How can I say thank you for the feats you performed in these mountains last night?"

In answer, Edith flung her arms around him.

"Well," he whispered, "there are still a few days before you must be off back to school."

Edith felt suddenly downcast. After all the adventures of the past weeks, the thought of school seemed completely alien somehow.

"Of course, there will be other school holidays," said Betty. "Won't there, Doctor?"

The Doctor said, with more love than Edith had ever heard him muster, "The doors of Forest Cottage are forever open to you, Edie. Why, I doubt we could do it without you now. And, if you weren't to come back to us, how would poor Arnold communicate his unending need for sausages?"

"And my parents, Doctor?"

"They will return. Your mother and father are as resourceful people as I have ever known." There was a pause, and then the Doctor said, "The yetis are saved, and Betty, my dear, your ride home awaits."

Together, they followed Betty to the waiting pegasus and helped her up on to its back.

"The one disadvantage of travelling without a passport is that you have to leave a country the same way you arrive," Betty said, wrapping a shawl around her shoulders. "I'm not sure I completely enjoyed the thrill of riding a pegasus over four thousand miles, at a ridiculous height and an incredible speed. But they do have a way of keeping you feathery and warm up there." Betty laughed warmly, her eyes having regained some of their twinkle. "Edie, my dear, I'll be waiting at Forest Cottage."

Edith and the Doctor stood back as the pegasi began to beat their wings. Then, with a whoosh of excitement – a hurrah from Francis, a solitary bark from Arnold, and a squeal of unease from Betty – the pegasi took off into the open mountain skies and were gone.

Edith felt the Doctor's arm around her shoulder. His cape fluttered behind them both.

"It is time for us to go back down the mountain, say farewell to our friends and start our own journey home."

Just then, the familiar shape of Rakshek strutted forwards.

"Where are we going next?" the bharal bleated, his chest puffed out.

Edith repeated the question to the Doctor.

"You may tell him," said the Doctor, "that I already have an assistant and the post is now confirmed – but that we do need a courageous warrior to take on the position of Guardian of the Yetis. Somebody to lead hunters astray. Somebody to raise the alarm if ever Arabella Spearstrike and the Syndicate were to return."

Rakshek arched his eyebrows as Edith relayed the words.

"I accept!" he declared. *"Those pegasi might have wings, but they still can't get up and down these mountains like a bharal – that's for sure! I'll be the proudest, most courageous, most dedicated and loyal Guardian these mountains have ever seen! And I'll even make sure to eat all those blue poppies, so we never have that terrible business*

with worms and snails ever again!"

"*Come on, Rakshek,*" Edith said. "*For your first job as Guardian, you can escort us down the mountain.*"

"*It will be an honour, Your Majesty!*"

Edith laughed and the Doctor asked, "What did he say?"

"Rakshek seems to have decided I'm a queen – not just a girl who'll have to go back to school in a few short days."

"You're so much more than that, Edie." Together, the Doctor and Edith began to follow the line of hunters and Sherpas down the mountain, Rakshek trotting alongside them, while, somewhere up above, the King and his loyal retainers kept guard.

"You're the most talented young lady I've ever met," the Doctor said. "You've been given a gift and, if you'll let it, it will take you to the places in the world where magic still exists, where creatures beyond imagination still make their homes among the countries of men. You'll see dragons and unicorns, phoenixes and serpents. You'll see werewolves and hippogriffs, giant mountain rocs. Oh, the wonders you're going to see!" The Doctor stopped. "But first," he said, "back to the Traveller's Rest. It's been a long night, Edie. I do believe there are plates of cheesy chips and marshmallows waiting there, with our names on them!"

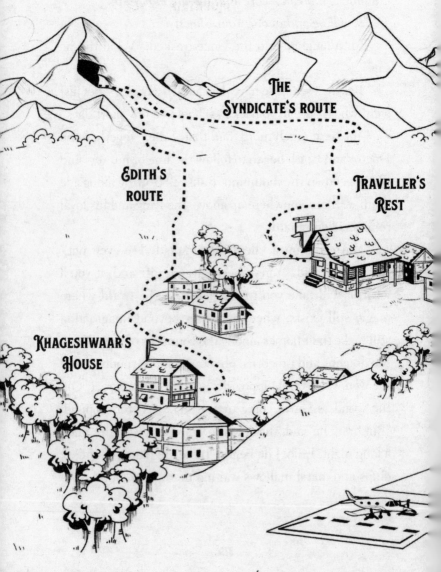

THE
SYNDICATE'S ROUTE

TRAVELLER'S
REST

EDITH'S
ROUTE

KHAGESHWAAR'S
HOUSE

ᴀCKNOWLEDGEMENTS

Every achievement I've ever managed has only been possible thanks to the immense support of a fantastic team around me – and writing this book was no exception!!!

Colleagues, friends and family always get leaned on, and without liberal encouragement, criticism, advice in equal measure, not to mention expert guidance – I'd never achieve a thing – let alone write this book!

Rob Dinsdale, who alongside Heather and the brilliant Elly at the HHB Agency (my agents for The Vet books), helped me hugely with an extremely heavy copy-edit, plot restructure and plenty of ideas to give me a decent shot at getting published. Rob is a brilliant author with his own books to focus on, goodness knows how he found the time to give me the support and steer I needed, but it was invaluable and I'm very lucky to have someone like him as a friend and mentor in this arena.

The charity team at Worldwide Veterinary Service

gave me the kickstart challenge to start the book –
writing a bit every day before I go to bed – and the eternal
patience and support of my wife Cordelia to take on
another side project has also been incredible.

Of course – my hardcore proofreading team of the
first draft – Noah (13), Robyn (13) and Damon (11)
helped me spot plenty of things to sort out – and the
inspiration and enthusiasm provided by Sheba (11), Giddy
(9) and Gabriel (6) has been a massive driver for getting
it over the line!

I'd also like to thank so many amazing children's
authors who have influenced and inspired me in writing
this. It is impossible not be influenced by the good
and the great – I'd hate to miss anyone out so I won't
fill this page with endless names – but having four
young children, you can imagine how many children's
books I have gone through at various bedtimes over the
years. I can only hope a flavour from some of them has
rubbed off in the text as it would have improved things
immeasurably!

I am also very grateful to the team at Scholastic.
A tremendous thanks to them for the opportunity to
join their stable of children's authors. I've been further
mentored and supported by Lauren, Yasmin, Ruth
and the eagle-eyed copy-editor Gen, who is clearly the

ultimate English teacher and would certainly banish me to the back of the class having spotted (and corrected!) how many times certain characters 'realized' something – even if it was 100 pages apart. Thanks to Aimee, the illustrator Jane Pica, and Hannah and Rebecca, who have driven all the publicity and marketing to make things win and really brought the book to life.

Finally – a big thanks to you!!! A book would never be written if it wasn't fun to do, and things are only fun if you can share the joy of them! Enthusiasm and support from readers adds so much fuel to the fire, and we need to keep that burning bright as the Doctor and Edie get ready for the many adventures ahead!!

SO, YOU WANT TO WORK WITH ANIMALS!

There are of lots of career paths you can choose from if you want to work with animals. I chose to become a vet: it's brilliant fun and, if I had my time again, I wouldn't do anything different – but there are a lot of options out there and they all have their own pros and cons.

Irrespective of the path you decide on, whether it is to become a vet, vet nurse, animal trainer, or even a wildlife ranger – one thing is universal: you need to show a passion for animals, be willing to study hard and be prepared to work long hours!

I think anyone working in the animal world will tell you there are many ups and downs. Animals can be unpredictable, it is sad when they get sick, it is truly heartbreaking when they die, but they can also be a source of unconditional love – and the sense of reward in helping a creature that is vulnerable and voiceless is unbeatable.

I think all of us can relate to why Edie and the Doctor undertook such a perilous journey to save a dying yeti. They wanted to champion a creature that had no one else to turn to – and whether it is nursing an injured bird, rescuing a baby hedgehog, stitching up a dog or pulling a bad tooth from the mouth of an unhappy baboon – it is awesome to be an animal champion!

Any experience you have with animals will prove your enthusiasm and help you get where you want to be. Work at a farm or stables, walk dogs, clean at a cattery, volunteer at a vets! It all adds up and will help you.

The key to becoming whatever you want is to be determined, not to give up and have the self-belief you can do anything if you set your mind to it! The right vocation is out there for you. If you don't get grades at first, don't be too disheartened – just have another go. We all fall down in life every now and again – it's the getting back up that makes us stronger. With the right mindset – anything is possible.

IF YOU LIKE ANIMALS, THEN WHY NOT JOIN THE WVS YOUNG VETS CLUB!

It is the perfect club for anyone who wants to become a vet, vet nurse or work with animals.

As a member of the Young Vets Club you'll not only have priority access to the latest *Secret Animal Society* news but you'll receive your own Vet Adventurer handbook and a biannual magazine packed with real-life animal rescue stories from our WVS teams around the world.

You'll also get to choose one of our rescued animals to adopt with quarterly updates from them to see how they are getting on. Your welcome pack will contain lots of stickers, bookmarks and fun-filled extras!

To learn more about the work of Worldwide Veterinary Service check out **www.wvs.org.uk** or head straight to **www.youngvetsclub.com**

LUKE GAMBLE

is a vet who lives with his wife Cordelia (also a vet),
his four children, four dogs, two cats, two ponies, a
snake and a fluctuating population of rescued chickens!
Having set up and run a mixed practice in the New
Forest for the best part of twenty years, most of
Luke's veterinary work is now with the international
charities Worldwide Veterinary Service and Mission
Rabies, which he set up in 2003 and 2012 respectively.
Sadly, Luke has never treated a yeti – but his eyes
are constantly peeled! Information about Luke, his
adventures and work can be found at
www.lukegamble.com